Best Wishes

Danny Tal

# Red Veil

·

## DEAN JACKSON

authorHOUSE™

1663 LIBERTY DRIVE, SUITE 200
BLOOMINGTON, INDIANA 47403
(800) 839-8640
WWW.AUTHORHOUSE.COM

First published by AuthorHouse 4/26/2006

ISBN: 1-4259-0104-2 (sc)

Printed in the United States of America
Bloomington, Indiana

This book is printed on acid-free paper.

*This book is dedicated to those people that selflessly give of their lives for the protection and enjoyment of others.*

# *Acknowledgements*

I would like to thank first and foremost my wife Karen who has provided total and utter love and support whilst I have endeavoured to write this book. My Golden Retriever Storm who has been by my side constantly whilst I have written and typed away. Even the companionship of a furry friend helps when things just aren't going so well.

I have an endless list of people that have read and proofed my book or given encouragement over the last few years and without that support I feel this book would still be in a dark cupboard never to be seen (And some of you might want to take issue with them for that encouragement!) My Mum and Dad, Roy Ward, Charlie and Nicola Beaumont, Derek and Janet Barker, Helen Staniforth, Vicky Sowerby, Hannah Compton, Matt Bolger, Simon Taylor, Debbie Stones and Julie Garnett. To you all, I just want to say thank you, you may not be 'editors' but you are all friends and in your judgement I trust.

I would also like to thank Ian White whose original Bronze Caricature provided the idea and inspiration for the front cover and authorHouse for their excellent support and guidance during the production of this book.

Lastly I would like to thank YOU, yes you, for reading this book, because that was the reason I wrote it, so that you could enjoy it.

Best Regards
Dean Jackson

# 1

It had been several months since the traumatic and unexpected break up of his marriage and there was now peace and tranquillity in his life after the emotional rollercoaster that he had not been expecting to ride. It will never happen to you, obviously, because after all we are perfect, goes without saying, but that doesn't stop the other party deciding to go and cut some other bastards grass! To describe Dom's emotional state as a car crash it would have to be 'fatal'. He had that empty feeling and felt incapable of love. A barrier had descended around his heart, an impenetrable titanium cloak that even Harry Potter would do well to lift. A girlfriend was not on the agenda, too tying and too much grief. Anyway, why piss a potential future girlfriend off because he was a bit of a 'grouchy git' at the present time. No, far better to get his head right before taking the next step. However, a man still has urges, and urges need to be dealt with appropriately. He could have gone out on a series of one night wonder shags that would have left him with a mobile full of numbers but he was trying to avoid grief. That was the last thing he needed. No, what he required was the services of a professional, highly illegal prostitute, which would not go down too well at work considering his occupation. However he felt it wouldn't have looked good driving around the streets where he worked trying to pick up a local Tom. Oh that was definitely a no-no. Dom had no problems reconciling his reservations with his emotions and his duty to the law. It even felt good flouting it, after all, laws were meant to be broken, speeding, under age drinking, seeing prostitutes and this was his way of giving the rods to the system and it felt bloody good. Not that anyone at work would take kindly to this arrangement and he was pretty sure he would get suspended and possibly sacked if anyone found out, but hey, life's too short and anyway who the hell was going to find out? It wasn't as if he'd picked her up in his car and they were shagging in the street.

So he was paying for the pleasures of life. Fate had dealt him an intriguing hand and it was obviously just meant to be. Dom met Sharon whilst at work. Fortunately he had gone to the job on his own and she had been a potential witness to a lad who had tried to steal a radio from a car. They had got talking and somehow, god only knows how he managed it they were both talking about their circumstances and the next thing he was a arranging to see her on a professional basis on his own time rather than works.

No matter how many times she heard the wrought iron gate crash back, it still sent a shiver down her spine. The sound had travelled clear as a bell in the cold damp night, and the anticipation as the footsteps scrunched along the gravel path to the door. She knew who it was this time; a quick glance at her watch told her that it was Dom, bang on time as per usual. Maybe it was just a function of what she did, sometimes never really knowing the person who was on the other side of the door and on some occasions not really wanting to open it, but tonight was different, Dom was more like a friend than a customer.

Sharon opened the door to be greeted by a huge bunch of flowers; Lilies, irises and carnations, tied with a big pink flamboyant bow, a box of chocolates and a bottle of wine. A cheeky smiling face appeared from behind the flowers.

"Now that's a cheesy grin, come on you soft sod, get yourself in here. Exactly what have I done to deserve this?"

Dom smiled affectionately, shrugged his shoulders stuffed the flowers into her arms and planted a kiss on the side of her cheek.

"You must have had a good day to be buying flowers!"

"I was just thinking this morning that it's been a long time since I've bought flowers for a woman and I got the urge to be romantic."

"I've come to the conclusion that you are rapidly losing your marbles, do you know that? What sort of a man buys flowers for a Tom?"

"Don't say that."

"But Dom, that's what I am!"

"You're a professional person just getting by like the rest of us."

"You know that a lot of people in your profession would not agree with that."

"Well that's up to them."

Dom headed for the kitchen and the corkscrew before sinking back on to the couch, with a glass in his hand. "Come on, sit down and join me, I didn't come to fight with you."

"No you saucy bugger you came to shag the arse of me." Dom paused and smiled "..............Well yes, of course. Seriously..., you have no idea how much therapy you've given me since my marriage went down the pan, the intimacy that you give me restores my faith in human nature. You ask nothing of me, you listen when I ramble on and from my point of view we have great sex. I look upon you as a friend."

"What about the forty quid?"

"Quite cheap really, I don't think a shrink would let me do what I do on your couch for that do you?"

"Err no."

"I could always pay by direct debit."

"Oh yes, and the tax man would have a field day with that."

They chatted about nothing in particular and time just flew by.

Sharon turned slowly to face Dom and put her finger to his lips. The time for talking was over, she'd helped massage his injured heart; it was now time to massage the rest of him. As she touched his lips she rolled around so that she could straddle him on the couch. His hands gently caressed the tops of her legs as the dressing gown parted. Her skin was smooth and warm and her fragrance was heady. Dom teased the cord from the dressing gown allowing it to fall open revealing a cream silk teddy. His hands moved gently from her thighs over the outside of the silk top to her breasts, as her nipples teased out the silk fabric. Sharon gazed down at the uniform.

4

"I love it when you're in uniform."

"'Been to court today and I know you like the officer and a gentleman thing."

"You bloody tease."

The buttons on the tunic where eased open with an accomplished touch. The belt and the shirt provided no resistance. Sharon kissed Dom lightly on the lips and then on the neck and chest as her tongue slowly worked its way down Dom's abs. Her hands had cupped him and were slowly massaging in a rhythm that was certainly having the desired effect, the pleasure immense, the timing perfect.

It was still only early when Dom stood to leave but he had really enjoyed the company. They had done the sex thing in about ten minutes but cuddled in front of the fire and talked about pointless shit like an old married couple for the next hour, but it was time for Sharon to go back to work, she had another customer at eleven. Dom kissed her and gave her a big hug as he walked from the door

"You take care and ring me if you want anything"

Sharon smiled to herself. Here was a gentle man, he was certainly too nice to be a copper. Who else would pay for her services and then tell her to ring him if she needed anything. She closed the door and looked at the clock. Ten minutes before the next one, she flung herself at the stairs; she had no time to spare.

# 2

$\textbf{M}$idnight Monday, and only three weeks to Christmas, the majority of working people tucked up in bed in anticipation of the busy shopping period and parties that lie ahead before the festive day.

Not this particular worker, Trish was a working girl, one that got paid by the trick or by the hour. It was all down to the negotiation, there were no business lunches here just a quick yey or nay in some one's car or a brief conversation as they walked past. The main bargaining chip in the deal were her looks as compared to most bags she certainly had the edge, plus what she was prepared to do for money, because there are some seriously sick people in this world that would take advantage of a woman who was selling sex.

Fortunately Trish didn't have a pimp, although she'd had one. He had been a mean and nasty bastard taking more than his fair share of the profits whilst taking none of the risks. It wasn't him that had put his heart and soul into the venture. Granted he had afforded Trish some protection, but it was normally after the act and not during. She was normally wearing the bruises, before 'Gripper' as he was affectionately known, found the punter. So in the end she needed to come up with a plan to prevent the punter getting heavy handed at the time. Trish and her working mate had taken a bus man's holiday to Amsterdam and, whilst sampling the delights of the local men, went on a shopping spree. Basically a dozen canisters of CS spray. The label on the front read THE PROTECTOR. Legal on the continent! Illegal in the UK. Trish had used it once spraying the sadistic sod in the eyes and then in the groin as he had dismounted. Boy, that would burn for days and the warmer it would get the more it would irritate as CS reacts to warmth and friction. Whilst he was writhing on the floor in agony his eyes streaming she had emptied his wallet and then punched him on the nose for good measure, after all she would have bruises for days so why shouldn't he. The pimp had been nowhere to be seen so now she worked alone and took all the profits. He had not been easy to get rid of, and then one day he just disappeared. When his body was eventually found it looked like he had bitten of more than he could chew as he was riddled with stab wounds. Trish was just grateful for the small mercy and that he was eventually off her back.

It had been a catalogue of errors that had led to a severe cash crisis and a fine that she needed to pay. The last thing that she really wanted at the present time was another fines warrant, which would just be the final straw. The problems had started early last year when she had got shacked up with this bloke called Jez who was heavily into the gear, quite the little drug baron. Jez had quickly moved into Trish's flat and used it as a Crack den. So it came as no surprise one day when crack was being cooked in the kitchen and several of Her Majesties finest booted in the door. Fortunately for Trish the tosser she was living with took the rap for it. The police looked upon his co-operation with some information as a means to an end for keeping Trish out of the mire. It did Jez no good at all as when the word got out he had grassed it was the beginning of the end, and once inside prison he fell victim to a nasty accident.

That had been Trish's first scrape with the law that year and her second was a complete brainstorm. This involved her building up huge catalogue bills and not paying for the goods. On this occasion however it did lead to a court appearance and a hefty fine and a drug rehabilitation program. The habit had been hard to kick when lover boy got sent down for a six-year stretch. The addiction had been her escape and hence all the goods ordered from the catalogues had been exchanged for drugs. Trish was unlucky as most catalogue companies build in an inherent loss factor to this kind of theft and write off the loss. But, alas, this particular company was struggling financially and as Trish had used her own name and flat and made no attempt to cover her tracks it was a fête à complis. Not the worlds brightest of criminal minds, but then again she was not really a criminal, well not in her eyes. She had not stolen from people and she was only in this predicament because of Jez who had got her hooked on drugs.

When she went on the rehab program, the decision was easy. Get off the gear, pay the fines and go straight. The only problem with the theory was that the fine amounted to five hundred pounds, and this was only a fraction of what she had got away with from the company. Trish was strong in mind and refused to do anything dishonest again. Her chosen profession may be illegal but certainly not dishonest. She looked upon it as a service to society. For the men whose wives no longer gave them what they wanted, sex! Or for the weirdoes that couldn't get it anywhere else.

Custom had been easy to come by due to the fact that she was one hell of a looker. She was not common, or tart like, almost classy in appearance, with exceptionally long legs and quite a bosom, plus lovely long straight dark brown hair, thick and glossy, which fell beautifully to the top of her breasts. Being 5'8 meant that she always wore flat shoes as men could be intimidated by height and if the need arose she could run faster.

To date Trish's career had spanned six months and she was beginning to grow in confidence. The first three months with the pimp and the last three on her own, which had allowed her to make big inroads into the fine, which was now down to two hundred and fifty pounds. Trish was easily making fifty pounds a night off just two punters and her life was returning to normal. She had even managed to start furnishing the flat.

Trish thought that her own speciality as a working girl was the blow job, because every time she got a blokes dick in her mouth, ten seconds later there would be that tell tale little spasm at the base of his cock and he'd explode. Either they were all ready to burst or she just had the Midas touch. Another of her favourite tricks would be to wear skirts just above the knee with no underwear, just suspenders! The rest just gets in the way. She particularly liked to bend over the front of the bonnet and take the short but brief frenzy from behind. This was quite the best way, as she didn't have to look at them or kiss them and she was in a position to run away if need be. Getting trapped in the car was no fun, plus it was plain old kinky and the punters loved it.

She had been standing outside the old school house for twenty minutes and business was slow to say the least, but the good thing about her job people wanted sex all the time. It was an especially cold tonight and the damp was striking through her clothing. She'd already had her obligatory two punters and now she was just chancing her luck, being greedy, trying to get a bit of extra cash for Christmas. Several of Trish's friends were out and about but only Trish had done any custom. Thirty seconds later and she would have been gone. She heard it before she saw it, as the car did a drive past. She spotted the gleaming large motor and was sure that she had seen it earlier in the night. That wouldn't be anything new; it takes a lot of courage to approach a woman in the street for the first time. It's like buying condoms in the chemist; we all do it, sex that is! We all know what they are for, but it's still embarrassing, you can guarantee that the cashier will wave them about like a trophy for all to see whilst you stand there wishing the ground would swallow you up.

Trish stood firm, just in case there was a bit of extra business to be had. The second time it came past her in the space of two minutes she was sure that the driver was out for a bit of extra curricular activity, but was just plucking up the courage to ask. The car came around again and cruised towards her and this time it was slowing.

Trish eased herself away from the wall and moved out to the edge of the kerb, just as if it was her regular boyfriend picking her up from the pub. The car crept alongside her, the passenger seat nearest to her and the window already wound down. Before she could even see into the car the smell of expensive leather combined with the sweet smell of after-shave filled her nostrils. The driver was certainly handsome, but what was distinctive about him was the fact that he was wearing a uniform.

"Get lost. You're bad for business so piss off."

"Hey I'm looking for a bit of action."

"So am I, but not with you, fuck off."

"Look if you think it's a trap we don't do entrapment in uniforms. I'll pay fifty quid for what ever you fancy!"

She paused leaning on the side of the car, with her head just inside the passenger window. It was certainly warmer in the car than it was on the street.

"Look, you pay so you choose."

"Are we on then?"

"Looks that way, but I want to see the money first."

"Trusting soul I see."

"What do you expect? You're a copper aren't you?"

The man slid across five new crisp ten pounds notes that were clenched in his leather-clad hand. "Get in the car and I'll let go of the money."

"Trusting soul!"

"Touché"

Trish eased into the front seat without questioning further what he wanted her to do. The seat was comfier than her sofa and it was nice to be in the warmth, that damp had chilled her to the core. It wasn't a bad night after all; three punters, hundred quid and she felt quite pleased with herself as she gazed from the car as they sailed out of Sheffield heading for the Moors.

As he drove she noticed him keep glancing across at her legs, and so she teased him by hitching up her skirt that little bit further and then running her hands down the inside of her thighs towards her pussy.

It was just after twelve-thirty when the car pulled into the lay-by at Hathersage. The car was lovely and warm and there was little point getting out of the vehicle into the cold, besides there was nowhere to run. The ambience of the car and the gentle tunes of Chris Rea meant that Trish was really in the mood for sex. The driver smiled at her and asked what she would like to do. She didn't argue with him this time and the decision was easy, doggy style in the back of the car.

Trish slipped between the seats of the car onto the back seat whilst her customer walked around the vehicle to the back door. She was knelt across the backseat and as he opened the rear door the interior light came on illuminating and casting a shadow across Trish. She erotically eased up her skirt to reveal a pert tight little arse and gently parted her legs. She knew that he was watching her every move, and he couldn't help but notice her gorgeous legs. She slid her hand between her legs and gently teased herself open so that she was ready to receive him. The light went out just as she heard the unzipping of his trousers. The sight of her had meant instant arousal and suddenly without warning she felt a warm swelling inside her as she was stretched. It was literally seconds, maybe thirty at the most, and unusually she found herself having an orgasm. The euphoria spread through her body and as the tingling wave ebbed there was a hot feeling deep inside as her customer unleashed himself into her. The feeling was different and she knew that he was wearing a condom. Most blokes tried to get out of wearing one and yet, Trish had completely forgotten. The first thing she would normally do is stipulate the ground rules. Wear one, or jack off. Fortunately he was a safetyman or so she thought. The real reason was much more sinister and Trish was just about to find out. This man hated women and moreover he hated prostitutes with venom.

As Trish rolled onto her back to face him, the attack was swift, merciless and without warning. As she started to smile, his fist hit her full on in the side of her face shattering her cheekbone and rendering her almost unconscious instantly. The punch between her legs was a full-blown hammer blow, a gruesome strike causing immense pain and damaging much of her lower anatomy. Before falling unconscious Trish grabbed at the door handle, her head reeling in pain, not knowing where she was or what was happening, the cold air striking her lungs at much the same time her face hit the gravel and the lights went out. The man was swift as he leapt from the car. Only two more strikes were made, one a full on punch in the kisser, splattering her nose across her face, and the second, a kick. Again this was pure evil itself as the steal toe capped boot found its target, the pelvic bone shattering on impact as she laid spread eagle on the gravel. Fortunately Trish was already out for the count but the damage was severe as she lay in her own blood, which was now beginning to pool around her face and nether region. Her attacker calmly cleaned him-self up discarding the condom and gloves into a bag in the boot of the car, and then, as if nothing had happened, drove out of the lay-by running over her hand as he sped off into the night.

# 3

It was a cold crisp sunny day
and the officers of 'B' group were arriving for the afternoon shift at
Valley Police Station. Everyone appeared in high spirits having just
had several days off. Dom sat in his car reading the headlines in the
local paper. 'Prostitute left for dead' He quickly scanned the article
to read that she was now recovering in the local hospital and was
in Intensive care as a result of her injuries. If it had not been for a

biker stopping in the lay-by to put on his waterproofs it would likely have been a fatal attack as she had sustained substantial blood loss and was in shock. Somewhere in the middle of the entire blurb it clearly stated that this was the third such attack on a prostitute in as many months and the ferocity of the attacks had increased. Dom sat there pondering the article thinking it wouldn't be long before one of them was killed. The banging on the car window shattered his thoughts, his mate snapped him back into the real world.

"Come on we'll be late for briefing."

V alley Police Station is situated in the heart of Sheffield's old industrial wasteland. Surrounded by a decaying steel industry, the area is a mixture of blue chip companies and retail outlets. The site is perfect with its close links to the motorway network and the millions of pounds being poured in by the government. This investment has provided a boost to the local economy and helped to reduce unemployment. There are massive tax incentives to companies locating within the area. The out-lying areas of the district are mainly old council estates that are undergoing redevelopment interspersed with the odd private housing estate. These estates have all the problems of inner city suburbs, high unemployment, high crime rates and a massively diverse ethnic population, which makes the Valley an extremely interesting and challenging place to work. The completion of the recent shopping complexes and stadiums in the area has also meant a massive influx of visitors to the area and hence this was going to be one busy day at the office.

It didn't take long for the twelve PC's sat around the briefing table to start the customary banter.

"'As the bloody proby med tea yet, or is it self service again?'

The fresh faced probationer attempted a retort but soon realised that he was skating on thin ice and what with the others heckling him and the Sergeant due imminently it was best he bow out now or get a good tongue lashing later. As the Proby left the room he was muttering under his breath.

"Tell us at training school that we are not here to make the tea."

"Well ya can do fuck all else yet!"

"Like you ever made the tea!"

"Hark at mono mash here."

"Calm down ladies and gentlemen," Bellowed the Sergeant as he walked into the room, "We've got a lot to get through this afternoon, including a little treat for two of you."

"What's that then Sarge? 'You buying the beer or have you got Claudia Schiffer to work with us?"

"The way some of you talk about cars this will be better than having Claudia Schiffer, although there will be a bit of paperwork to go with it." Derk leaned close to Dom and whispered in his ear.

"Ooooooh I've gone all goosy with excitement."

"Don't get too excited were not that lucky. More likely to get a social worker that looks like the 'She devil' like that last bird we had to take out."

The Sergeant scanned the room and noted that there was no tea on the table, and another reverse scan meant that Bed–Wetter was obviously the one that had been dispatched to make the tea.

"Oh for God's sake, will someone go and give him a hand, he can't find his dick with the light on, never mind finding fourteen cups." Several minutes later the tea arrived. "What the fuck's this?"

"Tea, Sarge!"

"Don't get smart, did we share one tea bag between all fourteen cups?"

"What do you expect Sarge, he's Scottish, he's just being frugal with the flavour."

"At least it's hot and wet,"

"Just like…."

"Leave it." Said the sergeant cutting Derk dead.

The car beats and associated meal times were quickly dispensed for each of the officers.

"Right then you two." As the Sergeants eyes met with Dom and Derk's.

"We've won the social worker. Bastard, I told you."

"Will you two shut up; you can have a social worker if you want, or, you can take the keys to the new Volvo T5 that we've got on loan from traffic. The car is fitted with a new device called ANPR and every advance driver within the force is to test it and report back on the system. Unfortunately for me, you two jokers are the only ones eligible on the shift. So get testing and don't bloody crash it because I'm not dealing with the accident."

Mush piped up "Dom's got plenty of form for that."

"Look the bus pulled out on me alright!"

"You blind bastard, you hit a bus."

"Oh shut up."

"And what about that wall, did that pull out on you too?"

"Shut up ladies it's like being in Kindergarten."

"What's ANPR?"

"ANother Police Reck" said Derk, emphasizing certain parts of the words.

"An intelligent question for once. ANPR stands for Automatic Number-Plate Recognition. The idea is still being developed and hopefully in the future the technology will be available so that the all Police cars will be fitted with it. The machine can read and scan a thousand car registered numbers per minute on the data base, so any with stolen markers or disqualified drivers or any other markers will be highlighted in the search facility and downloaded to the nearest police vehicle with the system fitted. At the present time however there are certain cameras at fixed points, mainly motorway bridges as it's easier to read the plates when the car is travelling in a straight line and there are more numbers for the machine to read. Plus the big advantage is that if situated just after a major junction it gives us several minutes to get in position for the vehicle's arrival at the next junction. These are state of the art machines and in South Yorkshire there is a camera located at Junction 36 southbound on the M1. That should give you time, if any vehicle is identified, to get to junction 34 and intercept it, and as such I would like you to stay close to the track." "What's the track?" Asked the proby.

"Motorway, Bed-wetter."

"In the trials the search criteria was too wide so today it's limited to stolen vehicles and cars used in crime. Your job, and hence the fast car, is to track them down and arrest the bad people. One last thing there are three other cameras in use in the area but you are specifically to concentrate on ones with the code M1S, which stands for Motorway one southbound Bed-wetter."

"I knew that"

"Yes of course you did"

"Alice, Jim, concentrate on the area around the cathedral and the university, obviously what with last night's attack things are starting to get nasty and the DI's convinced it won't be long before we're finding a body. Description's very poor, male white thirty- fifty average height and build in a nice car with leather trim."

"That it?"

"'Fraid so."

"Three attacks and that's all we've got to go on?"

"Look, don't shoot the messenger, CID are working on it, and apparently the witnesses are really poor. Give it as much attention until ten then I think they are trying to put a couple of under cover girls out to see who or what turns up. Mush what are you bloody whispering about?"

"Sorry Sarge, just saying it'll probably be a judge or a magistrate, they're always at it."

"Yes thanks for that little input, now shut up when I'm talking. Now get out there and fight crime or whatever it is you're supposed to be doing, and you two wait behind."

Dom and Derk sat there for another five minutes whilst the Sergeant gave them the low down on what they could and couldn't do. The fact that if they pranged the vehicle would mean they would be on foot patrol and this was reiterated several times. The two sat in silence as the car keys were dropped on the table and the sergeant turned and left. They sat there like a pair of school kids eyeing the keys on the table, cheesy grins on their face as if they had been left alone in the chocolate factory.

A chorus of "YES" was heard to ring-out down the corridor bringing a rye smile to the Sergeant's face.

"Who's driving first?"

"We'll toss for it, 'cos sods law say's that who ever drives first will get a prisoner and the other will miss out." The coin was tossed high into the air and Derk called heads. The thud of the coin as it hit the desk and bounced left both staring in anticipation, but there she was old Queenie facing up at them.

"You bastard."

"You can't talk about the Queen like that."

"Best of three."

"Not likely."

"Bollocks."

# 4

Skunk was a casualty of modern times, he found it hard to remember how he had ended up in the mess he was in but one morning he awoke surrounded by squalor. His parents had loved him once and deep down they probably still did, but they could never forgive him for the endless turmoil and what he had done to the family.

It had started with the petty crime, the shoplifting, and more often that not he had got away with it. This had escalated into theft from and then theft of vehicles, before moving into the removal trade. Well-moving other people's property out of their own homes without permission and then selling the goods for ridiculously low prices, just so that he could get a fix. One time Skunk had done a house and cleared ten grand's worth of jewellery but, because he did not have the contacts, he moved it onto a handler for a hundred quid's worth of heroin. His habit had steadily increased to its current fifty pound a day addiction.

In the beginning when Skunk had been a juvenile his parents were always out during the night sat in Police station foyers waiting for a solicitor and an interview and then the joy of seeing their son charged and fingerprinted, well it just broke his Mum's heart. Skunk's addiction became so bad that he had started to steal from his parents. Initially it had just been a fiver from his Mum's purse, but the temptation was too much when he saw the cash card. Call it love, gullibility or what you will, Skunk's Mum never anticipated this and had left her card number in a place so she would not forget it, alas Skunk also knew it and hence her account was systematically cleared. In a one-month period he had managed to obtain one thousand pounds in cash before the monthly statement came and his Dad had gone ballistic. Initially it was thought that someone else was responsible and that the card had been cloned. But once the matter was investigated, and CCTV evidence recovered from one of the machines, the culprit was soon identified.

Skunk had got wind of this and decided that he was already in the mire and so did a Linford Christie with the DVD and credit cards managing to get nearly another five hundred pounds worth of gear before being arrested. Skunk received a six-month sentence in a young offender's institute for his crimes, but it had not cured him of his habit as drugs were just as easy to come by on the inside. He even liked the lifestyle; he'd had his own room, TV, Play-Station and three regular meals a day interspersed with a bit of schooling. It was a good life style so he wasn't deterred and wouldn't have minded another stretch if it came to that.

This episode however had been the final nail in the coffin as far as his parents were concerned, particularly his Father, who had vowed never to have him back in the house. His Mum had written once or twice but he could tell that he had broken her heart and there was absolutely no chance of him going home, not unless he saved the world single-handed from mass destruction. Unfortunately the pull of the fix was too much for Skunk and he would never be able to kick the habit and hence he was now alone. He had cut off the hand that had fed and loved him and his options had become severely limited. He had made his own decisions when help had been offered to him but it appears that Skunk's decisions had been the wrong ones and he had thrown the offers of help back at the people who had loved him.

Skunk was now twenty-three years old and in the last two years had been in and out of prison for a series of similar offences. Skunk knew that should he appear before the judge again he would go down for at least two years, but if it were a serious matter then he would go down for a long stretch. He was no longer in the juvenile prisons and things had been grim the last time he had done time. Unfortunately the job seekers allowance that he was currently claiming did not go anywhere near paying for his three hundred pound a week habit. So, it was back to the same old status quo, burgling and fixing.

Skunk lay on his mattress in the one-bedroom flat that the council had provided. The room was cold and damp, overlooking the West Side of Sheffield. This didn't help, as the eleventh floor took quite a bashing from the harsh winter winds and rain, and the flats being in a poor state of repair let the cold flood in. When Skunk moved in, he moved in with his entire worldly possessions in one go. It consisted of him, the clothes that he was stood in and a bag of needles that he had picked up from the dropping centre. He felt cold and clammy. The mattress was damp and reeked, and there were no sheets on the mattress. There was one over blanket but that too was beginning to hum a little. There were no curtains in the flat and the condensation just streamed down the metal-framed windows and onto the floor. The block of flats that Skunk lived in should have been demolished years ago but they had recently been renovated and kept as part of the natural eyesore that forms part of the Sheffield landscape. The corridors and steps that run between the floors reeked of gentlemen's toilets but the smell was beginning to seep into the flat. Skunk couldn't tell anymore which didn't bode well as it meant he stunk too. The flat was also exquisitely decorated, with designer graffiti art on the walls. Damp crumbling walls over sprayed with Skunks tag and chasing the dragon slogans. Even the colours were horrid but he couldn't hang around to pick his favourites when he was high tailing it out of Halfords with several cans of spray paint stuffed down his top. There was no food in the flat but this was an added luxury that Skunk could well do without. At the moment he just liked the little white bags of powder and we aren't talking about the one kilogram ones with Tate and Lyle written on the side. Add to this general picture, dirty clothing discarded and strewn across the floor, intermingled with disused needles covered in blood and snot used as ornaments to adorn the squalor of the flat. After all a fix is a fix! As Skunk lay on the mattress he rolled over and tied the tourniquet around his arm in an attempt to find a vein. This was futile and Skunk had to resort to injecting into the only vein that he could find. His penis! The puncture marks around his groin and arms were just gross and Skunk was in a seriously bad way.

He often pondered his situation for many an hour, wondering what the cause of his own down fall had been, but he could never put his finger on it. His main theory had been the lack of discipline in modern society. It was too easy to point the finger at the people that were doing their best for you and cry wolf. "Mums hitting me, I'll get the social onto you." But all Mum was probably trying to do was instil a bit of discipline and the child had taken exception to this. Formal chastisement had gone from the schools and no one these days were allowed to hit a child not even as a form of punishment. Well, where's the learning in that? Skunk had soon realised that there was no pain to his misbehaviour and hence nothing had deterred him from the route he had taken. Society had gone soft. The reality was that he was in real pain now, how's that for progress?

The Police give out cautions like raffle tickets, especially for adults, a caution for theft, one for damage, and one for drugs, just to keep people out of the court system. A slap on the wrist, which really means jack shit in the great scheme of things. But if someone had the bottle to dish out some serious sentences then maybe, just maybe, a few people would sit up and take note. Word would soon get around that society was no longer prepared to accept and tolerate this behaviour and maybe the sentences would act as a deterrent. Sod their human rights, they shouldn't bloody have any.

The heroin was now beginning to take affect on Skunks system and this was the time for him to go out and get some money. He had been doing a lot of shoplifting recently to feed the habit and had been working with a team but they had all been lifted yesterday which meant he was back on his own. Skunk had been fortuitous though; he had gone back to the teams flat. Well, he was going to screw the place whilst they were inside but realising the Police would probably come and search he didn't hang around, especially when he found a hand gun wrapped in a tea towel under the bath and a clip full of ammunition for it. Skunk had thought it best to take it for safe keeping, before the Police found it. He was after all doing them a favour.

So there he was, all drugged up and no one to shoot. With this gun Skunk was going to make a serious amount of money very quickly. Well that was the general idea. Skunk picked up his jacket, slipped the gun and clip into his pocket and set out for the more affluent side of Sheffield. He felt as if he was invincible, the strength of ten men, and a criminal genius to boot. But he needed to act fast; the magic potion that gave him his powers would soon wear off. The heroin had gripped his senses and while he was super-human nothing could touch him, but alas in a few hours he would resort to a crumbling wreck of paranoia. The man behind the facade would reappear, but now, right now, he had the power to suck the life out of the well heeled citizens of Sheffield, and he was a parasite on humanity.

# 5

Dom and Derk made their way
down stairs and into the locker room. Both got tackled up, finally
both slipped on their stab proof vests which were a bit cumbersome
but it was better than joining the permanently dead club.

As the two strolled into the rear yard they both looked like
Robocop, fully laden down with equipment. Dom had his topper
box, which contained half the force stationary. The two were quite

giddy at the prospect of driving the new car for the day. After all, it was rare for uniform to receive such a perk. Fortunately it was still cold, but dry, which meant plenty of grip from the tyres, should it be required. Unfortunately however, it was clouding over and the forecast for later was not so good.

They both stood in the yard looking around searching for the car. On first inspection it was not there and both turned around to the parade room window to see if it was some kind of sick joke, but no one was stood there and so they walked another few feet. A step further and they spotted the beast parked in the Superintendent's bay. It looked as mean as fuck. This car had road presence and then some. It was amazing to think that this was one of the fastest production saloon cars in the world and it was all striped up and ready to drive. The advantage of the stripes and the woo wahs also meant that you could just about do what you wanted. Well, within reason.

As Dom walked to the rear of the car to put his box in the boot he spotted the badge on the back, which put an even bigger smile on his face.

"Hey Derk this isn't an ordinary T5 it's a T5R."

"What's that mean then?"

"It means it's even ruddy faster."

"Well how fast is it then?"

"250 BHP, does over 150 MPH and gets to 60MPH in less than 7 seconds, and I'm more than a little concerned that you're driving first."

As they jumped in the car it was apparent that this was no ordinary Police car. It had more gizmos and gadgets than Q. Two types of Police radios, satellite Voda-phone, Tracker device, video equipment, satellite down link screen, a rear illuminated screen that popped up in the back window, the ANPR and of course the normal wail whelp and lights.

"I wonder if the rear screen will flash up "Tosser" and the like."

"I'll look, shall I?"

Whilst Derk was attempting to get comfortable Dom spoke with both control rooms via the Voda-phone. There were too many scanners and Dom thought it better to be discreet and not advertise the fact that they were out with this car.

Within seconds of Dom pressing the Activate button on the ANPR a message appeared on the control panel.

'Stolen Vehicle. M1S Junction 36. Speed 75.6 MPH. Estimated time to junction 35 two minutes, Junction 34 three minutes and 40 seconds.

Vehicle is a white Ford Focus YN 53 NLB.

"Now that is clever."

"Never mind that, pull ya finger out then and get us to the motorway, you've got three minutes."

Derk turned the key in the ignition and the engine roared into life.

"What a beast."

"Will you fucking hustle?"

Derk eased the car from the garage and onto the side street. As soon as they were off the car park Dom hit the full Monty button, it's not selective it just puts everything on main flashing beam, sirens, blues, if it's got it that button turns it on.

This was one truly amazing car and the power surge was keeping Dom pinned in his seat unable to reach siren button to alternate the tone. The car was like lightening as they shot down the dual carriageway.

"I think we were supposed to put a video in the boot to allow us to record this you know."

"Oh great, now you tell me."

"We'll do it after this job."

"It's great testing this stuff but a little bit of a demo on the Gizmo's would help."

"Pull your finger out, Derk, the car will be here in one minute and thirty seconds."

A car well in front was obviously watching in his mirrors and swerved well out of the way. Dom dialled in the thank you sign to the rear screen and as the police car shot past the sign went up.

"Hope that bloke's a speed reader with good eye sight 'cos were doing 100 MPH."

"Don't get sarci with me; it's the thought that counts."

Three minutes had elapsed since the message and they now had forty seconds to get to the motorway, which was not going to be easy considering the traffic around the Meadwhall shopping complex. The tension rose as a bloke in a Vectra was playing silly buggers and the swearing and the gesticulation in the Police car was particularly unpleasant.

"Use your bloody mirrors you blind bastard."

"You really are charming when you want to be Derk."

"I had lessons. Anyway we're lit up like a fucking Christmas tree, how can he not see us?"

Dom turned to the Vectra driver as they went past to wave at the bloke's eyes, in other words use them, but by the time Dom had done the action the police car was two hundred yards up the road.

As the Volvo eased onto the hard shoulder at the top of the entry slip the clock said 10 seconds to spare. A million questions were going through their minds.

Had it come off?

Did it speed up?

Has it gone past already?

Before either of them could say anything, Derk Spotted the Focus in the middle lane.

"It's there." They both shouted in unison.

The Focus was in the middle lane of the Motorway, behind a coach doing nothing excessive, speed wise.

The Volvo roared into life and both occupants were firmly anchored into their seats. Within seconds Derk was situated right behind the stolen vehicle.

Dom picked up the radio set and began to pass a message.

"XS XS from Charlie India 3."

"CI3, Go ahead."

"We're approximately 50 yards to the rear of a white Ford Focus YN 53 NLB. Can you confirm that this is still a stolen vehicle?"

Always better to be safe than sorry as a false arrest can be costly both time wise and financially, mistakes do happen.

"XS to CI3, yes I can confirm it is a stolen vehicle, stolen from a hire company in Manchester."

"Yes Roger XS, does that mean he's forgotten to return it."

"It would appear so, due back yesterday, reported stolen at 5.00pm last night."

Dom dropped the handset in the slot.

"I hate these jobs, poor bloke will never have been in trouble before and we do the work for the Hire Company, because they have dropped a bollock, or they should have been more selective to whom they leased the vehicle to."

Dom picked up the handset again. "XS, just for your information this vehicle is stopping and we are at the 300 meter marker before junction 33 southbound."

"Roger, keep us informed."

Both Dom and Derk went to speak to the occupant of the car and returned a few seconds later.

"XS from CI3."

"Go ahead."

"XS, this bloke appears to be a businessman. He is going to drive the vehicle to the station. We'll make some enquiries at the nick before we arrest him. If what he's told us is true and checks out, he'll have good reason to sue the Hire Company."

"Yes Roger, I'll print the details of the job out for you at the station, if you can just let me know again when you're available."

"Roger, thank you."

"Well at least the ANPR works." Dom said resignedly

"Yes but this will tie us up till meal and then you'll be driving."

"Look on the bright side, if it's as effective as this I'll not be driving for long."

# 6

Paula Gabrielle Horton was what most people would describe as exceptionally beautiful, talented and rich. Her assets had been, and still were her stunning beauty and the ability to talk to anyone and instantly put that person at ease. She was a 'people person.' She loved to be with them and would do absolutely anything for anybody.

She was now the managing director of her own business, which she had built from scratch. Some would say that the foundations were from illegal means but that was just semantics. Paula had a first class honours degree in economics and languages, which she had studied for at Edinburgh University. This was followed by a Master's degree in French. The assumption had always been that within the European community a good translator would always be in demand. Also someone with a good grounding in economics could go far.

Her first job had been working for the civil service, liaising between agencies in France and Europe. She had then become the personal secretary / assistant to the Agricultural Minister. This came about due to the fact that the British government was always at odds with French Governments whether it is over sheep, eggs, beef, or what ever other commodity we could fight over.

By the time Paula was twenty-seven she was well accomplished in her field and had a very bright future ahead of her. It was at this point that things went drastically wrong. One night whilst at an Embassy dinner in France, the Agriculture Minister; Mr. John Alexander Fleming proclaimed his love for her. This came as a bit of a shock to her as he was a married man with three lovely children. He stated he was not receiving the attention he craved and that travelling men and women certainly needed the company of a partner. Paula was flattered by the whole romantic speech but was not flattered when they tried to say good night and he dragged her into the bedroom, gagged her, tied her up and then raped her. She had been scarred for life, and Mr Fleming was now languishing in a French prison near Leon. He had received a twenty-year jail sentence, and, due to the horrific nature of the attack, the Judge had stated that he would not get Parole. The press had a field day. Mr Fleming's family turned their back on him. Unfortunately for Mr Fleming it was inherited family money from Mrs Fleming's side. She had always supported her husband in his political career. It was ironic really because as soon as Mr Fleming went to prison she started running for election in the local bye-elections. Her main theme was family values and women's rights. She did well and the publicity and support for her went a long way and it wasn't long before she became an MP for Kensington, London. She often wrote to Paula, mainly to see if she was well and if there was anything that she could do but there wasn't and Paula had really wanted just to put it all behind her.

At the time of this horrific attack she had been called Paula Jennings. She had changed her name and moved from the city. That was five years ago now and nobody knew who she really was. No one could remember Paula Jennings and she looked nothing like she did when she was attacked.

It amused Paula, because out of the entire sordid affair, came the idea for her company. Initially she had hated herself and men but rather than completely avoiding them she did the opposite and started going on escorts with them, which she deemed an acceptable form of prostitution. She did not hate men but accepted that they had needs and decided to cash in on their weaknesses. In the beginning it was just herself working a lot of hours.

After several years in therapy that she had paid for herself, Paula had managed to get her head around the incident, compartmentalised it and moved on with her life. Her philosophy was not to get involved with men, not that she was a lesbian although she told people she was, it just helped keep them at bay and she did not want the added complication of love. She would know when the right man came along. She also believed that everything happens for a reason and that's why she started a dating agency, although in the beginning she hated herself for doing it, and it was more prostitution than a dating agency. Behind the dating agency was an escort business that was very profitable. She was a MADAM. Her clientele base grew rapidly, and, was now over five hundred in number. Most of her clients are very rich and influential people. Paula's top escorts went on extensive training courses in etiquette, languages, and self defence. This was a must and none negotiable. Her employees nearly numbered fifty and were of various ages, right up to the age of fifty. She only had a couple of men in her stable but she realised that to corner the market she needed to get some handsome men onto the books. Looks weren't paramount, being a gentleman and discreet was.

Paula's role as company director was to hook potential clients and she did that with her grace and charm. Once a client had been out with one of her escorts they often wondered how they had managed without one. Some of her clients were top solicitors, magistrates, businessmen, but all of them wealthy. Either their wives just couldn't be bothered or the clients were single and did not want the hassle of commitment. The clients paid Paula up front. The minimum was £500 a night and the average was a £1,000. In return the client was provided with a date that would have a verifiable cover story appropriate to the person and date they were on.

If the date were required purely for company and friendship purposes the escort would be given the client's hobbies and interests to study so that they could find something to talk about. The date would have time to prepare and do the homework. It was not just a freebie night out. They were doing a job, providing a service. It might be a business lunch and the man wants to appear with someone stunning to take his client's mind off the business in hand.

The date took forty percent of the initial fee, and then, should the client and escort decide to take matters further and sexual liaisons enter the equation, there was an undisclosed fee of £250. Paula did not take any of this and normally the costs would be recovered on the night, but if this were not the case then it would be worked into the client's next fee. Paula always justified the fee with the fact it was a discreet professional service. There had never been a complaint and the business had been up and running for three years. In the first year the clientele numbered about thirty. In the second year they had told their friends and via Paula's connections it was about one hundred. The Business was increasing at an alarming rate but Paula's aim was to top it out at one thousand clients throughout England and concentrate on the escort agency before the whole thing spiralled out of control. Her aim was to be able to provide a quality service and that was where she had the upper hand over any competitors, plus with the contacts she now had she was untouchable in respect of the law.

Last year alone the dating agency netted her £250,000 that was after the overheads, but the competition in this market was now fierce from internet dating agencies and her profits had steadily dwindled, not that she was bothered. The escort agency was a different ball game all together, it was her baby and with no real competition, profits were soaring, especially considering it was the same office space and hence no significant overheads. The training and the background stories were the only real costs. Angelo, a very camp New Yorker is responsible for the background fabrications and loves the role. It's like writing scripts for East-Enders and gives him full poetic licence.

Paula was sat at her desk when the intercom clicked. It was Angelo. "You haven't forgot about Mrs Sewell tonight have you darling?"

"No, I was just contemplating the best route home to avoid the traffic and get ready for the meeting."

"Give her the works honey, she's loaded."

"Been doing your home work on the Internet have you?"

"No not this time, this is a personal source."

"OK give me the low down."

"Just do what you do. She's the tenth richest women in England worth just short of a half a billion, likes riding, society do's and lost her husband ten years ago. She hasn't had a steady relationship since."

"It would be nice to get her onboard, that's my aim, to increase the women clientele."

"Well, hook her and I'm pretty sure she will have some rich acquaintances sweetie."

"You are a mercenary, do you know that?"

"Hey, I just love the work. I write the fairytale plots!"

"Well Shakespeare you better get ready to hook up a good one for this lady. Angelo, I'm leaving now so will you lock up?

"No Problem."

"Are you in or out tonight?"

"Oh it's my favourite TV night, the queer eye for a straight guy; I just can't get enough of the Carson bloke."

"See you tomorrow." And with that Paula was on her way out of the building.

The company was one of a number of offices, set in a little enclave around a courtyard on the edge of the canal. The building had been sympathetically restored to fit in with its natural surroundings. In the centre of the courtyard was a circular pond, a bubbling water feature that always made Paula want to go to the toilet when she saw it. The courtyard was secure and covered by close circuit TV that gave the feeling of added security.

Paula jumped into the Porsche 911. It was her baby, the one thing she had always promised herself when she had enough money. The smell of the opulent leather was divine. The key slipped into the ignition and at the first half a turn the engine roared into life and settled to a deep burbling purr. Paula eased her way from the courtyard and headed for home, she had a couple of hours to get ready, a soak in the bath whilst having one of her favourite tipples, a G and T, before going off to wine and dine Mrs rich pants. That should be fun.

# 7

Whirlow was probably the nicest place to live in Sheffield. The house prices on the streets in the area tended to start in the region of at least a quarter of a million pounds and that was just for a semi. Anyone who was somebody in Sheffield lived in this area. It was certainly the 2.4 children brigade or the 'DINKIES' (dual income no kids.) Most households have at least two cars, very long driveways and every child would have his or her own car parked on the driveway.

Skunk liked this area of Sheffield, although it was clear that he did not fit in, sticking out like a sore thumb, although strangely, he felt at home. The hoity toyti, rich snobs who looked down on people like Skunk, just did not want to confront him in anyway. He was an outcast but that suited Skunk just fine.

It had been a profitable afternoon. He had done a burglary on the low road near the park, a simple sneak in, the back door was open and as far as Skunk could ascertain the owner was either snoozing in the bath or asleep in the bedroom. He did not have the courage to stick his head around the door to find out whether it was a bathroom or the bedroom, besides the sound of the snoring indicated ether the person had a health problem or they were big. The jewellery was all laid out on the dressing table. One gent's Maurice Lacroix watch and a nice gold chain. There was also a gent's wallet, which was even better. Skunk just slipped out one of the credit cards and twenty pounds from the back of the wallet. On this occasion Skunk had his thinking cap on and placed the gold chain and the watch back on the table. He had seen this on one of those crime documentaries. The person who's card it was wouldn't notice it was missing for a while and hence he could have unlimited access to the funds. If he took the property the person would immediately spot this and call the Police. This way he could remain undetected for a while. The other plus was that the signature on the card was such a simple one and wouldn't even take any practice to forge. Keep the levels reasonably low and no one would even carry out any security checks. He had already called at the local petrol station and obtained forty fags, a bar of chocolate and a can of pop. EASY! If only everyone was so obliging thought Skunk, the world would be a lot better place. His second target was an old woman that had been walking towards him. He just walked straight into her. By the time he had picked her up and apologised profusely for his actions he had already relieved the women of her purse. Unbeknown to Skunk at that time it was quite a little haul. He was on a role; the women had got over a thousand pounds in her purse. She was often being told by her grandchildren not to carry that money, but she always said, "You never know when you are going to need it." Fortunately it wasn't her life savings. It was probably a good thing for both of them that the old lady hadn't spotted the theft until later in the day; otherwise she would have been likely to have a go herself.

Skunk was a one-man crime wave and so far nobody was aware that a crime had been committed. He had struck without arousing suspicion, and hence, in his eyes he was having one hell of a good day. The gun had not even left his pocket, no confrontation, just easy money.

It was now six in the evening and it was just about dark when the Porsche came past Skunk. Its indicator was flashing and the car turned left in front of him and headed up the long driveway to the beautiful bungalow at the top of the drive. Skunk watched with eager anticipation sensing another target and rich pickings.

The purring Porsche faded and there was the sound of the door clunking before stilettos could be heard on the cobbled driveway. Skunk casually walked past the end of the driveway glancing up towards the car. Skunk couldn't help but notice that she was a babe. It was what to do next that was intriguing him. Had she got a boyfriend or hubby in the house, or worse still, a dog?

Skunk had a bad experience with a Rottweiler once when he was trying to sneak a handbag out from the side of the front door. Needless to say, the handbag and house wasn't Skunks, and the dog had taken exception to this when it had seen his hand, appear around the door. What had really pissed Skunk off was the fact that the dog had not barked, but, just stealthily walked up and sunk its jaws into his wrist. It was then a tug of war, not over the handbag but the wrist. The dog won, hanging onto Skunk until the Police arrived. Four stitches and tetanus had been required, but no one had any sympathy. Skunk had regretted opening his mouth at the hospital when he had said he didn't like needles. The Policeman had fell about laughing. At Crown Court the Judge even praised the dog and sentenced Skunk to six months in a young offender's institute. Skunk had complained and appealed. That was his biggest mistake, judges clearly hate it when people are undoubtedly guilty and then deny the offence, dragging witnesses to court, so the judge doubled the sentence to a year on appeal.

Skunk had learnt a few valuable lessons from that scenario. One is, when clearly guilty, throw yourself at the mercy of those deciding your fate; they tend to be more lenient in their dispensation of justice and secondly, do your homework more thoroughly before wading in.

Paula was fighting with her keys and the briefcase. The Porsche was tooting and flashing as the alarm activated. Within seconds of Paula dropping her keys on the floor, Soapy the cat pounced at her feet, inter-twining between her legs.

"Soapy out of the way, let me get in and I can feed you."

All Soapy could do was purr and rub himself against Paula's legs.

"Thanks for your help Soapy." Paula scooped him up in her arms and bundled her way through the door heading for the alarm panel. 4455 was quickly punched in and the warning tone stopped. Peace at last as she dropped everything onto the large leather sofa.

Paula's home was very tastefully decorated. Based very much on a New York loft apartment, with next to no walls, all open plan and wooden floors. The kitchen was a beautiful handmade Swedish design, made from solid wood with black granite work surfaces. The kitchen opened out into a large dinning room that then dropped from a raised floor area into a sunken lounge with a central stone island fire. Paula had impeccable, but expensive, tastes. Soapy was now getting truly impatient as Paula opened her post.

'Soapy' had got his name after Paula had found him in the garage covered in oil. She had spent hours trying to clean him, so that she could take his photo and see if anyone had lost him. He was in a sorry state at the time but had been very amenable to getting into the soapy water to get cleaned up which in it self is unusual for cats. From that day on she nicknamed him Soapy never expecting for one minute that she would not find his owner. It had been some months later that she had found out that Soapy's real name was Herbert and that his owner had died. Soapy had run off on seeing the relatives coming to collect him. Paula always thought it had something to do with the three kids they had and Herbert's recollection of their visits when he was with his owner. As it turned out, the family, well the parents, didn't really want him anyway and were relieved when Paula volunteered to keep him. By then Soapy had become used to his name and so it stuck with him. They had been together now for three years and it was clear to see that he was at home with Paula and his lavish surroundings. It wasn't long before Soapy was delving into his favourite meal and Paula was sat in the bath, with a long Gin and Tonic in a tall glass at her fingertips, and her face set in a sea green facemask, which she had hastily applied with all the decorum of a trainee plasterer. Paula had a love for all types of music but tonight she felt in a classical mood and was humming along to

Delibes Flower Duet, planning her evening out totally oblivious to the danger that was lurking right outside the house.

Skunk had been circling around the block and eyeing up the bungalow, he was starting to feel a little edgy as the effects of his favourite sweetie were beginning to wear off. Skunk had decided that there was too much potential in this place to just walk away and he was really keen to see the woman that had got out of the car because she was gorgeous. Skunk had eventually managed to slip into the garden unnoticed by anyone and was beginning to survey his surroundings, planning his next move and an escape route should one be required.

Fortunately for the onlooker, Paula had created the perfect goldfish bowl effect, leaving the lights on and the curtains open. Everyone could see her, but she couldn't see out too well. Paula had never really bothered with the curtains, as she wasn't overlooked by anyone and with such a long driveway up to the house no one could ever see in from the street. Perfect privacy, well that is unless the person looking in is right outside the window.

Skunk had been around the house now several times readjusting the security light sensors. That's why Skunk liked bungalows as invariably the sensors could be reached very easily and now Paula's were all pointing harmlessly into the sky. Skunk had always dealt with the security lights at whatever job he went on, at any cost or risk to safety. One of the funniest things that had happened to him involved a security light, a hammer, a high roof and two Police officers. It had come about because the industrial unit at the end of his road had just had some super new security lights fitted. One of the lads in the Griff pub had offered Skunk twenty quid per light. No sooner had the offer been made than Skunk was off with a hammer and screwdriver to get the lights. The two lights were on each gable end of the building and Skunk had been able to shimmy up the drainpipe on the dark side of the building and then shimmy across the apex of the roof. Unbeknown to Skunk there had been a Police car tucked up behind a skip, with two officers finishing their fish and chips out of sight of the public. The officers were as surprised to see Skunk, the cat burglar, wondering across the roof with the tools of his trade, as he would be to see them. What happened next was even funnier and appeared to be something out of a Laurel and Hardy sketch. Skunk had successfully removed one light already, before the Police had seen him. Skunk had been knelt down, leaning out over the roof apex at the end of the building trying to prise the light off its bracket. Skunk got brave and was really pushing when the law of physics overtook, and gravity and metal stresses played an equal part. The next thing that happened was that Skunk catapulted himself off the roof still hanging onto the claw hammer, which was hooked, onto the light. Quite a gymnastic fete! There was Skunk hanging twenty-foot up in the air, praying the fixing wouldn't give way. By the time the officers had introduced themselves things couldn't get any worse, but they did. Before the fire brigade arrived the fixing broke and Skunk fell twenty feet, fortunately landing in a heap on the grass. To add insult to injury the only injury that Skunk sustained was a head injury when the security light hit him. The officers couldn't stop laughing and if Skunk hadn't have been so winded he could have escaped, because both officers were in tears. Skunk recalled it was the only time he'd had a really good rapport with the Police and he'd been able to see the funny side of it. Skunk snapped out of his little daydream. That was years ago and now he was not a nice person at all. He would rob his own Granny for a fix.

He was highly impressed with what he could see inside the house and realised that this really was his lucky day. The plan was, now he realised that there was no dog, to slip in and do what he had done earlier, pinch a credit card and a small amount of cash and escape undetected. All Skunk had to do was find a way into the house. After trying both doors and finding they were both locked his plan was not quite going as well as anticipated.

By now Paula was out of the bath and sat at her dressing table putting on her stockings when Skunk saw her through the window. What a turn on! This woman had a gorgeous body and in her matching under wear and stockings, Skunk's mind was racing, his thoughts and emotions way ahead of logical thinking. In fact, he had lost track of what he was doing and was quite content to just pike through the window. Skunk couldn't recall the last time he'd had sex. He knew he'd had it, but that was normally when he was off his head on drugs, and couldn't recall it after. Well, he did have a vivid picture of shagging his mate's Mum. She was twenty years older than he was and also on the gear, and she was just happy to get her leg over, as she had so delicately put it. Skunk regretted it as soon as he had done it. His mate had been laughing his head off shouting the whole time "Every hole's a goal! Ram her, ram her." Now Skunk couldn't face either of them and hadn't seen them for months. He was too humiliated and kept hearing the words "ram her ram her". What had happened to him to degrade himself in such a way? What about her he thought? It's the bloody drugs, it's degrading the very backbone of society, and morals have gone out of the window along with manners. Since that occasion, Skunk had sought self-satisfaction. The women were better looking in the magazines. The vivid pictures that he was now committing to memory would make excellent reference material later. Skunk needed to get a grip, his mind wandering and he was beginning to rattle.

Paula was totally oblivious to Skunk's presence and was merrily getting ready pulling up her shear stockings. Her legs were elegant, silky to the touch, and very long. Men would die to get their hands on those legs. Paula stood up and bent over to stroke Soapy. That sight was just too much for Skunk who was now certainly feeling horny. Paula picked up her favourite perfume spraying the Channel Number 5 behind her knees, on her breasts and then spraying it into the air and walking into the mist.

By this time Skunk had totally lost the plot, his mind was completely blown, and he was just about to make the worst mistake of his life. He walked around to the side door and rang the bell. Paula immediately went to the door and without even thinking or hesitating opened it.

SMACK. Paula was hit full on the side of the head with the butt of the gun and immediately reeled back, falling to the floor. The dressing gown that she had slipped on to open the door parted at the middle, revealing all her sexy underwear. Skunk was in the house, but he didn't really know why he was in there. Was it for her? He had just wanted to feel the power and steal something.

Paula was holding her head, but was conscious as Skunk bent over her. Paula returned the compliment. The pain was dispensed swiftly as she booted him between the legs. Skunk doubled in pain. His groin was already badly infected from the injections and Paula had reopened the wounds, and it started to bleed. Skunk stuck the gun to her head and ripped at her bra with his other hand pulling it off. He immediately started to grope at Paula's breasts squeezing them hard in his hand. This was satisfying, but Skunks groin was on fire and he was really pissed off. He wanted to fuck her for doing that, but he couldn't. The pain in his groin was so immense the thought of getting an erection made him feel sick. For once in his life he had the power to screw a beautiful women and he couldn't manage it.

Paula screamed at him "Get the Fuck off me. Take what you want and leave."

Skunk recovered his composure a little and stopped groping at Paula. She smelt and looked fantastic and in the right company, wow! The sexual stimulus would be intoxicating, but Skunk realised that this was not to be a relationship built around love. It was good old rape and pillage but he couldn't manage the rape so he was reduced to grope and plunder. The groping was now done it was time to plunder and escape.

"Where's your cash?"

"I have a twenty pound note in my purse and that's it."

"Bullshit you're loaded."

"That's as maybe, but I don't keep money lying around for exactly this reason, so little junkie shit heads like you can't get their grubby mitts on it."

"Fuck you. You're lying."

"Look for yourself and then leave; you've had your fun."

Skunk grabbed Paula by the hair and dragged her around the house, frantically searching drawers and bags without gain.

"I bet you've got a safe?"

"I have it's in the bank, I've told you, I have no money in the house."

The situation had rapidly deteriorated and Skunk had now added aggravated burglary and was about to add kidnapping to his repertoire.

"Get your coat, your cash cards and car keys. It's time for you to take me to the bank."

Paula dropped the dressing gown on the floor. She wasn't modest about this situation; it was too late now, as she put on her long fur coat. Paula looked at Skunk, who was waving the gun at her.

"Ready darling." she said sarcastically. "Oh and put that weapon down. The gun does work I take it unlike your dick?" Paula was a tough woman, and was not intimidated by this little twerp, but, she wasn't about to take a risk with her life over a bit of money in the bank, especially when her cash card limit on one night was only five hundred pounds. Soapy was hissing in the background but had decided to keep his distance. Skunk bundled Paula out of the house and towards the car.

"Get in the driver's side and slide across," He demanded.

As Skunk was pushing Paula into the car the gun could clearly be seen just as Paula's neighbour walked passed the bottom of the drive with his dog. The Porsche roared into life and there was much squealing of the tyres as the car shot off down the road. Skunk had only driven the car half a mile and had already clipped another car. This was a powerful beast but his driving skills were poor.

# 8

"Look on the bright side Derk, you drove the car, and you got a prisoner within five minutes, so that's got to be good."

"Not from my point of view. I drove the bloody thing for five minutes and now you, ya sporny bastard, have got the rest of the shift left to play."

"Look, stop your bitching, if it's quiet and I get bored then we will stop and swap over for the last hour."

"I'll believe that when I see it, besides by that time you'll probably have us face down in a ditch."

"Look its not my fault, I'm faster, smoother, and down right more aggressive behind the wheel."

"What ever!" Derk said with a resigned look.

Dom pointed the keys at the car and it blipped opening the central locking instantly.

"To be honest with you Derk, this is what the job's all about."

"Well let's have no red mist or they'll never give us anything on demo again."

As Dom turned the ignition key the entire car was an array of warning lights and instruments.

Dom was faffing about with all the seating controls trying to get comfy. As he depressed the clutch he instantly noticed that weight on the action. "You've got to have legs like Arny to depress this thing."

"Probably got some thing to do with the amount of power this thing has, but if you can't handle it then I'll drive for you."

Dom was just about to give Derk a few choice words when the radio crackled into life.

"XS to Charlie India 3 receiving?"

"CI3 go ahead."

"Yes, are you free from the previous incident and available to have a look for a car?"

"Yes, that's a Roger, can you pass the details?"

"Yes, we have just received a call from Whirlow, Sheffield. It appears that a woman has been bundled into her own car by an unknown male occupant and the car shot off at speed."

"Who's the witness?"

"It's a neighbour and he sounded genuinely concerned. He said she looked anxious and he forced her into the car via the driver's side and then made her slide across."

"Yes Roger, did they have sight of any of any weapons?"

"No not at this time."

"What sort of vehicle is it?"

"It's silver Porsche, 911 Carrera, with a registration of Mike Four Delta Alpha Mike."

"Interesting 'Madam' that's what it must stand for."

"Roger we've received that. Has a log been put on the computer for this tracking device to work?"

"Yes Roger, we are just updating it now."

Dom eased the Volvo out onto the main road, what a presence it had, instantly break lights could be seen, this was a mester's car, with loads of street cred; it was the cock of the road. There was silence in the car for a few moments, it was just at the tail end of the rush hour traffic and it was now dark. The streets were a sea of rear break lights and dipped beam. It would be difficult to spot anything at this time of night.

"Oh bollocks, it's starting to rain, that's all we need."

"Look on the bright side; I'd rather be in this with you driving, than in that Porsche in these weather conditions. Because believe me, that thing will be twitchy on the arse end if it's pushed, and at the end of the day if you get behind it, its going to get pushed."

"Do you think that the number plate on the car is going to reflect the character of the lady?" asked Derk

"Hope so!"

"That'll mean she'll be a right madam, a real cow."

"Not necessarily, it might mean that she is a Madam, you know a lady that is for hire, only coming from Whirlow she's likely to be wealthy and good looking."

"Now you're just dreaming."

By now the rain was easing off and Dom had headed towards town in an attempt to try and pick up the Porsche. The Police car was situated in the near side lane of the dual carriageway just approaching a set of traffic lights. Unfortunately the car in front had realised it was a police car and jumped on the breaks anchoring up rather abruptly on seeing the amber light when really it would have been safer to go through, but as it was the Volvo glided up to the rear of the car. A steady stream of traffic was pulling up to the offside of the Police vehicle. Dom looked in the mirror to see the passenger in the car behind pointing at the badge on the car, Dom was watching his lips and although he was unable to lip-read fully, it was obvious what the man was saying, "fucking hell, I bet that flys?"

Derk chuckled to himself as he too had been watching his mirror.

"People just don't realise how lucky we are!"

"The job does have its down sides, you know."

"Yes I know but on days like this it's just great to be alive."

At that precise moment in time, neither the car behind, nor the two officers could have anticipated what was about to happen. The driver of the car behind was about to watch a spectacle that he would enjoy.

"XS to Charlie India 3."

"Go ahead."

"Yes there's been a report of a fail to stop Road traffic accident in town two minutes ago heading towards the Motorway."

"Yes Roger." said Derk

"OH FUCK."

"What?" said Derk nervously looking 'round.

"Look onto the opposing carriageway three cars back in the offside lane it's the Porsche."

"It's a pity that car stopped quickly in front of us we could have gone and blocked him."

The lights were about to change and Dom needed to get the car out of the jam.

"As soon as the lights change to amber hit the full Monty button." The lights went to amber and the car in front on this occasion helped as he had started to creep. Derk hit the full Monty Button and the world erupted.

The Porsche driver had obviously been watching the police car to see if he would be detected and as soon as the lights went on the police car the Porsche shot out of line into the junction. At the same time, the police car was doing a hand-braked pirouette to fall in behind the Porsche. This was game on, who needed the new ANPR; good old observations had found this one. The cockpit of the police car had gone from serenity to instant overdrive as the two worked overtime, Derk was passing a commentary to the control room, whilst Dom was attempting to give chase to the flying silver Bullet.

"XS from CI3 this vehicle is presently doing 70 mph in the offside lane of the carriage way approaching Oldham Road, the lights are on red, and he's breaking, breaking, breaking, and he's through the lights on red. Is the helicopter available to assist with the pursuit, as we will be on the motorway in less than two minutes at this speed?

"XS to Charlie India three be advised that at the scene of the accident in town the driver of the vehicle you are pursuing produced a hand gun, so proceed with caution and try not to corner him until we can get an armed response vehicle (ARV) to you."

"That's easy for them to say but staying with this lunatic is not easy and he's dictating the route."

The controller in the control room caught a glimpse of the downlink from the CCTV; wow they are absolutely flying. It's going to take ages for the ARV to get to them at this rate.

"XS to Charlie India three what's your present location?"

"Yes, we're just coming up to the Valley Island and fortunately he's not got blocked, the last thing we want is him out of the car with a hostage and a gun in a crowded place."

"XS to CI3 unfortunately the ARV is struggling to get to you due to your speed please update ASAP at the island and we'll try to send an intercept from another area."

"He's heading for the motorway, he thinks he's going to out run us, well he'd be wrong."

"XS from CI3 he's gone left under the viaduct, we are heading north at the present time to junction 34 northbound entry slip, can you position the cameras on the motorway for evidential purposes?"

"Yes, Roger."

The tarmac under the viaduct was dry and both cars were doing 120 mph but rapidly approaching the breaking zone for the island. By now the pursuit had been going just over a minute. The actions in the cockpit had started to calm down into a well oiled machine. The car and the two partners were working well. The initial surge of adrenaline had gone and although their senses were heightened the pursuit was now in a safer and more controllable state. They were both going the same direction albeit at high speed, but at least the roads were less crowded and the sirens would give fair warning to unsuspecting motorists. They had to stay reasonably close because it was the Porsche that would hit everything first, the congestion that is, but they too had to be careful it did not appear as if they were pushing the car in case of accident. It was a very difficult situation to call and had it not been for the fact that there was a women in the car who it now appeared was a hostage, a man with a gun, the pursuit would probably have been called off on safety grounds.

The island was not a problem as both cars flew up the long slip road to the motorway. Both cars were doing 80mph as they came off the island and the growl was immense from the Volvo, as Dom pushed it all the way to the rev limiter to stay with the Porsche.

"Knock the sirens off Derk no one will hear them at this speed coming from behind." Derk was struggling however to fight the inertia on the seat belt and the G force to reach the button. The sirens fell silent which just made the car howl even more, and by the time they had got to the top of the slip road the car was doing 140 mph. The Porsche was about 100 meters to the front of the police car and as he hit lane one he immediately veered into lane three of the motorway, followed by the police car. 155MPH the Speedo read and the Porsche was just steadily eking out a bit of a gap. At this speed Dom knew that he needed to be looking half a mile down the road because something would pull out not realising that the car behind was doing twice the legal speed limit.

"At least he'll get a ban if nothing else. You know what the Government's policy is, heavy on the motorist easy on the terrorist! He might even get a verbal caution for the kidnapping."

The humour was welcome, as driving at this speed was tense and fraught with danger. The road spray from the rain earlier was not making the job any easier. Derk was still commentating on the pursuit and they had been advised that the helicopter would be above in moments. This would then provide the control room with a microwave down link so that the Operations Inspector could control the pursuit a little better and at least he could see the road conditions for himself. The ARV was still attempting to cut across country and play catch up.

"Derk, tell the operations room to put the matrix on for the motorway, flashing speed limit signs of 50mph."

"Why?"

"Why? Because someone will jump on the brakes up ahead and we'll be able to catch up a little on him, this distance is too much."

The matrix went on and the success was instantaneous. The motorway slowed down by some 20- 30-mph and this had the immediate effect of some one balking the Porsche. The break lights went on and the Porsche was in a nosedive to shovel nearly one hundred miles an hour off to prevent running up the arse end of the car in front. Within seconds the Police car was on him again and the gap was down to less than fifty meters.

"XS from CI3. Remove Matrix at this time it did the trick we don't need too many scares." At this time the Porsche started to swerve in the carriageway.

"He's toying with the idea of coming off Derk. He's running for the hard shoulder and the slip road, get ready I think we're coming off."

The Porsche dropped a gear and grunted as it hit the entry slip, the car being slammed into third gear.

"He's missed a gear."

As the police car nearly ran up the back end of the Porsche. The Porsche swerved and shot down the embankment back onto the motorway and into the outside lane again, the police car continued onto the island and back down the slip road falling in behind the Porsche as the pursuing car had maintained its speed and momentum. The growl of the engines was deafening as both cars accelerated back up to 150 MPH. Fortunately with the traffic on the motorway it naturally allowed the police car to stay with the target car. The one-mile marker shot past in a blur for the Barnsley turn off taking just twenty-three seconds to hit the entrance for the exit road. The Porsche was still in the outside lane and it was suddenly clear that the tactics had changed. The Porsche driver jumped on the brakes and fortunately the Volvo was just far enough behind to brake in time without running up the back of the Porsche. The back stepped out on the Porsche as it headed for the slip road, virtually doing a ninety-degree turn and narrowly missing several other vehicles. The Volvo weaved its way through the almost stationary traffic, and up the slip road, just in time to see the Porsche turn left on to the main route out onto the Pennines. The Porsche driver was now desperate, he must have thought he was going to outrun the Police, but with no such luck, and if truth be known the longer it stayed like this, the greater the chance of all the other units closing in.

The fine drizzle had stopped but the road was still damp and there appeared to be a slight mist in the air. It was an eerie scene as both cars sped along the main A628 towards the Pennines.

It was stalemate and the Porsche needed to do something special to escape. Things had become routine in the Police car and all the training was beginning to pay off. The Armed Response Vehicle was still playing catch up, but the helicopter was now locked onto the target vehicle, which took the pressure off Dom and Derk. They had done an excellent job in hanging onto the car to allow other specialist units to come and help.

The plan was about to change again. The Porsche veered hard left down a dirt track heading towards some woods. The driver had obviously realised the helicopter was above him and had decided he would take his chances in the wood. Little did he realise that the heat seeking infra red pod on the helicopter would track him and he could not escape. The road was a mixture of dirt and gravel and it was starting to become over hung with trees. The speed had dropped off and then the dirt track opened out into a large gravel car park. The Porsche started to spin as it skidded to a halt. The Volvo had stopped at the entrance to the car park to prevent its escape. Dom and Derk could see some frantic movements in the Porsche, which was turned sideways onto them. The offender was attempting to drag the woman from the car by her hair, and she was putting up more than a little resistance to this. The helicopter was hovering high above, and the entire car park was lit up with a million-watt candle bulb from the Police spotlight. Once Dom had realised that the driver of the Porsche was getting out and attempting to make a run for it he started to creep towards them. The scrunching sound of the gravel under the wide tyres could be heard in the car, however, from the frantic minutes before everything was serenely calm in comparison. Skunk probably couldn't hear the car moving due to the noise of the engine on the helicopter.

The offender appeared from the car and both officers would have described him as a stereotypical drug user. He had long greasy blonde hair in a ponytail and looked very thin and gaunt in his face, wearing extremely scruffy, dark clothing.

"I can see the gun." Said Derk

"XS from Charlie India Three be advised. I can see what appears to be a small handgun, Silver in colour, and looks like a modern gun with a clip. Unable to tell whether real or not but the offender looks well agitated."

"CI3 that's a Roger. We can see him from the TV satellite down link, you are too close to him back off just in case."

"Roger, but what about the hostage?"

The gunman's arm was swaying, pointing first at the woman, then the police car and then the helicopter although every time he looked skyward he seemed to get blinded. The gun was pointing at the helicopter and then there was a single crack. The gun was real, and he had fired. This man had lost the plot, and he was prepared to use it. The woman was still kicking and screaming as he started to drag her away from the Porsche. By now the helicopter had retreated to a safer distance, but the light that was bouncing off the trees was casting an eerie shadow over the scene.

The gunman levelled the gun at the car and several single cracks were heard. The windscreen exploded as several bullets ripped through it and struck the intended targets. Either he was very lucky or an expert shot. Derk was hit in the shoulder and Dom was hit in the head, a glancing blow, although there was a lot of blood. The gunman was desperate to escape, and his attack on the woman clearly ill thought out. The woman fell to the floor still being dragged by her hair and the Volvo was steadily inching towards the gunman, although he obviously did not realise it. Doms face was covered in blood and his vision was blurred by the cracked windscreen and the blood in his eyes but he could make out that the gun was being levelled at the women's head.

Red mist had descended, flight or fight? This was definitely a fight to the death. High stakes. The accelerator was floored; the growl was immense, like a wounded animal that had felt the pain, the roar of the attacker, gravel fountains as a result of the charge. Man and machinery with one sole intention. Death. Whether the woman had sensed the instant dual or Skunk had refocused on the car, but the result was Paula broke free. The gunman was startled, like a fox caught in the gaze of the headlights, turning the gun on the Police car again. Skunk got off several shots. Dom however had got one shot and his bullet was a lot bigger. The impact was hard and low on Skunks body, as he attempted to dive out of the way. No such luck as the Volvo collected its prey and rammed it, crushing the life from Skunk against a large Sycamore tree. The air bags exploded in the car protecting its occupants, but the team had done its job. The hostage was alive and in one piece, if not a little traumatized. The two police officers were alive, just; Derk was unconscious and slumped in his seat. Dom was fighting it, hanging onto the images, he couldn't be sure he had taken the gunman out, but he had. The Volvo had rendered the killer lifeless, scrunched, crushed, and pinned to the tree. Swedish engineering meets English forestry.

Dom was trying to hang onto consciousness; a red veil of blood running across his eyes. He could hear his Sergeant's voice, "Don't prang the fucking car." But he'd more than pranged it; He'd killed it! In an eerie kind of silence as he could hear the helicopter droning above the door to the car opened, he turned and tried to focus, the smell of Channel wafted into the car, but it was the face of an angel, this was it, he'd died as his slumped forward into her arms.

"This isn't going to T-cut out!" was all he said before he too could not resist the tranquility of unconsciousness.

# 9

The buzz had been tremendous, he had played her like a cool cat, he'd stalked his prey driving past several times so that she would know he was looking for business and also think that he was too scared or nervous about approaching her. The encounter with the uniform had been a stroke of genius and the Police would start to feel uneasy about the investigation and what it was going to unearth. Would they go at it full throttle or just back off for a short time so that they could re-check the facts and look at the evidence pointing at an enemy within.

He'd been so cool with Trish at the first encounter when she had thought he was a Police officer and he had done nothing to dispel that theory or encourage it. Well okay maybe he had embellished it a little but so what, he could. He was the bad guy!

He had soon realised that bad guys don't have to play by any conventional rules they just do what they want to satisfy the lust for gratuitous violence and sex. He presumed it was the same for a robber or a fraudster. They did their own thing weaving delicate and intricate plan and plots to achieve their own goals.

He had read with interest the article in the paper that morning about the girl being left for dead and the story of how she had come to be on the streets although every different paper had a slightly varying account. He did not care, she was scum and that was that. It had gone onto say that this was one of several attacks that had occurred recently. He was so pleased he was getting some recognition for his work. He was pretty sure that the public would back him. They were vermin after all, selling their souls to scum. Obviously he wasn't scum but he needed to pretend to be so to be able to get near to his prey. His hunger for another attack had come from the satisfying victory and the sound of bone cracking when he had kicked her the previous night. Delicious! Tonight would be the special one, the one that was going to be his first example of how disgustingly cruel he could be. The others had just been a warm up, practice run although he was ruing the missed opportunity the previous night. He knew in his heart of hearts that he should have finished the job off properly but he needed for her to tell the police about him.

He was deep into the territory of the Yorkshire Ripper as these where his old stomping grounds. In fact he was pretty sure that the officers that caught the ripper still worked round here. What a challenge, could he do it? Could he really become an equal? He knew he would have to be far more careful due to the advancement in crime investigation techniques and evidence. That DNA stuff was a real bind.

He had gone out early and decided to park up near to the Fat Rascal pub. His car looked like it belonged to one of the punters in the pub. After finding a dark and secluded spot with a decent vantage point he watched as the working girls went to work, plying their trade. It looked like it was a busy night with plenty of punters on the street. This concerned him greatly, there were too many witnesses, if he struck now someone would spot the car, or give a good description, no, to strike now would be reckless. He was thirsty for another attack but not foolish enough to get caught so easily. He was about to leave, the prowling attacker had surveyed the scene but did not like the hunting ground. It was at this point that he noticed a new girl, some what removed from the others. Perhaps it was her first time he thought to himself, now that would be an intriguing proposition, first time and she gets blooded, beaten to a pulp, now that would make a nice little trophy.

As he started the engine he looked again just to confirm where she was stood before he worked his way down towards her. She appeared nervous but that was not what was concerning him. What was she doing? She was talking to herself; perhaps she was singing or something? The attacker turned the engine off and waited. Something was not as it should be. As he watched intently he soon realised that she was no sewer rat, but the rat-trap. He watched her closely and every time a car pulled up she immediately spoke after they had left. The attacker moved location and sure enough there they were, two cars tucked up the back street adjacent to her pulling the punters as they left.

The sneaky fucking bitch, the man returned to his initial vantage point and continued to watch the proceedings. He was having bad thoughts now, dirty thoughts about what he could do to this young sexy policewoman. Before he'd even realised it he was cuming into his own hand. He had spent several minutes working up to frenzy as his little plot unfolded in his head. The final twist of the knife in his head had lead to the first involuntary spasm as the waves of euphoria and pleasure washed over him. It was time for him to go home and back off for a while. He would play them at their own game, cat and mouse. He knew who would get bored first, they needed a result, he could just bide his time, but one thing was for sure, they would regret making him wait. He knew that his next victim would be a sacrifice and he would show no mercy.

# 10

$\text{T}$hud, thud, thud, thud was the dull feeling that Dom had as he started to open his eyes. His head was pounding and he felt extremely groggy, probably a combination of the anaesthetic, drugs, and all the excitement. As he tried to force his eyes open and focus, he was confronted with a mirror image. It was Derk in the opposing bed to him, but he was still asleep. Dom's mouth was dry and he felt sick all of a sudden, as he realised the horror and the enormity of the incident and how lucky they both were. Well considering he thought he'd died this was a definite improvement. Dom pressed the buzzer and a nurse came in, all smiles. 'Hero for a day' thought Dom; best make the most of it.

"Could I have a nurse, please water?"

"Of course would that be a fizzy nurse or a still one."

"A fizzy one please............ I think that came out wrong didn't it?"

"Yes, but that's just the anaesthetic wearing off."

"How's Trouble over there?"

"He'll live, besides he won't be able to compete with the number of injuries that you've sustained."

"Typical?"

"He's got one bullet hole, albeit very nasty and you, my boy, have three."

"Three............that's just down right careless."

"I was speaking to the policeman outside. He say's that when you hit the man with the car, it would appear that the gun has gone off again, and a round shot through the radiator grill, bounced of the engine bay and hit you in the chest just to the right of your lung. Fortunately it had lost that much momentum it just hit your rib and got lodged."

"Lucky old me! Well head and chest makes two what about the third?

"Oh it's a mere flesh wound." Dom could see by the bandages, easy presumption as to which arm, his left one.

"Great...........lucky me!........... What day is it then? How long have we been here?"

"It only happened yesterday and it's now ten at night."

"What, twenty four hours?"

"Yes."

"Has he woken up at all?"

"Yes, but he's on morphine as the bullet broke a bone in his shoulder. He woke at three this afternoon and then dozed off again."

Dom looked ashen, the thought of nearly getting his mate killed was sinking in and the shock of the incident started to set in. The nurse must have seen the distress in Dom's face and put her hand on his.

"He'll be fine, you're a bit of a celebrity you know, both of you are. You're on the front page of every newspaper."

"How's the woman?"

"Very upset and worried sick."

"How do you know that?"

"Because since the Police finished taking her statement last night she's been permanently camped outside the room."

"This room?"

"Yep, this room."

"Wow I've never had a fan club. "

"She's been keeping the Policeman Company that's guarding the room."

"Why have we got a guard?"

"Reporters have wanted to talk to you, and to prevent any of this and their sneaky little tricks, you've got a guard."

"I bet he's pissed off, baby sitting"

"No, say's it was his day off and he's getting the overtime."

"Good for him."

"Would you like to see the lady?"

"I'm not sure I look my best."

The nurse fixed Dom a drink and helped him with it, she was right. He had been shot in the chest, because when he tried to move he could certainly feel the pain.

The nurse left and the room fell silent. There was then a feint knock at the door, as it was eased open. Dom was instantly stunned by her beauty and thought it was a dream. She was about thirty-five, tall, 5'7 maybe, and slim, but with a curvy figure. Beautiful, straight dark hair, with a gentle face and sparkling eyes. Wow, she was elegant and stunning. Other than any mental scars she may have had endured, she certainly appeared to be in one piece.

As she walked towards the bed Dom couldn't help but notice that she was starting to cry. A tear fell from her face.

"Come and wipe your tears on my bandages."

The woman smiled and sat beside the bed and took hold of Dom's hand; she was half laughing, half-crying. The shock was also affecting her, and Dom could feel her shaking like a leaf.

"I've thought about what I would say to you all day, and worded it many different ways. You don't know what it means."

Dom took his hand and put it to her lips as if to stop her saying what she was about to say. Dom smiled at her and shook his head slightly.

"You don't have to say anything."

Dom tried to ask if she had been injured but Paula just sobbed, no one had ever risked their life to save hers and they were strangers at that. Her emotions were in turmoil; she felt proud, safe, protected and loved, something which she had not felt for a long time.

She took hold of Dom's hand and pressed her face into the palm, kissed it gently and rose to leave.

"Your friend is very gracious."

"Who? Derk."

"He say's if anyone else had been driving I might not have been here today."

"You can't say what if, just be thankful we're all alive. You've spoken to him then."

"Yes of course."

Her voice fell to a whisper as if no one else should hear and she lent back over Dom and whispered in his ear. "You're his hero too."

She gently kissed him on the cheek and turned to leave

"Your name? I don't know your name!"

"Paula." She cleared her throat and tried again. "It's Paula"

The door closed and the room fell silent, bar the odd monitor, checking on blood pressure and heart rate that was merrily beeping away. At last he was on his own with his emotions. Dom replayed the conversation in his mind and was overwhelmed by her beauty. Never before had he felt so proud. Maybe neither Derk nor he would ever say it to each other's face, but in Dom's heart, Derk was his hero too. After all he was his best friend.

Dom was laid in bed pondering what had happened to his bullet-proof vest. He was sure that he had been wearing it at the time of the incident, but he couldn't remember whether he had zipped it up as he'd got in the car. It was normal for him to travel in the car with it unzipped because it was uncomfortable to drive in. The real answer was that his vest had been partially zipped but as the car had struck Skunk the gun had gone off. Whilst the bullet was travelling through the engine bay the airbag had exploded on impact with the tree which had catapulted Dom forward into the airbag. At the moment he had hit the airbag with his head, the angle of his body had been tilted totally forward and the bullet had travelled down the inside of the vest towards the chest cavity. An inch either way and the bullet would have been in his head or his heart. He was a very lucky man; he just didn't realise it yet.

# 11

Paula hesitated as she stepped into the corridor; she wanted to ask a difficult and personal question but just didn't quite have the courage or know how to phrase it. Paula had been at the hospital on and off for the last few days and had seen Derk's wife on several occasions but not Dom's, her foot was just about inside the ward door when she heard voices. She could not be seen due to the curtains and slipped inside and sat at an unoccupied bed. She pulled out her mobile and put it to her ear just in case someone looked in and wondered what she was doing. The fact of the matter was that she was ear wigging.

"Come on tell me?"

"Tell you what?"

"Why you've got fucking suicidal tendencies and why you got me shot?"

Derk was smiling at his friend.

"Dom that was a really close call."

"And another thing the next time you go trying to get us shot, I want the low down on why your marriage went tits up first, else if you're dead, how will I know the gossip."

"Do you really want to know?"

"Well there's bugger all else to do in here!..........Come on then tell me the juicy stuff. My impatience has got the better of me. What really did happen between you and Claire?"

"This isn't easy you know just bearing your soul. As I've told you before it's embarrassing and degrading."

"I'm sorry mate, I don't mean to pry."

"Yes you do, but its okay...............Well you know the sort of hours she works, she's up at six thirty and back anytime between seven and ten at night, and okay, I suppose it goes with the territory, director at thirty, which is bloody good going, but where do you go from there?"

"Downhill?" interjected Derk.

"We have no kids, good wages and to be honest we had a good lifestyle and to a certain extent I always accepted that she needed to put in the hours. It was a function of who she was and what she did. That aside it did not mean that I liked the situation. In the end it must have been the old classic tale of everyone else knowing apart from the injured party, Moi. And to be totally honest I had no idea. With Claire being the young up and coming executive I always accepted the travelling, the business meetings, the courses and the time spent on conferences in London. When you work for one of the leading Blue Chip companies in the telecommunications area you accept it, even if you don't like it. It's all job related you tell yourself. You know no better, and never have cause to question the obvious. Do you know what really pissed me off?"

"What?"

"Well considering it was a communications company, she would go away maybe twice a month, saying 'oh I'll give you a ring when I get there.' This would change sometimes to 'I'll give you a ring after the meal in the evening.' And do you know how many times she contacted me? Not once! I should have seen it coming. Always the same bloody excuse the phone didn't work or her battery was flat. Or she thought it was too late to ring. I was sat at home, whittled silly thinking something had happened, when really, she was getting boned silly. And what really hurts, I always believed her. I suppose the last thing you want to do whilst shagging the boyfriend is break off and ring the husband, kind of breaks the atmosphere I would have thought. Oh just hang on a sec while I ring my Policeman husband. Not really the turn on you're looking for is it? But I was so bloody foolish and blind. It couldn't happen to me, not charming little old me. The, 'all action cop hero husband'. I must have been looking the other way when the bus hit me. But that's life. I used to go to bed at one am in the morning, and then at seven am she would ring me, always with a good excuse. I never thought anything of it at the time; it's amazing that all the phones always appear to work in the morning. I always accepted without question the reason. I trusted her. I suppose when you have a good sex life, you think you love each other and on the face of it you're both pulling in the same direction and appear happy you never question it, why should you?"

"So how did you work it out?"

"I couldn't really believe it myself, but there I was sat at home with a Stella watching some program with Samantha Janus. She was a woman who was seeing a man behind her own husband's back. The sister found out and she started seeing Samantha Janus's hubby and everything just went pear shaped. So there I was sat thinking, I appear to be missing something here. My mind was off into overdrive. Even a Pentium 4 would have suffered attempting to assimilate all that was going through my mind. So off I went upstairs. Well because Claire had gone on a course she had not taken her brief case. A quick delve into the back revealed two very interesting receipts, hotel receipts, and both for dates when I was on evenings. The receipts showed that the invoice was paid in cash with Claire's registered number on the bottom. I was like a guided missile straight to the evidence like I was supposed to find it. It was one of those really horrible sinking feelings. I can hardly describe the turmoil it puts the body through, but feeling instantly nauseous, the stomach churns. I would imagine it's like holding a valuable ornament at Christi's that's worth two million. Then, just before it goes on sale, you pick it up, and in full view of everyone you drop it on the floor. Time travels in slow motion and it feels like its taking ten years to impact. You can see it falling, but no matter what you do you just can't stop the vase hitting the floor and shattering into a million pieces. Shame soon falls upon you, and your life is scattered everywhere. You can stick it back together but it will never be the same again. So there I was stood in the bedroom and I'd just dropped my life on the floor and it was in pieces, to be honest I had no idea what on earth to do next. I tried to ring her mobile with no joy. I felt like shit and I had instant diarrhoea. I sent a pager message that remained unanswered. I wanted to fight but I had no one to fight with. They were the longest hours of my life just waiting. I had no idea who it was, only my suspicions. Nervous energy, shock, call it what you like but rest assured the body will not allow you to rest under those circumstances. So it was time to act. The messages being unanswered just convinced me of the infidelity, but at that time I had no proof. The receipts could have been explained away with a little effort. But I still had this gut feeling I was right. Like the time when you get behind a stolen car, you know before you put the blue lights on what is about to happen. Trust your natural instincts, they're usually right.

I rang the hotel where the receipts were for, and explained that I was due to meet my colleagues in the morning and that they said they were travelling up the night before only I had forgotten which accommodation they were stopping at. I gave Claire's name and the man who I thought it might be, but to no avail. I tried all the local hotels and travel lodges in the vicinity without gain. So I then got the car out and physically went and checked the car parks just in case they had used a different name. Everything turned out negative, until I was just about to give up, when, out of the corner of my eye I saw her car parked in the corner of the Trust House Forte Hotel at Worksop. She had obviously used a false name as they were paying cash. And this was the one that they had used on the previous occasion. I used the mobile and again rang the hotel. I spoke with the same girl who was very helpful. I told her that I had found my notes and that this was definitely the right place. I also explained that the reason I had not given the right name was due to the fact that they had just got married and I had given her maiden name and I couldn't remember for the life of me what her husband was called. So I made it easier for her and gave her the registered number of the vehicle. Straight away she said "Oh Mr and Mrs Timms." They have just gone to bed.' I thanked her and said I would be there shortly. So there I was sat in the car park wondering what on earth to do for the best. Do I charge in and beat the crap out of him or do I do nothing? I was aware that I might really lose it and put my job on the line. Funny really, I wish I'd hit him. But the professional in me came out, and this inner calm took over. When I walked into the foyer I thought the receptionist was going to give me some hassle about giving out the room number but as soon as I showed her the badge she let me through. I explained we were operating a sting operation. She must have thought I meant that they were my colleagues. She didn't realise I meant with her. I stood outside the door, initially I was trembling but then again I recovered my composure and knocked on the door. I disguised my voice slightly, saying I had a message for Mr Timms. I was trembling and excited at the same time, it must have been the adrenaline buzz. On one hand I just wanted it to be someone else. Just a great big mistake; yet on the other hand I wanted to find out the truth. I hate deceit and lying. I can take anything but that. I always prefer the truth no matter how much it hurts, then at least you know where you stand and you can go and get on with your life, and ultimately they can get on with theirs without having to go behind your back. John as he was called shouted out "who is it?" Game on, I thought, because I certainly recognised the voice. I'd met this bloke before remember. Some works do at Christmas as I recall.

I'd shaken his hand and thought what a wimp. "It's Mr Simkins the hotel manager." I replied. "I have an important message."

"Hang on a minute," Was the reply. Well what must have been going through their minds god only knows? Well when the door opened you should have seen the complete and total look of shock and horror. It was his worst nightmare and I just waltzed into the room. He went so pale I thought he was having a heart attack there and then. I nearly called the paramedics. Well these older guys, they might be able to take one kind of pressure but when it comes to the crux of the matter he was done for. Literally caught with his pants down.

"Oh shit," was all he could say.

"Surprise, Oh, I think you better buy a map because you're supposed to be in London at a conference. Can't miss it, it's that big capital thing at the end of the M1 or were you just stopping for fuel?'

Claire's head appeared from under the sheets. She went to get out and it was then that I noticed that she was wearing a baby doll outfit that I had never even seen before. I couldn't help myself then and ended up having a go at her.

"You lying deceitful cow." I blurted at her. "How long as this been going on then?"

John made the mistake of telling another porky or two trying to convince me it was their first time. It didn't bode too well when I produced the receipts from the previous occasions, which silenced them both.

"Would that be the same man then or different ones on the previous occasions?"

There was stunned silence in the room.

"All I want to know is why?"

"He was there and you weren't!"

"But he's twenty years older. It's like shagging his daughter for him. Or do you love each other?"

He was just sat on the bed shaking his head. I'm sure he was expecting me to knock his head off. But I was totally composed. Gutted, but, with it.

So at this I produced one of those all situation grabbers, so that it makes it easier when you go to court. I took out the camera and before they knew what had happened I had taken two pictures.

'Don't bother coming home tonight. Give me a day to clear my stuff out. Buster comes with me. The house is yours I hope you will both be very happy together.

With that I turned my back to them and walked out. When I got in I opened the bottle of brandy, read the Sheffield Telegraph and saw the cottage advertised. Got up the next morning made a few phone calls and the rest is history. Left my wedding ring on the table on the way out. I toyed with the idea of trying to patch it up but I would never have trusted her, so it was best to call it a day and move on. Get on with my life."

"What did his wife do?"

"I honestly have no idea. I never told her. Why destroy her life too, she's done nothing wrong. I found out it wasn't his first affair and if she would have found out he would have been homeless. I suppose what you don't know can't hurt you, and you never know if I had not found out then things would have been different, but you certainly cannot live on what ifs, only facts.

Paula was distracted by the nurse who was pushing the medication trolley into the room; this was the perfect opportunity as she had the answer to her question. Paula dropped her phone in her Prada handbag and made like she had just swept in behind the nurse. "Ah my hero's are both awake and looking better than ever," as she planted both of them a kiss on the cheek and then started to devour the bowl of grapes that was on the side. Paula's mind was in turmoil, she almost wanted to cry as she left the hospital that evening. She was stunned at the tale of a fallen marriage and lost love.

# 12

Dom had been off work a month and he was bored, he needed to get back to work and soon. Buster had been walked off his little legs and was ready for some peace and quiet. Dom had called on Sharon on several occasions just for a little TLC, but at forty quid a chuck he had to be careful with the money, so he had limited himself to one visit a week. Unfortunately he had only seen Sharon last night and all of a sudden it felt like it was going to be a long week. He couldn't even go for a pint with Derk, as he was a way on holiday recuperating in the sunshine on some beach in Tenerife. That's what he needed a holiday. Dom decided that maybe a trip to town, admire the sights have a beer and maybe bump into a few friends would be the order of the night. Thursday night in town was always good for a bit of totty spotting. That was the unfortunate thing about living so far out in the countryside that Taxi's cost a bloody fortune and hence he was forced into having to drive.

I f Dom had of been at work then he would have known about the new GATSO camera that was situated at the end of the parkway. He wasn't speeding excessively but he was speeding. He was sure he'd been doing 47 in the 40's but it was all academic. The quick flashes in succession told Dom he'd just spent sixty pounds and accrued himself three points on his licence. Could anything else go wrong? His appetite to go and have a drink was diminishing and he was definitely low on cash now. His mood had gone from being quite bored to despair and depression. He didn't feel up to socialising or the ribbing he would take for going through the camera. No he had other plans and headed away from the town.

# 13

The desire was back and stronger than ever, the urge to purge the streets of another sewer rat, to inflict some serious pain was overwhelming but now he just needed to pick himself a suitable target. It had been a while since he had cruised the streets but after his last attack he had felt the urge to strike again but the sight of the Police operation had made him cautious. He had realised that the heat was on and it would be best to lay low for a while. There had not been any attacks now for nearly five weeks and the police were probably sure he had moved out of the area and he was also sure that the attempts to track down the attacker had become pretty low key. He was sure that they would not associate the prank he had played on the WPC with the attacks on the prostitutes and felt confident that that little rouse would have been one of her colleagues playing a nasty trick on her. The sight of a blown up sex doll with a chocolate dildo stuck in it's mouth on her doorstep would be more in keeping with a childish prank than an act of a deranged sex attacker, but he knew deep down that the officer would have been disturbed by the finding. Of course no one would admit to it, how could they? But she would have doubts, well, that was the whole point and should she continue to play her games on the street then he would consider her to be one of them and she was entitled to the same treatment.

The rouse of the attacker had failed miserably and the police had been more professional than he could have believed. The Doll had been recovered instantly and examined forensically. Alas there was nothing that would give them a lead. The doll could have been purchased in a thousand different sex shops or via any form of mail order, believe it or not they were very common items, normally sold for stag parties so it had been a dead end. The police had issues that were concerning them. Was it a hoax and the offender just didn't have the balls to stand up and be counted or was it genuine? Until the former could be proven then it had to be treat as a real potential threat to one of the officers. It had already been muted that the offender had worn a uniform and as such this lead them to their own front door.

Covert cameras had been fitted at the officer's home and although she didn't know it she had a surveillance team attached to her 24/7, she undoubtedly would not have been impressed at this but it was for her own safety.

The main dilemma for the officer in charge was whether he should leave her in the field, so to speak. If the attacker was an officer then he would not go near her in the street and it would be more likely an attack near or at her home. If the attacker was not an officer how had he tracked her to the house, had he followed her straight from the street, had he followed her from the station? Fuck, did he know she was an officer or did he think she was a prostitute? Detective Superintendent Ross sat with his head in his hands rubbing his forehead trying to second guess what was in the mind of an unknown attacker. He had decided that he couldn't take the risk of using her again.

If it was an officer he would know her and steer clear. No this time he had called in a couple of girls form the undercover vice unit in West Yorkshire.

The girls had been out there three times a week for the last five weeks but not a sniff, nothing and the frustrations and costs were escalating. Maybe they had been isolated attacks? Or maybe the attacker was just too closely attached to the police and knew every move they were making.

Imagine the surprise of the attacker to see yet another police officer purporting to be a slag of the night. He had been convinced that by now the intensity of the search for him would have waned, they were only scum after all, and who gives a fuck if a prostitute gets beaten? The error on his behalf had been the prank, this had given the police the incentive as no one attacks it's own.

Again it had been the way she had talked into thin air that had given her away, but rather than him getting excited he had become frustrated and angry. They have no idea who they are messing with. Knowing exactly which station they would be working from he went and parked up near by, he would wait, imagine what little scenario he could and would play out. The only thing he needed to be was flexible and bide his time. It was only a matter of time as he watched the two girls walk from the station. This didn't look too promising as they were both heading for the same car. Bollocks, no wait they've stopped next to one if they were leaving together they would be in one by now. Perfect now it was just a matter of which one. Imagine the power to know that some one's fate lies in your own hands. One will get home safely, the other, well, who knows?

# 14

By the time Dom had read the evening paper it had already been on the news and the police had not been able to hold back much of the story. That would really frustrate the investigation, but the attack had been in such a public place. All that was known was that an off duty Police officer had been travelling home along the M1 back to West Yorkshire, and for some reason, stopped just prior to the slip road at junction 40. The reason was unknown but the body of detective constable Louise Reagle had been left at the bottom of the embankment. She had been badly beaten (No details divulged) but she had not yet recovered consciousness and at the current time was lying in a coma in hospital.

The Police had been careful not to divulge what she had been working on but initially they were not sure whether the operation in South Yorkshire was linked to her attack. It was best to assume nothing at this time but work on it as if it was. The news had been a hammer blow, totally unexpected, but more perplexing was why had she stopped on the motorway?

It had taken several hours for the Police to come up with a plausible theory but it was only when the accident investigation officer had been asked to attend the scene in daylight that a reason for the detective stopping was put forward. The assumption was that she had been followed, and if that was the case then they could now link this case to the attacks in south Yorkshire as that was what she had been working on. But, if she was being followed then she would never have stopped on the hard shoulder if some one was flashing her, nor would she have pulled over to a parked car. No, that was definitely not it. She was a Police officer; she knew the risks of stopping in your car on the motorway. No, the only reason she would have stopped is if she had witnessed some incident and had stopped to help, or had she been stopped by a marked police vehicle. The ramifications of that were too dire to even contemplate.

The AIB officer had found tyre marks on the road indicating a car losing control at speed, swerving violently in the middle and offside lane of the motorway, and heavy breaking veering across to the hard shoulder. The tyre marks on the road were broken which would be consistent with a vehicle fitted with ABS, pulling straight into the hard shoulder. The theory hence that she was followed and at the appropriate time the car has sped in front simulated a blow out or what the officer would have thought to be a blow out or some other emergency and she stopped to help, Viola! It would have all appeared innocent until she was struck at point blank range.

One could assume that other vehicles should have passed them and there may be witnesses, but at three in the morning who knows?

Another theory put forward was that there were two attackers. The attack had taken place else where and the vehicle driven to its current location. The body quickly dumped and both then left the scene in one vehicle. Initial forensics had refuted this as an option as there was no blood in her vehicle which would have been expected unless the blood was in the offender's vehicle. Too many theories and not enough answers. The investigation was leaving too many unanswered questions. The only thing they knew for definite was that the car that had swerved on the road had ABS breaks due to the broken skid pattern. So they had that and a tread pattern but that could have just been a genuine incident over the last few days, maybe they had a record, but worse still maybe they didn't.

This investigation was under the jurisdiction of West Yorkshire but by the end of the day a team of detectives had been sent to work in South Yorkshire. The series of attacks linked and a sadistic bastard out there that could be a Police officer. The attacker had made a mistake and that was that he had left the poor girl alive. There was a professional witness; however in her current state when that information could be gleaned from her was an open question and that's if she would ever recall anything.

# 15

Click................The operator was stunned by the call she had just taken and sat motionless for what seemed like an eternity. Pam was an experienced Police control room operator and had worked in the force operations room for nearly ten years but this call had spooked her because she knew that without question, the call to be genuine. The office was a hive of activity, with people beavering away at the phones and computers all oblivious to the call.

"Inspector Woodward, I think you better come and listen to this call "

"Is it urgent? I'm just going to the loo."

"Oh yes, I think you'll want to hear this."

Pam was already reloading the taped phone message from the digital encoder and placing the audiotapes in to make a copy of the call.

"Come on Pam, play the message, I'm busting."

Ring ring …….

"Good morning South Yorkshire Police, Pam speaking, how can I help you?"

"This is a message for the officer who is investigating the series of attacks on the prostitutes."

"Would you like me to put you through to him?"

"No, no, I haven't got the time to hold on, just tell him that there will be another attack tonight on another prostitute, and that the person responsible is an officer"

"A police officer?"

"Yes police officer!"

"Can I have your name and telephone number as we will need to speak to you further?"

"Sorry, I cannot give you those details, making the call is dangerous enough and if he finds out then I dread to think what he'll do to me."

"How do you know it will happen tonight?"

Click……

"That's it Sir."

"Right, find me anyone with rank connected to this and preferably yesterday, while I go to the loo."

Not more than twenty minutes later they were all together in the conference room and the tape was played again for the benefit of the new listeners. The voice was, without question, frightened, hesitant, and there appeared to be nervousness in the way she spoke, but maybe that was just due to the nature of the call. The voice was very softly spoken; she sounded almost angelic, of an innocent nature. She sounded as if she was middle aged and the voice was accent less, possibly as a result of a lot of travel when she was younger and, or, a good education. The tape ended and the assembled listeners sat motionless and stunned.

"Oh bollocks," said the DI.

"What is it?" asked Inspector Woodward.

"Well without doubt there was something about that call that just screamed at me that the information was genuine, don't you agree?"

"Yes that voice was screaming for our help if you ask me!" said Pam.

"Well my lot will love this, everyone's going to be on overtime to catch this bastard, and we haven't got a clue where he's going to attack next in Sheffield, and boy, is it a bloody big area to cover."

"Look on the bright side, at least it should be a face someone will recognise." said Pam

"Oh I hope the voice is wrong, because whoever is responsible for those attacks is going to be in for a real hard time. They will be lucky to get out of prison alive. Imagine. Being a copper in prison is bad enough, but one that has nearly killed a Police woman and then four Toms. Oh well, think of the detection's, five serious assaults, this boy could get twelve years for this little lot." The DI was talking and moving at the same time now as he had an operation to plan and quickly.

"I know I haven't asked, but do we have any way of contacting the women or tracing the call at this time?"

"'fraid not."

"Thought not, oh well, let's hope we can nail him." Said the DI

Detective Chief Superintendent Ross was sat at the back of the room. He appeared to have the worries of the world on his shoulders. He said nothing, but something was not right.

# 16

"Good evening ladies and gentlemen" bellowed the Detective Inspector at the assembled group of detectives.

The wall behind the inspector showed a large map of the area to be covered. Surrounding the map were pictures of the first four victims and an arrow pointing to the first point of contact with the attacker.

"Right then, listen in. I know it's been nearly a week since DC Reagle was attacked and you've all been working flat out, but things are about to change. As you well know we have an unknown male attacker out there and the descriptions that we have been able to gather from the victims suggest that he is male white, approximately six foot tall, about thirty five to fifty five years of age, and considering that he has had contact with four women and they have all lived, the description is pretty fucking thin to say the least. Well ladies and Gentlemen, as of three pm today, the list of suspects narrowed dramatically to 2556. And by that I mean we have received information that it is a police officer responsible for the attacks. I know we have known about the uniform for a while and we were concerned how the attacker knew about DC Reagle? But this may just help tie it all together."

The room was silent before the statement but then the mutterings began, that is until the tape-recorded message.

"So no daft questions you all now know as much as I, however the twist is that the press have got a whiff that something is in the air so they will no doubt appear if an arrest is made so be on your best behaviours. We can only cover so much of the area so we have ten fixed observation points all to be double crewed and three mobile units again double crewed. No Police radios are to be used at all unless in extreme emergencies and at the point of arrest other wise we could spook him. You have all got mobile phones, but again, do not use them unless it is an emergency or you have seen a possible target. If you sight a target in a particular area ring the nearest observation point in sequence of the direction in which the person is travelling and try and obtain photographic evidence if possible. Hopefully any arrest should be without a struggle considering who we are potentially dealing with, but at the end of the day take no shit. Any questions?"

"How reliable is the information? Have we been able to confirm the info by some other means?"

"Unfortunately we have not been able to do either but due to the serious nature of the crime we must assume that the information is reliable at this time, possibly from a frightened spouse or girlfriend. Lastly get your self a drink and I want you on the plot by 7.30pm. and for fuck's sake be vigilant we might only get one shot at this. Oh and word of this does not leave this room or you'll find yourself back in uniform for the rest of your service."

"Sir, you said a limited suspect field of 2556. I take it then you are assuming he's from South Yorkshire or do you know something we don't?"

The Detective Inspector did not respond, as he walked off to his office, he couldn't. This was one aspect of the case he had not even had time to really consider, but he knew that he should have. There was the West Yorkshire element and now he was beginning to worry that the reason why the young DC had pulled over on the motorway was a simple answer. She had known the attacker. Then there was GMP or Derbyshire Police, they both bordered South Yorkshire and had easy access routes to the city and the areas where the girls had been attacked.

He sat in his office pondering the question but it was no good. It was too late now to get any spotters from other forces and anyway it would be a chance occurrence that the offender would be seen. No they would have to go with what they had got, and pray for a little luck.

# 17

Maybe Dominic had just been unlucky, because it was not he that was recognised, but his car parked on St Swithens road. A quick call to the control room revealed that it was Dominic's car, and that he lived some ten miles away. So why was it parked in the street in the middle of town adjacent to where the majority of the Toms work? The call was made to the Inspector. In view of the fact that it was now eleven-o clock at night and no one else had been seen, it was time to decide whether to concentrate in this area.

The decision was an easy one, and after a few quick calls to the intelligence office, seven addresses were given out to the teams for observations. Unfortunately only two of the fixed observation points covered these addresses, which meant resorting to mobile observations.

Another hour passed and without a sign of their new suspect and fortunately they had not taken any calls via the control room to say that some one had been assaulted elsewhere. The tension was mounting and the DI feared the worst that some one was about to become another victim. He was frustrated that there was nothing else they could do.

"SOD IT," shouted the DI. "Total change of tactics. Lets send a couple of officers to each address, we don't need a search warrant because we want to arrest the bastard and if he is present at any of the addresses, arrest him for GBH and rape."

The decision was a decisive one and acted upon swiftly. It wasn't long before the police were knocking on Sharon's door.

Dom was spread eagle on the bed, whilst Sharon tormented him by playing typewriter on his head and chest.

"Shit," said Sharon "Who is it at this time?"

"Are you expecting anyone?"

"No you're my only customer tonight!"

The bell kept ringing.

"Persistent whoever it is, I think you better go and see before they wake the whole street."

As Sharon wrapped her silky bathrobe around her she bared her cheeky bottom to Dom as she left the bedroom laughing at him laid star shaped in the bed.

"Don't be long its cold with out you."

"Oh shut up, you know that I don't charge by the hour, you've got me all night."

Sharon slipped back the bolt on the door but left it on the chain. As she opened it slightly, she could see two men in suits and one showed her his identification badge. Not that any was required, we all know CID when they knock on the door.

"Sorry to trouble you Sharon, but we fear that you may be in danger." Said the DS

"What do you mean?"

"Have you got someone in with you?"

"You know I have, you bastards. Been spying again?"

"It's for your own good, can we come in?"

"Have you got a search warrant?"

"Sharon we don't need one as we believe you to be in real danger so it would be better if you co-operate with us, we're not here to arrest you."

"You better come in then."

"Sharon is Dominic Veil here?" That hit home hard, a police officer in her house, a direct hit and they had said she was in danger. What the hell was going on?

"Yes he's in the bedroom."

"Has he assaulted you in any way?"

"Don't be silly! We are talking about Dominic"

"Well unfortunately we need to speak to him and we will need a statement from you stating your relationship with him and how often you have seen him, if you have seen him before including dates and everything."

"What is this all about?"

"It's about a series of assaults on prostitutes and at the present time we need to speak to the man in your bedroom."

"Oh this is just a load of pants and you know it."

"I hope it is Sharon because I know Dom very well."

DS Evans and DC Rudge made their way to the bedroom where Dom was now sat on the side of the bed fully dressed.

"I heard all that downstairs fella's so don't bother repeating it. You'd be wasting your breath."

"Sorry Dom but you know how it is we have to do it officially. Therefore, I must tell you that you don't have to say anything but it may harm your defence if you do not mention when questioned, something which you later rely on in court, anything you do say maybe given in evidence, do you understand?"

"Of course I understand. I've probably said it more often than you two."

"YES WELL YOU'RE UNDER ARREST ON SUSPICION OF ASSAULT AND RAPE ON FOUR SEPARATE OCCASIONS."

Dom was silent and stunned, that had knocked the wind out of his sails. He sat frozen on the bed, he had not expected that and he obviously had not heard all the conversation downstairs.

"Is this a set up, are you winding me up?"

"No afraid not Dom, this is for real."

As they made there way down stairs Sharon looked utterly perplexed by the whole proceedings. "I'm telling you gents, I am a good judge of character and you have got this one all wrong."

Dom leaned across holding her hand and kissing her gently on the cheek "It's okay, I'll see you later, tell them whatever they need to know."

As they left the house the Flash was telling and immediate; the press was already there.

"You bastards, you have set me up." Dom gave the royal wave to the press, which would probably appear on the front page of the local daily paper in the morning.

Dom was whisked away to the nearest Police station and at the present time it appeared as if he was in a whole load of doo doo. He had been arrested for four serious arrestable offences, but most of all, he hoped he would be given the opportunity to clear his name, because there was definitely some weird shit happening and he didn't yet know why but someone was pointing the finger at him.

# 18

The interviews were interesting if not very enlightening. Dom co-operated fully telling them everything he could about the nights in question. Fortunately when the police went to take a statement from Sharon she had kept an accurate record of whom she had seen and on what nights which took Dom out of the equation for at least two of the attacks.

Dom could clearly understand why he was in the frame and although he was with Sharon on the dates he also knew it would not totally clear his name. He was the number one suspect at the minute. His brief had been given some disclosure and Dominic read from the pad. On the face of it he agreed he did look guilty.

I was all circumstantial and although a good starting point for the police they were along way from making a case with real evidence. But Dom had easily been able to account for several issues but others had left him unable to give a reasonable account. He was a Police office with a uniform. Well we are no good without them! One of the attackers had specifically mentioned a uniform. Dominic's car was a saloon, with full leather. He was now car-less whilst the police did all the forensic tests on it.

He was in town the night DC Reagle was attacked. This was known due to the speeding fine and the GATSO picture of his car. No one else could assist with his whereabouts. He knew where officers would live, collar numbers and be able to gain access to such details although there was nothing on the system to say he had checked, no audit trail, but that didn't mean it hadn't happened. It would have been so easy for him to leave the Blow up doll at the officer's house.

No attacks whilst he was in hospital.

He was found at a prostitute's house.

T hey had not told him about the tip off, that might put someone else in danger and the police really needed to find the source to have any chance of making any allegations against Dom. It all fitted apart from the fact they had no concrete evidence, was he being set up? Was he a part of it? Was there more than one attacker? It was no good; they were simply just finding more questions than answers. The good news was they had a suspect and hopefully forensics would turn up something. From Dominic's point of view to prove beyond all doubt that he was innocent.

Complaints and Discipline had also been quick to attend at the station and suspend Dom from duty and ban him from any police building; he was now on the other side. It did not help when the superintendent dropped the morning paper on the desk, and the morning Headline read.

POLICE ARREST ONE OF THEIR OWN FOR RAPE.

Underneath was a beautiful picture of Dom giving the rods to the local photographer?

"Bet he earn't a pretty penny from that shot? Said Dom quizingly

"Even if you didn't do it sunshine I think you're out of a job." Said Superintendent Marsh from the rubber heelers.

"Any good news?"

"No not at the minute."

There was a gentle knocking on the interview room door and the DI walked in. "Can I have a quick word with you Sir, there's been a development." Dom couldn't help but notice the angst in his face.

It was shortly after that Dom gave a sample of DNA and was released on bail to return to the Police Station at a later date although they could arrest him at any time should they find something concrete.

Dom left the Police station in a state of shock. He had been suspended on full pay, well at least for the moment he had an income. His actions last night had been foolish, not the Sharon thing but rodding off the press and he knew it, but that wasn't the reason he was stunned. It had been the last thing the Detective Inspector had said to him before he left, that had been the news that had really pole-axed him. Dom was deep in thought as the man bumped into him. Dom turned to look at him and was just about to walk into the trap.

"You're Dominic Veil?" The man said.

Dom was in no mood to play games with this man.

"Yes I am."

The man instantly stuck out his hand towards Dom as if he was going to shake hands and then pushed a letter into his hand. It was from Claire's solicitor. It was funny really when Dom read the letter. It was a non-molestation injunction that had just been served on him. An injunction, which meant he couldn't go near Claire or assault her in any way. Dom didn't even want to speak to her, let alone see her, but Claire had seized the moment and she was intending to make him pay the solicitors fees and use this incident against him in court. By now she would have told her solicitor he had assaulted her on several occasions. It was a real crock of shit. She was now intimating that Dom had been seeing prostitutes before she had started seeing the other man.

Dom stood in the street laughing at the man who turned away from him and walked off. The laughing turned to sobbing. The injunction was a joke, the fees were a joke, it meant nothing, he was glad to be rid of Claire and now he was at the point were he didn't even mind paying. None of it mattered any more. No, he was sobbing because of Sharon. The Police had returned to see her this morning to find her body at home. She had been murdered, how? Why? What For? When? He did not know. At least he wasn't the suspect. But at that moment in time Sharon had been his only emotional tie with any one. He was on his own isolated and emotionally wrecked.

Dominic's thoughts were not for himself, but for Sharon's two little boys. What the hell had happened, and how could things have gone so drastically wrong, the police were with Sharon until 2.00am taking a statement to get him off the hook, but she really did get him off the hook when she was murdered whilst he was being interviewed. Dominic was hoping that the murderer had left some form of DNA at the scene, linking the series of attacks and explaining what the hell was going on, but he was unsure if the Police had any forensics at all. They hadn't pushed the DNA with him in interview, in-fact they hadn't said anything which probably meant they didn't have any. If they had the attackers DNA and suspected an officer they would have already run it and cross referenced it with the officers DNA already on file, so that wasn't going to save him.

Had she been killed because of him?

Was it connected to him?

Had the police jumped too soon thinking he was the offender?

Why was the press there so quickly, and who tipped them off?

And how did the offender know that the police had left Sharon's house?

Something was seriously wrong but now he had been suspended he would not be privy to any of the investigation.

The DI was equally perplexed by the night's events but he knew deep down that Dominic was now innocent, and he also knew that the caller had been extremely accurate with the offender's intentions. The main concern was, would the caller be the next victim, because things were certainly getting out of hand, and she was probably the best witness they had if they could only find her.

# 19

Detective Chief Superintendent Keith Pemberton Ross, better known as Rossy to his friends, was sat at his desk, feet on the window ledge looking out over the city centre of Sheffield from his fourth floor office. Today had not been a good day and valuable time had been lost messing around with Veil that had caused the attacker to kill and make the entire force look dilatory. It was not the Police's finest hour and he was really pissed off. He threw down the evening post on his desk with disgust.

The phone rang and after two rings his secretary picked up the call.

"Mr Ross it's your father."

"Oh fucking great," thought Rossy, "that's just what I need."

Most people would only be too pleased to talk to their own fathers however in this instance Rossy's Father was also the Assistant Chief Constable and his Boss.

Arthur Ross had been the ACC for the past five years and was well past his sell buy date, he should have retired before he even got the post. It had been a job for the boys, and greed had got the better of him. Unfortunately it had held the force back years. He was out dated, not up to speed with the current trends in management styles. The only thing he could do when the chips were down was to pull rank and shout louder than the other man. Today it is called bullying. Fluster the opposition even though he was normally in the wrong. All wind and piss. It was well known that Rossy just wouldn't spare his father the time of day at work, yet out of work they were the best of friends. It was an agreement they came to, else they would have long since fallen out and that would have been the end of the relationship. At least once a week the two of them liked to go fishing and then for a pint together. Work issues are just not discussed and this relationship works well.

Rossy, unlike his father, was actually a very talented Police officer. It's the norm for most people to get promoted on the back of other people's success but not in this instance. Ross's successes over the years had given more power to his father's elbow and actually it was role reversal. Rossy junior should be the ACC, but at this rate he would definitely make Chief Constable before he retired and it would be on his own merit and achievement. If Rossy had been a criminal he would have been a very rich man, because there was deviousness to his mind that gave him the lateral thinking ability to second guess the opposition and attack them. He came up with motives that people would never have thought of, which invariably would shoot enquiries off at a tangent. Crime held no boundaries, no frontiers, in his field as a modern criminologist he was way ahead of the rest. But still the bosses would be reluctant to go with him due to the costing implications of the investigations, but invariably he was right and he got results. Call it a gut instinct but he had the mind of a criminal, and it was fortunate he was one of the good guys else he would be sat on a Bahaman Island with his own yacht by now having conned a few people out of millions of pounds. It was his destiny though to champion the course of justice.

"**G**ood morning Sir." said Rossy.

It was unusual for him to call his Dad Sir but they were at work and it sets a precedent and shows respect. Well that had been the theory. Most of the time it just depended on what mood he was in, as to what he called him.

"You can call me Dad this morning; I'm ringing about our day off. Do you fancy a game of golf this week?"

"It's a bit difficult at the moment this Veil thing is causing me some grief and now it's a murder, well, I just don't know when I'm going to get the time."

"I've got a meeting with the Chief in an hour about this; I'll ring you later when I have briefed him. Anything new I should know about?"

"No Sir," It was work again. "I'm literally baffled on this one, I thought we had him."

"Maybe he's got help."

"Yes, and maybe we are barking up the wrong tree."

"Speak to you later son, bye."

"Bye "

Rossy spun around on his chair to see the picture of his wife on his desk, Abby. Boy she was gorgeous, but things just weren't going too well at the moment. It was a function of the job. Police officers and marriage just did not mix well. It was a volatile mix of cocktails, which normally ended up in divorce. There wasn't one of his friends that he had joined with that was not on their second or third marriage.

Most would be using their pension lump sums to pay off the mortgage or would have to work after retirement to pay off their debts. Rossy had been reasonably lucky. His first wife had run off with another Policeman whilst he was knee deep in a ten million pound fraud investigation. This was one thing he had never even seen coming. It would have been difficult to see it coming however, when he wasn't at home. That enquiry had taken the best part of him for eighteen months. Constantly travelling onto the continent and working long eighteen-hour days. It had done him two favours, got him promoted and he didn't have to pay the solicitors costs of the divorce. It was a lot better in the long run. His wife had been lonely, what was she supposed to do? They went three months without sex, and that can be hard on both parties, so she had looked elsewhere, and ended up doing more than window-shopping.

It had worked out well though, because his secretary at the time made an immediate pass at him. Eighteen months on they were married. In the beginning things had gone really well, especially as there were no big cases for him to work on. The trial had come and gone from the fraud job and all parties involved had got five years imprisonment. It was only when the appeals started that problems had begun at home. Abby had left the job with the Police and had taken a course in interior design. She had her own business that was doing very well.

The pressures of the appeals had really taken their toll and Rossy had hit the bottle. He was disguising it well and no one knew, apart from Abby, who had been on the receiving end of a drunken stupor brawl, and after fighting like cat and dog he had done something he had never done before. Struck her. Rossy shook his head, it was no good sat at his desk wallowing in self pity he had to get on with sorting things out. They needed a break on the attacks and now the murder. He set about the statements again, just in case there was something that he had missed. That was why he was so good, most investigators would rely on being briefed, but Rossy always went through the statements with meticulous detail, and invariably he would spot something that everyone else had missed.

The phone rang again and this time he picked it up. "Superintendent Ross speaking."

His secretary was ear wigging at the door; she hated missing the phone call but on this occasion she was on her way back from the canteen, she liked to know who was calling. Just nosey, but it's always nice to be in the know. It's amazing how much you can learn from a one sided conversation.

"Yes I Know, I'm sorry."

"Did I?"

"Have you told anyone?"

"I don't remember doing that."

"I'll make it up to you I promise."

"I'd had one or two but not that many."

"I'll see you later then."

The phone had gone dead before he had the chance to say goodbye.

His secretary knocked on the door. Well seeing as how she was stood with her ear just about on it she thought it best to see if the man wanted a coffee. Especially since it had sounded like he had just been given a bollocking and had to eat a bit of humble pie.

"Can I get you a coffee?" Marge said as she stuck her head around the door.

She immediately saw Rossy with his head in his hands. He looked pale and sweaty.

"Are you alright Sir?"

"No I feel shocking. Can I have a glass of water and some headache tablets please?"

Marge dispatched herself without hesitation and was back in less than a minute with the said items.

"Come and sit down on the sofa Sir. You really do look terrible."

"I'll be fine in a minute, it's just." Rossy couldn't speak he was quite shocked.

"I'll go and get you a coffee as well. Don't you move Sir."

Rossy just sat on the sofa stunned by the last conversation. He remembered arguing the other week and getting into a physical fight with Abby but that was two sided. This time he couldn't even remember what they were arguing about. 'A black eye.' She had said. He really did go over the top.

Rossy needed help and quickly. He couldn't even remember getting drunk last night.

Arthur Ross was sat in his office flicking through the paperwork on his desk when the Chief buzzed him to say he was ready for their meeting. Art, as the Chief and the other ACC's knew him, was not really looking forward to this. The previous Chief had appointed Art before he had left. It was nailed on for him and life had been easy living on the successes of his son. The previous Chief had only been too happy with the situation. Unfortunately the new Chief was big into Best Value and everyone pulling their weight. Unfortunately, Art did not understand the modern day politics of policing. He couldn't go to a meeting without shouting at someone if things weren't going his way. Yet he was also too far detached from proper policing. It had been twenty-three years since he had been on the streets. Pre PACE (Police and Criminal Evidence act 1984). The days of putting the prisoner in the cell until they confessed to something had long since gone. Art had always been brave in a group of Bobbie's but he had never arrested anyone on his own, a startling fact, but true. If that were to happen today the officer would be on reports for lacking moral courage and motivation. How things had changed.

Art picked up his paperwork for the 'morning prayers' as they were called with the Chief. He hated this, because the Chief would ask him all sorts of questions he couldn't answer, and the Chief would know he couldn't answer them. That's why he asked them. Art also knew what the Chief's ploy was; he wanted Art to ask for his retirement. Well that wasn't going to happen. Art would go when he wanted to. Regardless of the fact that he was useless at his job, he still enjoyed the status of the role that he played and frightened all the staff, a true bully. Alas things had backfired at home because he had treat his wife the same way and in the end, after thirty years of marriage and without warning his wife just upped and left. Not before she dropped the divorce papers on the kitchen table and told him he was an arse. Art walked into the Chief's office. It was like a lamb to the slaughter.

Rossy sat there nursing his headache and the panic attack wondering what on earth was happening to his life. What no one knew, absolutely no one, was that he knew the murder victim. Explaining this one could be very difficult. Maybe he never would have to explain that he knew Sharon. He had to hope that his detectives weren't that thorough and would miss the fact that he used to see Sharon on a regular basis. The only thing in his favour was that Sharon had taken a liking to him and had put his name down as someone else in her book. He would be impossible to trace in the enquiry. He knew she kept the book. He had met Sharon when they were carrying out the fraud investigation. One of the offenders, a solicitor, had plenty of money to throw around and he threw quite a bit in Sharon's direction. He had seen her maybe twenty times over a three-year period. But now the person on the tape had said it was a Police officer, things were going from bad to worse and the net was closing in on him. Due to the publicity surrounding the attacks, he had been throwing money at the case to try and solve the problem. He had thrown as much money at the problem that you would a murder, and then all of a sudden it was a murder and they hadn't even started on that properly. This case was going to be costly in more ways than one. If it ever came out he was seeing Sharon suspicion would fall on him. At least he could kiss goodbye to his career prospects and probably his marriage. People were expecting miracles on this case and they had their best man on it. Unfortunately the best man couldn't think straight because he was trying to keep himself out of the mire.

His own private world of 'thoughts' were shattered when the door flew open.

"Dad, Sir." Stammered Rossy

"What the fuck's going on?" shouted Art.

"What do you mean?" Rossy was flustered, was the game up so soon? Had he been spotted? All the time trying to put all his thoughts to the back of his mind, at least so he didn't look guilty.

"What do I fucking mean?" This was an Art speciality "I'll tell you what I mean hot shot. Fifty six thousand pounds, one arrest, one innocent man released five assaults and now one FUCKING murder." Art was really screaming and any signs of Rossy's headache abating had just gone out of the window.

"Tell me we have something up our sleeve on this one because from what I can see we have Jack shit. The costs are escalating and we have no answers and no plan."

"Well we have a plan, or should I say had a plan, only it's gone to rats."

"Well you'd better get on the job and sort it. And quickly before there's a post for ACC advertised. The Chief's just chewed my nuts."

"It's............"

Art cut him dead. "I don't give a flying fuck who you think it is, just catch the bastard and put it to bed." Art turned on his heels and marched out of the office. Rossy shouted after his father but it was wasted, he was already gone.

"We have to have evidence unlike in your day when you made it fit."

"Marge can I have some more tablets please? Just fetch the bottle."

Rossy just needed five minutes to get his thoughts together, he needed to think clearly, like he used to, it just required some lateral thinking. Rossy was playing the tape over and over in his mind. The voice was familiar but he couldn't place it. He'd known last night that something was out of place…….. But what?

"Oh Fuck no…!"

Rossy ran over to his desk and played a copy of the tape again. He was distraught. His day was going from bad to worse. Just take all the pills he told himself, it would be easier than this. The voice on the tape, although disguised somewhat, was Abby. He now knew that she doubted him. She thought he was the attacker, the man doing the assaults. He had listened to that tape a thousand times and only now did it all fall into place. He was in a bit of a tight squeeze on this one. Abby doubted him and he'd even assaulted her last night after the call was made, she must have found out somehow that he had been seeing Sharon. He couldn't even push the point with her in case she called the police again and this time gave his name. Rossy was walking a tightrope. The sort of tightrope that makes people do silly things. No! Suicide wasn't an option, he would be announcing himself as the clear suspect and the pieces put in place after his death would just nail him. It would ruin his reputation and his Father's and he had done nothing wrong. Well apart from working too hard, drinking too much and punching his wife maybe once or twice which was the problem because he couldn't remember last night. God he wished he could remember. It was down to him to catch the killer now because if any of this should get out then he was ruined, clearing his name would be impossible. Shit sticks.

It had to be Veil, or, surely he was the key. The enquiry was now in it's infancy as a murder enquiry. He had twenty detectives on the case working around the clock. The bill for this one was going to be huge. It was no good he would have to go to the murder scene. It was risky in case someone recognised him, but no one would be expecting the Detective Chief Superintendent to be involved, no one would be looking at him. Well that was the theory. It was a well known fact that most people could not pick the offender out of a line up just after the incident had happened so if they thought he was a police man then they would not and could not assume he was involved in the whole nasty proceedings. It was a risk he would just have to take. The big advantage was that if forensics found anything he could claim he had contaminated the scene. Certain evidential matters may however be difficult to explain, very difficult!

# 20

The Detective inspector was fuming. Nothing was going their way. They needed a break in the murder case and nothing was forthcoming. The report from the science laboratory had been inconclusive. Well it had been conclusive in many respects but not in the way the Police wanted. The profile was shot. The DI had just spent thirty minutes speaking to the

Professor on the phone. It had been explained to him but he was no scientist, it was way over his head.

"Get DC Ward in here," shouted the DI. He was in a reel grumpy mood.

DC Ward was on the fast track promotion system; he would be an Inspector within five years and possibly a Superintendent within ten years. But it was his degree in Microbiology and his clear knowledge and understanding of DNA that the DI wanted to talk about.

"How can I help, Sir?"

"Tell me about DNA."

Wardy lunged into an explanation of the human cell; its genetic makeup and chromosomes.

"The fundamental building block of cells and the key structure to all cells is the DNA. It controls everything about us. DNA is short for Deoxyribonucleic acid. A DNA structure is made up of a three dimensional double helix."

Wardy was drawing pictures on pieces of paper and had everyone's attention.

"When people suffer from certain disorders like haemophilia, it has been proven to be a break or fault in the genetic code. The makeup of each individual is unique and more distinctive than any fingerprint. Because it is in all cells, it can come from anywhere that was made up of a cell, saliva, blood, faeces, hair and skin. That is why it's so good evidentially. The method that we use involves a process that allows the double helix to part. Depending on the type of DNA it can be done by heating the DNA and then adding an acid or Alkali to ionise it bases."

"What the fuck, are you on about?"

"It's like Ice Sir. You heat it up and simply the structure breaks down. There are many different ways to do this procedure but the main aim is to build a map of each person's little nucleotides."

"Like a computer program."

"Just like a computer program, without one little part there will be a defect. It truly is an amazing thing and now we are that advanced that we can manipulate the genes and alter the DNA structure, making crops stronger or more disease resistant. The structure is sequenced and shown on an Auto radiograph."

"Like a bar code?"

"Exactly, like a bar code."

"Okay Einstein, what does this report mean in respect of the two samples that were sent to the lab?"

Wardy studied the scientific report and then concluded. "Right, the sample from the attacks on the prostitutes is that of a males DNA. Veils sample does not match this. The sample taken at the murder of Sharon Norburn, from under the fingernails is only a part code, but it doesn't appear to be the same as the first one"

"How can you have a part code?"

"Well over time DNA breaks down, the cells disintegrate but in this case the victims hand had fallen onto the sun bed. Cells mutate and break down under UV or Infra red light and hence in this case you have only got a part DNA sequenced code. However what you have got tells you that it was not Dominic veil."

"Well we knew that, he was at the Police station when she was murdered."

"Oh and one other thing." Said Wardy.

"What's that?"

"DNA will instantly show what sex your assailant is. That is due in part to the X and Y Chromosome."

"Enough, stop right there while I still understand what you have just told me."

The DI wasn't as daft as he was making out, and he had understood in chief the main components of the report. It was the part about the incomplete sample that had foxed him but now he had it sussed, and besides Wardy had explained it much better than he ever could to the rest of the team.

The DI turned to his DS, "Just confirm with the lab that they will be cross referencing all the officers that work for the Police, and any partial match we need to know ASAP"

"Boss you do know that there is still a loophole?"

"What fucking loophole."

"Well everyone that joined after 1996 has it taken as a matter of course. Anyone that joined prior to this meant it was not compulsory. We had no power to take it and although some gave it voluntarily many refused."

"How many will we have on file?"

"Best guess thirty to forty percent, but remember the age of the attacker is not likely to be a recent joiner if it is one of us, hence unlikely we will have his DNA profile. Gut feeling boss it's just a wild goose chase, I think our man's too cute for that."

"Just make sure we check what we have got, tick it off the list. I better ring Rossy and tell him the good news, we have two attackers! But the big question? Are they working together, because that would certainly help explain the attack on the West Yorkshire Detective? Sometimes the more we find out the worse it gets."

# 21

Dom was sat in bed. Curtains open, looking out across the open countryside reading the morning paper. The Thursday edition of the Independent always had a jobs section, but nothing seemed very attractive. He hoped that he would keep his job but he knew it was extremely doubtful. At the side of the alarm clock was Dom's bail sheet. He was due to answer his bail on Monday at 10am. It was not particularly something he was looking forward to, but he hoped that the matter in relation to the assaults would be sorted one way or the other. The Police were probably waiting on the DNA tests before taking the matter further.

Dom had spoken to Sharon's sister yesterday on the phone and she was now looking after the children, she now had custody of the children. Dom reflected that it was best that they move to Cheshire with Linda and start over and try and rebuild their lives. Dom had been surprised when Linda had told him what Sharon had left in her will. Obviously her occupation had paid well. Oh well at least the kids could be taken care of properly. Linda had explained how she had put some of the money in trust for when they reached eighteen, which would allow the investment to grow and the rest was to be used for their education. Dom had only met Linda at the funeral but she had promised to keep in touch and keep him updated on how the kids were doing. Deep down he knew he would never hear from her again, why should he?

The knocking at the door interrupted Dom's thoughts. Buster erupted into a string of barks that were merged into one. Dom peered out of the window to see the unmistakable image of a CID car. Dom's heart missed a beat. Now what? Had they come to arrest him again?

Dom opened the upstairs window and looked out over the two officers. The Detective Inspector investigating the assaults was present and Superintendent Marsh from Complaints and Discipline were now staring up at him.

"Down in two seconds just putting my clothes on."

"No problem, we'll wait in the car."

"Does that mean a trip to the station?" asked Dom tentatively.

"No, not at all, take your time."

Dom was caught off balance at how co-operative they both were. They must have a hidden agenda thought Dom.

Two minutes later the men were sat in Dom's lounge drinking coffee.

"Dom, the results of the DNA have come back and you will be pleased to know that you are no longer under investigation for the attacks on the prostitutes, and you are certainly not a murder suspect." said the DI

Immediate relief set in, at least they had told him straight, no stringing it out, and obviously some DNA forensics had been found somewhere. At least he was in the clear, well from any criminal proceedings.

"May I ask then what's happening with the enquiry?" After all he was still a Police officer at the moment even if he was suspended, and Sharon had been a friend, a very close friend.

"Basically son, very little, descriptions of the actual offender are poor. We know he wears what we believe to be a Police uniform, drives a big car with leather upholstery."

"Might be a Police officer but the chances are it is someone impersonating an officer." said the Superintendent

"Problem is Son, we now have a different issue. The DNA from the murder scene and that which we obtained from the sex attacks are different. They are different people. The reason why Sharon was murdered is a mystery at the moment, the motive is unclear, well it's not unclear, we haven't got one. We all thought they were linked and worked off that assumption, but now it looks like our job has escalated into two jobs."

"Oh" Dom was wondering what possible motive anyone could have had to kill Sharon. It simply did not make sense.

The Superintendent broke Dom's train of thought.

"As you are now no longer under investigation for a criminal matter we can deal with the disciplinary aspect of your suspension. The conduct un-becoming of a Police Officer in relation to the press pictures and likewise, with the Sharon issue. In view of what you have been accused of I have got to advise you that you are entitled to seek legal representation to represent you at the hearing. The date has been set. Three weeks today. Here's your formal notice of the hearing. You have fourteen days to reply to whether or not you will be legally represented."

"The fact that you have offered me legal representation for the hearing intimates that the Chief is considering sacking me or asking me to resign! Is that correct?"

"Yes I am afraid it is."

"Then I can tell you now that I will be legally represented."

"By whom?"

"I haven't got a clue yet but I'll find one. Do you need to know prior to the hearing who he or she maybe?"

"No, that's not important. However, should you choose legal advice then we normally consult with a legal representative prior to the trial so that we are not disadvantaged in any way."

Dom thought, 'well you're holding all the aces anyway.'

The Superintendent asked if he had any questions about the hearing, which he had not at that time, but was advised that he could contact him at any time if he needed to know anything.

The Detective Inspector thanked Dom for his co-operation in the other matter and both men excused themselves and left, thanking Dom for the coffee.

As the door closed behind the two men, Dom reached for the Yellow Pages. It was time to find himself a solicitor. He had a trial in three weeks, and the odds were looking decidedly dodgy.

# 22

The knocking on the front door was persistent if not bloody annoying

"I'm coming, keep your hair on"

Bang Bang Bang

"Are you completely deaf? I'm coming."

Bang… "Give me a minute you impatient sod."

Dominic opened the door to be greeted by a huge cheesy grin from his mate Derek

"Good morning." Derk said, barging his way past Dominic and heading for the kitchen.

"What's good about it? The bastards are going to sack me"

"Oh stop being so positive, you never know they might make you stay and that would be worse."

"At least I'd be paid."

"Look you can't be so sure that they're going to sack you, there's plenty of other options open to them."

"I don't think so especially considering what happened and the incident that they couldn't prove in West Yorkshire. They've just been waiting for me to trip up."

"You might just get a fine and a slap on the wrist."

Derk was by now rummaging around in the kitchen looking for the coffee to put in the coffee machine. "Where's the coffee?"

"In the fridge, it keeps it fresher."

"Silly me why didn't I look in there?"

"Because you're uncouth and you drink instant, not the real stuff"

"What's this one then?"

"Colombian, it's a dark, rich, smooth coffee, two things we'll never be."

"What Colombian and dark......... you've not seen my tan."

"No you pillock. Rich and smooth."

The coffee pot grunted as it was switched on and within seconds a delicious aroma filled the kitchen. Derk by this time was in the biscuit tin.

"I love coming here, you always have them nice cookies, the big chocolate ones with the gooey middles."

"They don't last long when you get here."

"Do you want one then?"

"No I don't feel up to eating at the minute, but a nice cup of coffee will be just the ticket."

The two of them sat at the small pine kitchen table that Dom had taken from the house when he left his wife. She had cursed him but he didn't care. They sat in silence for two minutes waiting for the coffeepot to do its stuff. Derk then jumped to his feet stating he ought to make himself useful and saying "You don't take sugar do you?" He was soon sat back down and they both had mugs of steaming coffee.

"How can you be so sure they are going to sack you?"

"I got the obligatory notice twenty two days ago advising me to get legal representation."

"What's that mean then?"

"I'm fucked"

"Apart from that?"

"Well you know how the police discipline code works, bollocking, fine, sack or resign. It's all about degrees of severity for the offence.

"Well they might just fine you."

"No because they told me to get legal representation, there are only three options available to them, a reduction in rank."

"What to, a cadet?"

"Thanks, you're not helping."

"Sorry."

"It would appear its PC to P45 for me, I don't think there is another option available to me."

"I told you to get promoted and at least they could have made you a PC again."

"Well they can't reduce my rank so it's either resign, or let them sack me, with no references."

"Well you've asked me to go with you so I'm assuming there's a game plan."

The pause in the conversation spoke volumes as they looked sat each other over the table.

"Absolutely NOT." said Dominic

"Thought so. Come on, get your suit on."

"Look they might still have jobs at the end of the day, but at least I'll still be a handsome bastard, and they'll still look like overgrown puppets with ponsey haircuts."

"That's not going to be your opening gambit is it?"

"Bit ruff at the edges?"

"I'll say."

"Well actually that's my closing speech. Thought I'd hit them with it and leave a bit of a lasting impression."

"Oh good, I'd hate us to ruin any chance we've got before we start."

"What's with the we? It's my little arse on the line."

"Is that little? Figuratively speaking."

"Oh piss off, you are here to play the chauffeur and buy the teas."

"Thought so."

Derk was about ten years older than Dom and he looked like Bobby Ball, the comedian, short cropped dark hair with a moustache, quite rugged looking bloke, he once got mistaken when working undercover for a hit man for the Mossad, and nearly got arrested under the prevention of terrorism act. A better friend Dom could not have, he had a heart of gold and a deep sense of loyalty to his friend. The two had one hell of a good run at work, prisoner wise before the shooting incident. It had been five months since that fateful night in January. Dom had never returned to work as he had been suspended just as he was about to rejoin the shift, whereas Derk had been back at work a month, although it had been difficult for him. He was missing his mate and things just weren't the same. They had been close friends and partners at work for almost two years and their workload put the others to shame, but it had been a partnership, and that had ended the night they hit the tree. This, however, was probably not their finest hour, well not Dom's.

Derk asked "Tell me again why I'm your friend?"

"Cos we go out on the pull together, get pissed, sing badly and fall down."

"No you pillock, I mean your work Federation Friend?"

"Because my dear friend, I'm fucked. I have about as much chance of escape as a wax cat running through hell being chased by an asbestos dog. So I'd rather walk out of the door with my head held high, with you, rather than some pompous Federation rep and besides, we can then go and get drunk, pull a couple of tarts and fall down."

"Oh I see. But wasn't it the tarts that got you into this mess in the first place?"

"Only partly."

Derk began to notice that the house was in a complete tip. There was clothing strewn everywhere and he was beginning to wonder whether Dom had a clean shirt to wear.

"I know what you're thinking, but the house keeper is under the weather."

"I didn't know you'd got one."

"I haven't, it's me. Like I said I'm under the weather"

"I'm the injured party here and don't you forget it." The voice screamed from the bathroom. Virtually un-intelligible but that was due to the toothbrush impeding the flow of verbal bollocks. Within seconds Dom appeared at the top of the stairs in his best suit and tie looking like the proverbial dog's dinner. It was clear to see that Dom was extremely nervous and rather anxious about the day's proceedings but Derk quickly ushered him out of the door and towards the car.

It was an absolutely glorious day for June. The leaves on the Acer outside the front door of the cottage had fully opened and its beautiful variegated two-tone foliage shed a dappled and mottled shade across the pavement. The skies were a heavenly blue and it was just the most perfect walking day. Dom would have given anything to don his boots and just disappear. It would have been a good day to gather his thoughts but it was a little late for that.

"Come on ya miserable sod, get in the car."

Dom was jolted back into the real world and as he looked into the car saw the child seat anchored into the back and he suddenly thought of how Derks life had changed over the last eighteen months since the arrival of little Ross. He was the world to Derk and not far off for Dom as he was a godparent. Funny he thought to himself. Not really setting the best example at the moment. The drive into the town centre seemed to pass ominously quickly and they were soon parking in the multi-storey car park adjacent to the main headquarters building. The mood in the car was somewhat sombre and for the first time Derk was not really sure what to say or how to approach Dom. They had been the best of friends for a long time now, but this was just one thing he could not help with. He was there for support, but that was about it. They walked across Lady's bridge, which passed over the river Don.

"Do you remember when we used to do the mile and a half jog around this block as part of the entrance test?"

"Before my time. We used the nice playing fields at Graves Park."

"They don't even get out of the gym these days, just do the shuttle runs. I tell you what though. I used to hate the smell of the hops from the brewery plant. Especially whilst you were running, it used to make me feel sick."

"I'd hate to have to run around here now, I mean look at all the cars and the fumes, it would kill you."

"You must have been reading my mind. I bet it would be a health and safety issue now."

"It's ironic really, I ran around it to get in the force and now I'm walking back round it to get out. Great."

The two walked down the steep front slope to the main doors and made their way passed the reception officers, Derk showing his warrant card. Dom had to be signed in.

"Morning gents."

"Morning." In chorus was returned.

"It's a lovely day."

"Depends on your perspective I think, weathers great, but the rest of the day could be better."

The main HQ was now corporate, everything in matching colours, with statements of promises to the public, scattered all over the wall like a PR campaign.

"That's what really pisses me off." Said Dom

"What?"

"All these bloody badges we keep working for, yet it never really changes the way we police. I mean an officer should work hard and be professional, but yet we've had the Seven Peak Pointers, the Charter

Mark, Investors in People, EFQM, Best Value and all for what? It's political crap. Soon we will be wearing the uniform with the badges on the arm. We'll look like Scouts. Well you'll be wearing it, not me."

The elevator stopped at the floor with the canteen on. Both stepped out and into the foyer. Stood waiting by the double doors to meet them was Taylor QC.

"Oh good morning gentlemen."

Derk shot Dom a glance that spoke volumes and basically meant I'm not impressed.

"I'll get you boys a coffee, do take a seat. Back in a jiffy."

Taylor was back in two jiffies, but blamed the canteen staff.

"Could not operwate the machine. Anyone for qweam?"

Derk stifled a smile; Dom just put his head in his hands and thought to himself.

"So your it, a 6ft beanpole, one strong gust and that would be it, trousers that are too bloody short and to top it all with a bloody speech impediment."

"So what's the game plan?"

Taylor almost looked lost and stunned by this question.

Derk whispered under his breath. "He has done this before?"

"I think he's just given in."

"Well what I thought, was we'd emphasise your good work wecord.

That it was your first time. It is a pity about the picture in the pwess and then you giving the wods to the weporter, which I must say was caught perfectly on film."

"The Paparazzi love him, perhaps a career in Hollywood," suggested Derk

"Piss off. Anyway have we found out who made the phone call and gave the tip off to the press?"

"Well we're not sure." Taylor said tentatively.

"Good, good." Dom's temper was beginning to fray at the edges.

"Can I ask you Mr Taylor, have you done anything to save my ass? You see, I don't think so. You look like your wearing your son's suit, you don't look the part and you certainly do not appear to be on the ball, and if you're my best chance, I'm fucked."

"He's edgy," Derk said putting his arm around Dom's shoulder to reassure him, and attempting to calm the situation.

"No shit," Said Taylor.

This certainly caused a few raised eyebrows from those within earshot and a rye smile from Derk.

"Look I'm sorry okay, but the way I see it, is if I don't resign, they're going to sack me. Yes or No?"

"Well, erm, yes you could be wight. It might be better to go out with some dignity and a weference. Look the picture of you two in the papers a few months ago made you weal heroes but that was all undone when this blew up in your face."

"I'm still a hero."

Both turned to look at Derk as if to say will you shut your face, but the glance was sufficient enough.

"They even got my name wrong when I was the hero."

"You can't expect them to get everything wight."

"They got it wight, right this time when I dropped one."

"Unlucky odds I guess."

"I tell you what; I'd love to meet the man that really is doing all this shitty stuff to the prostitutes cos I'm certainly taking what could be classed as the public rap for this."

Dom gazed from the window over the city he had policed for ten years and turned to the other two. "Gentlemen I have reached a decision, I intend to resign from my position of Constable."

"Are you sure?" quizzed Derk.

"No, but I'll do what I do best. Wing it."

"It's time gentlemen, are we weady to go?" Asked Taylor QC

"What's this we shit, you're getting paid a fortune. I need the loo!"

"You OK?"

"Yep. Nope, my guts are rumbling, my knees are shaking and I feel like I'm going to shoot myself. Other than that I'm fine."

The room was a large corporate looking conference suite in a milky blue colour with lovely beech tables and a deep royal blue carpet with some kind of emblem on. The room was laid out with the good guys on one side angled at 45 degrees towards the top table which was elevated, and the bad guys on the other side again angled at 45 degrees, bit like a triangle. As the three entered the disciplinary hearing, sat on the opposing side of the room was Superintendent Marsh, who was putting the case for the disciplinary hearing along with the force solicitor. Sat behind them, were the bag carriers, a couple of inspectors neither of which Dom recognised.

All parties then took their seats and awaited the arrival of the Chief Constable.

Dom took a brief glance at the Superintendent who appeared more nervous than he did. An unusual situation for him he thought, prosecuting one of his own.

"Oh well," thought Dom, "at least this is not a criminal proceedings and I won't be going to prison for this. My anal virginity will remain intact along with my good looks and sanity." A feeling of sudden terror and then absolute calm came over him. He smiled to himself.

Very soon he would have no wife, no job and no security. Oh well, a clean sweep, at least he had his dog and trusted friend.

There was a quiet knock on the door and all in the room stood. In walked the Chief who was a tall distinguished looking gentleman with a beard, wearing full uniform with all pips and whistles on his shoulders. Only twice had the Chief's decisions been challenged, and appeals had been futile, as the home office had instantly backed the decision made at the time by the Chief. And rightly so! The Chief took his position as the presiding officer at the centre of the uplifted horseshoe table.

"Good morning gentlemen." He was allowed to say that, as there were no ladies present in the room on this occasion. There were a few moans and grumbles from the others in the room, mostly because they feared him but generally they were just being rude.

Dom stood up coughed slightly clearing his throat and said, "Good morning sir, I'll greet you even if the others won't."

It was a clever ploy; it appeared arrogant but was testament to Dom's nerve as the Chief smiled and the others looked shocked and flustered for not having had the manners to greet the Chief properly. It was ironic really because Dom was onto a loser anyway. The Chief eyed Dom over the glasses that he was just putting on. The Chief had never seen such balls out behaviour in his presence and under such circumstances.

The Chief replied, "Good morning to you Officer. Is there something you want to say?"

"No sir. Well I just remembered your speech on standards and how you hated walking into rooms and people ignoring you or just grunting. I too think it is bad manners and whatever the charge laid against me today bad manners is not one of them."

Dom glanced over to the Superintendent on the prosecuting side who now appeared even more uncomfortable despite being on the winning side. If Dom would have had a chance of winning today then this little stunt would have helped him pull it off but alas there was no hope anyway.

Derk leant forward as Dom sat down and whispered in his ear.

"It's a pity the Chiefs not a woman because with charm like that and those blue eyes we would have been onto a winner."

"My Mum says I'm a charmer and a ladies man."

"In your dreams!"

Taylor QC was now giving them both the evil glare, which tended to suggest they behave and start taking this seriously. The superintendent stood and was setting himself to read out the charges against Dom.

"Sir, I am sure that you will have no doubt read the papers and know what charges are to be put to PC Veil as this is a much publicised incident but the charges are as follows."

Taylor QC was already on his feet and shot the Superintendent down instantly.

"The papers have no relevance to this hearing and I would suggest that you stick to the facts not to hype up any glorified bunk-am, otherwise my client will never get a fair hearing." It was soon apparent to Dom that when Taylor was in full flow he pronounced his R's properly, amazing.

Derk whispered. "He might look like a Pwatt but he's on the ball."

Superintendent Marsh continued. "Yes, so sorry sir, I was setting the scene a little."

"Well don't. Just get on with the facts in the case," said the Chief.

"Firstly, on Wednesday the 7th May 2003 at 2200 hours you were arrested at 40 St Swithens Rd, the home address of Sharon Norburn who was using the address for immoral purposes and making a living from immoral earnings and you were found frequenting the premises for sexual purposes, and secondly, whilst being taken away for questioning, you brought the service into disrepute by giving a visually obscene gesture to the press who put this picture of you on the front page of the papers. Both acts are that not becoming of an officer within the Police service and are not acceptable."

The Superintendent dropped his pen on the desk and then fumbled

"He's a bit edgy for a man on the winning side," quipped the QC

Derk answered, "He's either up to something or hiding something."

Superintendent Marsh regained his composure for the first time during the proceedings and continued.

"Furthermore, as you are well aware, there have been four violent assaults on prostitutes and at the present time it is intimated that a Police Officer is responsible for the series of atrocious assaults. At the time of PC Veil's arrest there was an operation in force to capture the person responsible, and although forensic evidence is available, none of which matches to PC Veil, until the attacker is caught, he may in some way be linked to the incidents."

Taylor QC "May I just interject at this point and object to the complete and utter rubbish that has been put before the Chief this morning."

"Please continue," asked the Chief.

"Before you find that my client or infer that my client was responsible for the Lockerbie bombing can we stick to the facts in hand. There are currently two charges of bringing the force into disrepute, and at the present time my client has intimated that he will plead guilty to these. Surely Superintendent, a man with your experience should be able to tell the difference between fact and hearsay and prosecute a guilty plea."

The Super stammered badly, "Err yes yes."

Derk added his wisdom, "He's always been a yes man, the arse licker. He's absolutely fucking useless."

There was a chorus of "Tosser," by Dom and Derk.

At this point Dom stood up, "Sir may I speak. The prosecutor appears to be making a total…"

There was a pause. Everyone in the room was thinking cock-up or bollocks of the case but Dom had behaved exemplary to date and was not just about to blot his copybook.

Dom regained his composure and thread and inserted the word "hash" when everyone else had already inserted others.

"The circumstances are these; I have recently split from my wife in acrimonious circumstances. I had a bad week and was purely looking for sexual gratification not a girlfriend, my life is complicated enough at this moment in time. I went to what I knew to be a masseur that considered the extras and it would appear walked into a trap that was not intended for me. There was an anonymous tip off, and the Police and press turned up. I regret my actions towards the press and realise that it was totally unprofessional, but I do not regret going to see the lady or the masseur or what ever you want to call her. I know they offer services that we deem to be against the law, but this is my view, I would rather see someone get paid to provide a service, than have some sexually frustrated bloke running around the streets with a hard on looking for sex, because the consequences of this are tragic and we see it everyday. The sooner it's legalised and properly controlled the better and it's no good the 'do gooder's' or the 'non approvers' with their 2.3 Mercedes, three ex-husbands and the social life of a coffee morning, dictating to the Police complaints authorities about Policing issues like they always do. Every time we pamper to those with the most clout that are likely to affect our careers and make the most noise in the papers and to the MP's. We then use the get out of 'it's against the law' to the rest of society. We are weak and we waste time and valuable resources on such crap. I always find it ironic when we stop the doctors and the magistrates or the solicitors that have been using the ladies of the night. Ironic in that they don't want to be with Mrs Round table.

I can only apologise for my views and do not wish to categorise people or pigeon hole them, it's just the way I see it. I am also in full agreement with the Chief's decision to sack anyone that fetch's the Police service into disrepute and under the circumstances I would like to tender my resignation if you would accept it. In my support and defence to being allowed to resign rather than dismissed I have ten years exemplary service and two awards for acts of bravery. I have always upheld law and order; my honesty has never been in any doubt although I have been misguided recently in a view of my personal choices, which have lead to conflict for the service. In respect of the assaults I would like to say on record, that I have been totally exonerated of any involvement. I wish you all well and that concludes the defence."

The Chief appeared stunned more than anything else and turned to Superintendent Marsh.

"Have you anything to add?"

"Err yes," Stammer, "well no, no," stutter

"Good I'm glad you put us clear on that." The Chief was clearly playing with the Super, as his part in the proceedings had been a fiasco.

The Chief turned his gaze to Dom, rubbing his temples and stroking his beard. He appeared to be struggling with something but then said "Rather unorthodox for a hearing but I will retire and we will convene again in one hour."

All rose while the Chief exited stage left. The room was filled with the sound of shuffling papers and mumbling. Poor old Superintendent Marsh looked like he was the one on trial and actually did not appear to be looking too well.

The hour soon passed and all quickly reconvened.

The Chief took no time at all in announcing his decision. "Having considered the case and all the circumstances surrounding it, I believe that you were caught in somewhat of a compromising position."

Derk whispered, "He means with your trousers down."

"And although you may not have been the quarry on this occasion, you were captured. I have no sympathy with the resultant fiasco with the press and media attention. Your exemplary record does you credit and it is this, and this alone, that will allow me to accept your resignation as opposed to you being dismissed. Your actions may have lead to the police resources being focused on you, allowing a killer and or an attacker the opportunity to strike again whilst we were clearing up the mess with you. For that there is no charge brought against you, but the repercussions of your actions are clear to see. In any other circumstance you may have kept your job, but not today. I will clearly accept your offer to resign and your references will only reflect the positive aspects of your work. It has been an unusual hearing to say the least but I admire your honesty. This hearing is now adjourned. I wish you well in your future endeavours and thank you for your hard work over the last ten years. After the hearing Mr Marsh will take care of the administrative procedures relating to pay and pensions."

The Chief stood and all rose whilst he had left the room.

Dom turned and shook Taylor QC's hand thanking him for his efforts.

"Actually," Taylor replied, "you did handle that very well and should you ever be interested in taking up work with the legal profession I can tell you now that I would take you on as a solicitor's runner to make representations to the clients at Police stations."

"It's a kind offer but you'll have to let me think on that one. Representing the criminal fraternity was not what I had in mind."

"Well, the offer's there, and don't forget we are all innocent until proven guilty."

The superintendent was packing his brief case and appeared to be looking down his nose at Dom. This was too much for Dom to take and as he was no longer one of the rank and file the Super was no longer a senior officer to him so Dom walked over to the man. Derk was anxious and sensed trouble. Dom looked the Superintendent straight in the eyes, flaring his jawbone and setting a steely gaze on him with his piercing blue eyes. Marsh appeared uncomfortable and was beginning to wish he had not appeared so smug in victory. The team behind the Superintendent were fidgeting and looked anxious. Dom stared straight at them and said, "Someone better go and get the loo roll because one of you needs to wipe his arse, oh and I'll send you the bill for the prosecution because that was shite boys." With that, Dom turned on his heels and headed for the Personnel Department. Derk immediately put his arm around Dom's shoulders ushering him from the room before the situation deteriorated any further.

"Hell of a day, you always do it in style."

"Yep that much style that you're still employed and I'm unemployed."

"We need to get shit faced, what else can we do?"

# 23

Dom had resigned himself to
the fact that he was now unemployed. He had spent the last two
days down at the job centre and the benefits agency trying to get
him-self sorted out. What a fiasco that had been. More forms to
fill out than he had dared to imagine, bureaucracy gone mad. How
many O levels, A levels, courses have you been on. Surprisingly the
Police train you in all aspects of life. You can clean shit up of the

streets. Paperwork by the ton and real silly working hours with the minimum of financial reward, just a good pension! In fact now Dom thought about it he was lucky to be unemployed. The British justice system would just have to survive without him. He doubted it would cope, but what the hell if they, the public, pleaded for his return then he would have to think long and hard about it.

Since his first day of unemployment, and the initial two job offers there was nothing imminent on the horizon, the second job offer had been working at the pub where he and Derk had got hammered. Dom had a science degree and was actually well qualified in the exam department stakes, but it meant nothing when there were no jobs to be had. The only saving grace was that the social would pay the rent on the accommodation until he found work. At the minute it was a toss up between working in the pub for Gregg and, or working for Taylor QC. A few weeks behind the bar appeared the most appropriate choice until Dom found his feet. Besides, that would be cash in hand, which would suit everybody down to the ground. And as far as Dom was concerned the company was better and he could just about work the hours he wanted to.

On the way back from town Dom had stopped off at the off-licence. A bottle of wine was in order. He was going to put his feet up and relax in front of the TV. One of the Lethal Weapons trilogies was on, so a bottle of his favourite plonk would go down a treat. A bottle of Jacobs Creek, a lovely velvety red Shiraz Cabernet from Australia, £5.49! Such extravagancies would have to stop when the funds ran out. But what the hell, Dom had no other vices to speak of, well not now, not since the tragic death of Sharon.

Dom had spent the last few days when not at the benefits agency trying to get on top of the housework. The house was just about spick and span. There were still a few items in boxes but on the whole things were looking pretty good. In fact Dom had got one of his cookery books out and made himself a fancy beef burger accompanied with a summer salad. Suddenly there was no end to this man's talents. Since the split with Claire, Dom had found plenty of time to indulge in the things he wanted to do. Like for example Sunday afternoon. Dom would watch football on the TV and then retire to the bathroom with a good book and the radio. He could listen to the top forty for a couple of hours whilst sat in a steaming tub. He always came out looking like a shrivelled prune but what the hell, it was totally relaxing. Not a care in the world. Dom could only see his worries easing because now he was unemployed there seemed less to worry about. None of that there keeping up with the Jones!

After tea Dom went for a walk with Buster and then went and settled in the Bath for a soak. Oh that was the other good thing! You don't have to wait until Sunday to chill out for an hour. Dom had just about steamed up all the windows and was into the second chapter of his new Grisham novel. The wine was going down a treat. In fact this was a great night. All of a sudden Buster went berserk. It was his job to, and anytime anyone went past the front door he would play merry hell. On this occasion he did not calm down and seemed quite agitated that someone was outside. Dom dove out of the bath and tried to peer through the bathroom window. All that could be seen was the top of what appeared to be a sports car, he was sure it was a Porsche with the whale tail fin on the back. Dom quickly wrapped a towel around his waist. "Hang on I'm coming." Dom's shout was inaudible, as Buster appeared to be winning on the decibel stakes.

"Will you give it a rest?" Dom opened the front door half dressed and dripping wet to be confronted by someone he had not expected to see ever again.

"Paula!" There was no way that Dom would ever have forgotten anyone so beautiful. Paula looked at Dom rather shy and sheepishly.

"I'm sorry to intrude. Have I interrupted anything?"

"No not at all, you probably saved me from pickling myself."

Paula smiled. She was kind of looking at the floor. She appeared embarrassed to be there, yet she wanted to be there. After all it was Paula that had found Dom.

"Come in, before I freeze to death and you start laughing at me when my knee's start knocking together."

"Thanks. Are you sure I'm not interrupting anything."

"No there's only myself and Buster, if that's what you mean." Busters woofs were now muffled due to the fact he had a big soft cuddly toy in his mouth. He appeared hinged in the middle as his tail was shaking his body so violently, whilst stuffing the teddy into Paula's knees.

Paula had done her homework and she knew full well that Dom was now in the process of getting a divorce. She just wasn't sure whether anyone else had crept into his life.

"How did you find me?"

"I have my sources, and money buys answers."

"I do hope you didn't part with a lot. I'm not sure I'm worth more than a fiver."

As Paula stood before him she wanted to blurt it all out, there and then, get it off her chest, but it was too soon. She just needed to bide her time.

"Make yourself at home while I get dressed."

Dom ran off up stairs just hanging onto the towel as he hit the landing. Paula had tried not to watch but ended up laughing at him as he nearly lost it all on the top step and this little bare bum went round onto the landing. Paula was surprised to see the house in such a tidy state. It was very clean and everything had its place. (Timing is everything!) Dom had obviously got his act together. Paula was admiring a lovely oil painting above the fire place when Dom came downstairs wearing a pair of purple and pink cotton walking trousers with elephants embossed on them and a long cream fisherman's style woolly jumper. Dom certainly had the rugged handsome look. He was also carrying wine.

"Care to join me?"

"Absolutely, yes please. Love the oil painting." It was a moonlit coastline with a village on the mountainside all lit up.

"It's an original, I inherited it. My Dad painted it for my Grandma and when she passed away I inherited it. Doubly sentimental."

"Does your Dad still paint?"

"When he gets the time. It became a bit of a chore for him not a hobby, but I think he will do some more soon, especially since he has just retired."

"Have you anymore I could see?"

"Yes, see for yourself."

Dom gave Paula a quick-guided tour. She loved everything about the little cottage. It was so homely and cosy. Quite unusual for a man's house!

Paula picked another lovely picture, which was a recent one that Dom had acquired, although it was not an original it was stunning. It was a Spanish village on a mountainous hillside surround by vineyards and mountains.

"What a beautiful picture. It evokes such feelings."

"You mean when you look at it you are there. You can feel the sunshine and smell the fresh mountainous air."

"Exactly I couldn't have said it better myself."

Dom was stood directly behind Paula and couldn't fail to notice how good she smelt. Her hair was silky and shiny. It was ages since he had been this close to women. It was funny, Dom had not seen Paula since the day at the hospital, and yet they were stood talking like they were long lost friends.

Dom handed Paula a glass of wine and they went and sat in front of the fire.

"Can I get you anything else?"

"No I'm fine. I bet your wondering after all this time why I've looked you up."

"I would be lying if I said I wasn't curious."

"I've wanted to see you since that day at the hospital. There was, and is, so much I wanted to say to you, but I found out you were having marital problems and I felt that if I came around it may cause trouble for you."

"You must have had a sixth sense because it was a little acrimonious in the end."

"I'm glad I left it until now, but then I nearly missed the opportunity, especially since you left the Police, my source could have dried up if you had moved out of the area and hence that is why I have appeared today."

"Well all I can say is that you look fantastic. Much better than the last time I saw you."

"You too, you were the one with the bullet holes, not me remember?"

Dom could sense what Paula was trying to say. She was upsetting herself like she had the night at the hospital.

"Do you have any idea what it is like to want to say something to somebody and yet the words you use will never amount to anything like the depth of what you are feeling or want to convey?"

"Paula it was my job."

"No, there was a cut off point, when, at some moment that night, you risked everything for me; you crossed the line. Yet you didn't even know me. How selfless."

"People do it everyday, Policemen, Firemen, Paramedics, Doctors, Soldiers."

She stopped him and put her fingers to his lips. "Yes, but only you saved me."

"I'm not going to win this argument am I?"

"One day Dominic Veil I will sit you down and tell you what I want to say about it. At the minute it still just makes me want to cry when I think about it."

Trying to make light of the serious conversation Dom spotted the TV.

"Hey Lethal Weapon is on. Would you like to stay and watch?"

"Are you sure, I feel like I'm intruding on your evening."

"Hell, I'm sure I can cancel the hot date I had lined up."

Paula glanced at him and smiled.

There was only a two-seater settee in the room and a large leather beanbag. The two sat slouched into the sofa, sharing the hugest bag of cheesy puffs and Dom polished off the majority of the wine. Dom was so pleased to have some female company. It was nice and intimate, yet somehow it felt different, like they had been friends for a lifetime.

Paula was sat there thinking she was in the safest place in the world. After all she was sat with her guardian angel. Well, at least her own, personal, bodyguard. Dom noticed that whilst the film was on whenever a gun was produced Paula sank deeper into the sofa and squeezed tighter in towards him, and considering the film this happened a lot.

Paula angled her head onto Dom's shoulder and whispered in his ear. "He was going to kill me."

"I know."

"Even before you saw us that night and before the pursuit he had told me he was going to kill me. I was so frightened. I could see it in his eyes. But it was funny, because when the Police car started to chase us, I thought you wouldn't have a chance. But by the end when it all got messy, I was prepared to die, and yet I was, happier to die, if that's the right way to say it because I had hope, and I knew I wasn't going to die alone in the middle of nowhere, and even if he had of killed me someone would have got him."

Dom put his arm around Paula. She shut her eyes and appeared to relax and fall asleep in his arms. It was obvious to Dom that neither of them had received any stress counselling and this should have been done months ago when everyone involved could have spoken about the ordeal.

As the subtitles went up for the film, Paula awoke.

"I must go its late."

"Will you be alright?"

"Oh yes, I feel a lot better and I haven't really said what I wanted to say."

"It can wait."

"Will you come and see me at my house Saturday night? I'll cook you a meal, play you some of my crappie records whilst you can tell me war stories and your life history."

"I'd love to."

"Oh and don't forget your chaperone."

Dom looked puzzled, "Buster?" Dom said, "Do you mind?"

"Don't be silly, my cat likes dogs. And besides he's your family?"

"Thanks, what time?"

"Eight-ish. Fetch a bottle and I'll put you up for the night."

"It's a deal."

"Oh and come with an open mind, I may have a proposition for you if you are still looking for a job."

"Intriguing!"

Paula kissed Dom on the cheek and closed the door behind her. Dom heard the Porsche purr into action, and then silence, she was gone.

Dom slipped off the sofa and onto the floor at the side of Buster. "What was all that about Buster? She's beautiful. She can't like me. It didn't feel like that, you know sex stuff, it felt like old safe Love, friends like a brother or a sister or Mum and Dad. Oh well it looks like we will find out on Saturday. Better give you a brush." Dom turned out the light in the lounge, let Buster out for his nightly pee and they both retired. Buster was snoring at the bottom of the bed before Dom was out of the bathroom. He didn't have the heart to move him. Dom picked up his Grisham novel again but within seconds his eyes were done for. It was a good night's sleep.

# 24

It had been an ordeal finding out Paula's address. Fine, when a woman says 'come around at eight, I'll cook you dinner.' Normal people leave their address. It makes it that much simpler. Dom had never been to Paula's house as he was off sick when the investigation had been wrapped up. Fortunately Dom still had his old mates and he was never going to forget the registered number of her car M4DAM, so a swift phone call, and hey presto, an address. Naughty really but in this instance Paula wouldn't have minded her details being passed out to Dom. Still illegal but Dom couldn't give a shit, what could they do fire him? Dom had also been a burden to Derk who had been giving him lifts since he had sold the car to pay his bills. He was in no rush to go anywhere and didn't have a social life to speak of. Well not up until now that is.

Derk pulled up at the bottom of the drive and looked up at the bungalow.

"This woman has some serious cash. Ask her if she'll marry me will ya?"

"Derk.................... piss off, too bad you're married already."

"Only kidding, have a good night and don't do anything I wouldn't do."

"Great, free reign then."

"If you need a lift back in the morning give me a ring."

"Cheers Derk, see ya later."

Buster was half way up the path with a bit of a spring in his stride wagging his tail. He had started to bark. Not that he was chasing anything; he was just announcing their arrival to the street. "Bust give it a rest, this is a respectable neighbourhood." Buster duly obliged and decided to pee on the hosta instead. Dom walked up the long cobbled driveway towards the double garage and the front door. Paula was already stood on the doorstep with the front door open and soapy in her arms.

"Hi, I'm impressed."

"Whys that?"

"Well, I realised about half an hour ago I hadn't given you my address and secondly you are bang on time."

"Never keep a beautiful women waiting!"

"Why, thank you kind sir."

Buster was sat patiently on the doorstep eyeing Soapy who was peering out of Paula's arms with more than a little trepidation about the visitor.

Paula bent down to stroke Buster and Soapy was off into the house. Buster did not give chase and after a few seconds Soapy reappeared when he realised he was not about to be dog food.

"Come in. Don't stand on the door step."

Dom produced a bottle of wine from his bag and handed it to Paula.

"One of my favourites she said a Rosemont Shiraz, an excellent choice."

Dom was stood in the entrance hall admiring the large open hallway and wooden floors.

"You have some beautiful paintings."

"Alas these were not painted by my father!"

"Pity."

"You're telling me! He'd be worth a fortune if he'd painted these."

Dom walked into the kitchen, which gave views into the lounge.

"Wow, this is gorgeous. Love the kitchen; you can't beat a large kitchen. This must have cost a fortune?"

"Thirty six thousand!"

"Was that for the house?"

"No, that was for the kitchen."

Dom paused "Wow, I couldn't earn that amount of money in two years. Now I couldn't earn it in ten years. The DSS are real bad employers, there's no chance of a rise and the promotion prospects are shocking." Paula laughed. "What's funny?"

"You are! And the fact that I'm a crap cook and I've got this all singing and dancing kitchen. It's just for show, really, I haven't got a clue what I'm doing."

"What's for tea then?"

"Well to be honest I haven't even started cooking yet, I've not long since got in. I'm not even showered or dressed."

"Brill, well would you mind if I cooked whilst you got ready? I'd love to cook in this place."

"Be my guest, are you sure you don't mind?"

"Paula, I'll be in my elements. I take it how ever; you've got some food in?"

"The fridge is full, please yourself, I bought absolutely everything. Forgot to ask you what you'd like."

"Oh I'm dead easy to please. Have you got enough ingredients for me to do a Spag Bol."

"Oh yes… that's my favourite. Look I'll leave you to cook and I'll get cleaned up. Stereo's in the lounge, put some music on, I'll be ten minutes."

Paula was shouting back across the lounge, "I'm sorry about this you must think I'm a shocking host."

"Don't be silly."

Dom walked into the sunken lounge. The sofa was a wrap around leather affair, which surrounded the central feature, the fireplace. Buster had made himself at home. He was laid fast asleep on the rug in front of the open hearth fire. Soapy had a newfound friend, and was asleep snuggled up to him.

"What a pair you two are."

Dom found the stereo easily. Choosing from the two thousand CD's was a little bit more troublesome. Eventually settling for Celine Dion.

"Great choice," was the cry from the bathroom.

Dom was soon back in the kitchen. He found a beer in the fridge, and, was in no time at all browning the mince, and throwing in all the other ingredients. Garlic bread was popped in the oven and the pasta onto boil. It had been ages since Dom had cooked a proper meal for anyone and he was having more fun than he'd had in a long time. He was so wrapped up in the cooking and his singing that he had failed to notice that his host had returned and was happily sat watching him dancing around the kitchen like a lunatic.

"I love this song said Paula." Dom stopped singing temporarily, embarrassed. "Don't stop, you and Celine just had it together then."

"Thanks."

"It always reminds me of you this one."

Dom started listening intently to the words. The song was, "If that what it takes," he knew instantly why Paula thought of him when she heard this song. He just smiled at her, "Fancy a beer?"

"You're a mind reader."

"I've noticed that you've got a flash security system."

"Yes, since my little unexpected house guest, I have this place fully wired. Even the panic attack buttons are wired up to a calling station. If I accidentally set it off I have to call them within two minutes or they notify the Police."

"Excellent system."

"It makes me feel safe, gives me peace of mind to know that help is at hand so to speak and I think in some ways it has helped me to recover a little. I wanted to move at first, I did not feel safe but now I'm settled again. The perimeter is also covered by cameras so anyone coming to the house will be caught on film."

Dom laughed. "That was my downfall, being so photogenic."

While Dom put the finishing touches to the dinner Paula set the table and lit the candles. Both sat down to a Dom special Bolognese, which left Paula wanting to hire him as her chef. The two just spent hours exchanging stories and by the end of the second bottle of wine both knew the others innermost secrets. Neither had had it easy, and Dom had certainly learnt a lot more about Paula than he would have ever guessed. Dom had completely forgotten the fact that Paula had invited him because she had a proposition to put to him. The two went to sit on the large sofa in front of the fire with a pot of coffee. They both needed a little caffeine to take the edge off the alcohol.

Paula went and put on her favourite Barbara Striesand album and prepared herself for what she was about to ask Dom. If it came out wrong he would not speak to her again. It was all down to the delivery. So a small glass of brandy to go with the coffee might just help and she thrust the glass into Dom's hand.

"Dom, are you aware of the type of business I own and run?"

"A very profitable one looking at all this."

"Well yes, but that aside do you know what the actual company does?"

"Well, I thought it was some kind of dating agency."

"Close, you see many years ago I realised that many people went to prostitutes for pleasure, to relieve their frustrations, or purely for the hell of it. Many have regular clients and some can be very well paid executives, professional people with money. So I came up with the idea of a discreet agency with quality females on hand to provide company. Hence I became the Madam."

Dom was sat in stunned silence on the sofa hanging on every word. This is interesting stuff. But what had this got to do with him? His initial thought was that of a bodyguard.

"The company took off and the word went around and we quickly started building a client base. I had help from a police friend who was discreetly vetting the girls and the customers to see if there was anything sadistic in the past or something that we needed to know about. The last thing I wanted was one of the girl's pick pocketing one of the clients and then losing them or even worse trying to blackmail them. We were extremely careful and the business just took off. Then about two years ago one of the clients came to me and asked if I could provide him with a proper escort, not just a girl to meet and bed. A no ties situation, he wanted an escort, well educated to take out or escort him to certain functions. This man was single, his wife had recently passed away and he wanted a beautiful woman to talk to, have fun with, and be seen with but purely on a level without emotional commitment, basically pretty women without the risk of picking an unknown commodity off the street. Initially I was a little sceptical about this kind of relationship fearing it could be too risky, so I did it myself. It worked well, and the financial recuperation from this job was huge. Again, word got out. Well actually I made sure that word got around, and the next thing there were people from all over the country ringing me. Rich people with money to spend. Either lonely, divorced, wife somewhere else, whatever, there are a million reasons. The costs went up and people were prepared to pay and I mean really pay. The problem I had was finding suitable women, or should I say suitable women with the intelligence to consider being an escort. At this time there were three tiers of customer base. The ones that purely wanted sex and as you are well aware, prostitution's illegal, especially if you consider that I was the pimp. Crude I know but I was. The second tier was those that wanted an escort for the night and then sex later. This is not such a problem now because I can work from an escort / dating agency principle and anything that the client wants like that is a private arrangement, financially speaking, with the girl. Actually it's not at all and I am fully aware of what the customer wants, else I could send the wrong girl. Confidentiality is paramount. The third tier, are those that want the company but no sex. This particular clientele are growing in number but these are the most expensive clients to fund from my point of view. The girls have to be good looking, available at short notice, intellectual, well spoken, well mannered and have excellent communication skills. In view of the cost involved I use models from agencies and then send them on courses, language courses, so they can get by in French, German, and Italian etc. One girl is even studying Russian. I pay for the training. They go to New York to a friend of mine that used to be a butler. He now owns a restaurant in Manhattan and they learn about food, wine, etiquette, and whilst in New York fit them out with a new wardrobe. Each individual customer is researched thoroughly. All the girls have cover stories on every outing. The homework is paramount. I have a team of five just creating cover stories for the girls so that they don't embarrass the client or themselves on the date."

"This is absolutely fascinating," said Dom whilst Paula took a sip of her coffee.

"Good I'm glad you think so, because that just about fetches me up to date with the history lesson and the state of my business." Paula was in full flow and she had Dom's attention.

"But, you are now wondering what the proposition is that I have for you."

"I've got that sussed. Bodyguard, escort for the girls on certain outings, safety aspect since your attack."

"…………..Not exactly."

"You want me to help with the background checks and cover stories."

"No, nothing like that."

Paula was hesitant but she had to take the plunge and just tell him.

"You see, Sharon Norburn was a very good friend of mine. She was one of my original girls but when I put an end to the purely sex based clients that were obviously putting me in a difficult position, lawfully speaking, well Sharon asked if she could take those clients with her and hence she did. It helped me out beautifully and Sharon was making a packet. You might not have thought so to look at the house but she had a quarter of a million stashed away in various funds. She was going to retire in a few years and go and live in Spain. Life is full of coincidences or maybe it's just fate. Your marriage breaks up, and you start seeing Sharon, who was one of my best friends. She used to tell me how you took her flowers."

Dom looked suitably embarrassed.

"Then you saved my life, the hero. Your picture was on every newspaper cover and hence Sharon and I made the connection with you and us, like I said fate. She described you as a charming young man, gentle, considerate, well spoken with lovely blue eyes and very handsome. I know you already have a degree in engineering. So really you're ideal." Paula paused to let that last sentence sink in.

"..................For what, exactly?" he enquired.

"..................Being an escort," she said sheepishly

There was along silence and neither of them spoke for several seconds. Paula was now convinced she had blown it."

"....................A male prostitute?"

"No not at all, that side of my business is finished; I only deal with the second and third tiers."

"Yes but that still includes sex."

"Sometimes, yes, maybe………….. Look, I would never have made the proposition if you had still been employed and if it had not been for Sharon telling me what a really nice guy you are with women, and anyway you're already my hero."

"That last parts cheating."

Dom was stunned. He sat on the sofa brandy glass in hand looking like he had just been slapped across the face by an alien, while Paula meanwhile paced in front of the fire waiting for some kind of reaction.

"Look you can say no, really, I won't be offended."

"Just out of interest, what is the deal?"

Paula smiled at him and came and sat back on the sofa next to him. She took hold of his hand. "For you, and only you, I have a special deal. You see for a while I have had several women approach me requiring an escort. I already have one guy that works for me but I would describe him as a model. Its all sex for him, he's not really a charmer and that's why I need you. You do have a way with people. That's clear for all to see."

"Stop creeping and tell me the deal."

"One thousand pounds a night split fifty-fifty."

"Five hundred quid a night!" Spluttered Dom

"Yes five hundred, and at least three nights work a week. Normally, Thursday Friday and Saturday."

"Fifteen hundred a week, six grand a month, seventy two thousand a year." Dom was talking out loud and he couldn't help but smile.

"There could be a lot more work, but that will be the minimum. Alternatively I will pay all your bills, house, car, food and pocket money and I will invest your wages along with mine. The more money there is to invest the quicker it will grow and in five years time I will give you a contract that guarantees a sum of one million pounds."

"You're kidding me. Do you do this for your other staff?"

"No just you. It's a once in a lifetime offer and I'll even put it in a contract."

"Is that when you plan to get out, five years?"

Dom between you and me I will have made at least ten million from my investments and it will be time to start spending it and touring the world."

Dom was in a state of shock and needed to take some fresh air.

"Do you mind if we take Buster for a little walk, I need some fresh air?"

"Mais Oui."

Within minutes the two of them were walking, arms linked along the darkened and deserted streets of Whirlow. "It's really nice around here." Said Dom

"It can be. Some people think they're a cut above the rest but other than that it is a lovely place to live. It's right on the edge of the countryside, great for walking the dog."

Dom was very quiet and pensive.

"What's the matter? Is it the thought of living off immoral earnings?"

"No it's nothing like that.............. To be honest I'm stunned by the offer. It's a really good one."

"Nothing to do with the sex then?"

"By the sounds of it there isn't that much to worry about, most want discretion and an escort for the night."

"Do you think less of me for offering you the job?"

"No this is business. Outside of that I want us to be what we are, friends. What if the job was not for me?"

"Simple. I either pay you up front like a job or I will pay to the nearest two hundred thousand for each year of work if I invest the money for you. If after a few weeks you were to decide that the job wasn't for you I would pay you in cash for the jobs that you had done."

"What about Buster if it's an overnight job? I'm just thinking out loud here!"

"No problem he can stay with Soapy and me. I don't work in the evenings at all unless it is a dire emergency.

They looked like an old married couple, Paula almost willing him to join her in the business as she clung to his arm.

"Have I told you about the fringe benefits?"

"Very funny."

"No I'm serious, there's more."

"Like a health scheme and a pension plan."

"Close....... membership to a fitness club, with a gym and sauna, which, I will expect you to go to daily in order to stay in shape."

"Remind me again who these women are. Where do they come from?"

"Professional women requiring company without any hassle, rich executives, bored very rich housewives, socialites. In some instances the man hires us to give self esteem back to the women, but that one is very carefully planned."

"Old ones then?"

"No not at all, the ages vary, but many are in there forties. Is that a problem?"

"I've a knack with the old ones; it's the young ones that I struggle with. Not trendy enough." There was another pause "Sounds good to me."

The two had completed the tour of the block and Buster had peed on just about every tree in sight. As they approached the drive, Paula stopped Dom tugging at his arm as he headed for the door. "There is one other fringe benefit; well it's a gift really"

Dom thought she was about to kiss him but then he heard the noise. The electric doors lifted on the garage. Dom couldn't quite see that clearly at first, but as he walked closer he could see sat at the side of Paula's Porsche was a brand new Volvo C70 T5 coupe in Silver, closer inspection revealed it had beautiful black leather upholstery.

"It's fully paid for the keys are in the ignition. However the car is yours regardless of whether you take the job or not."

Dom was again for the second time tonight speechless.

"Er.........why.........Er..............thank you, it's fantastic."

"No................ Thank you, and don't ask me why, because you know why!"

"I wish I was sober."

"Never mind it will still be there in the morning."

"Just give me a second." Dom walked over to Buster who was now rolling around on the damp grass and doing back rolls. Dom appeared to bend over and whisper in his ear. Buster barked once. Paula was laughing at the two of them. "You're mad."

"Only a little............. You'll be pleased to know that having consulted with my pensions advisor and guru that I would love to take you up on the offer and I would only be too pleased for you to invest my earnings."

"Brilliant..... Welcome to the company. I'll get the contract made up straight away."

"Buster would just like to know if Soapy snores."

"You are crazy"

Dom put his arms around Paula and gave her a big kiss on the top of her head. "Thank you for this."

One arm slipped around her waist and they went into the house to celebrate.

. The deal had been struck and they both needed another brandy or two.

# 25

Dom was sat at the breakfast counter mulling over the previous nights revelations trying to put everything into perspective. He was comfort eating. Well he must have been because nobody eats two bowls of Alpen for breakfast! The tea was mashing and Dom was staring into space. He had been offered a once in a lifetime deal. It would set him up for the rest of his life. But what was taking some real soul searching was the fact that Paula had told him she was a lesbian and she had not been out with a bloke for four years, well other than for business purposes. She had slept with the odd one in the course of her business, but that was the sum total of her involvement. Paula had started seeing women when a female client asked her to go on an escort. Dom was gutted because she seemed so perfect. 'Oh well' he had thought to himself, 'that will save me from fucking up the friendship. My mind will be focused from the start.'

Dom looked up to see the delightful Paula walk into the kitchen. She was wearing what appeared to be riding getup. 'Very raunchy,' thought Dom.

"Good morning," they both said simultaneously.

"Sleep well?" asked Paula.

"Not really, too much on my mind.....You?"

"Like a log, it's the best I've slept in ages. Probably got something to do with having a man in the house."

Dom was struggling with the concept now, if she liked having a man around. Oh well it wasn't worth worrying about.

"Do you ride?" Dom enquired.

"Very well, thank you. Lucky for you that you're going to New York this afternoon or else you would be having your first lesson."

"Sorry, who's going to New York?"

"We are!"

"I've got to find a dog sitter."

"Sorted it, spoke to Derk who spoke to your Mum and Dad."

"Wow, you don't mess around do you?"

"Nope, and I've even spoken with my solicitor about a contract. It will be ready when we get back from the Big Apple."

"I've never been to America before...........It's Sunday morning and you've spoken to your solicitor."

170

"He's one of my best clients and good friend so I can talk to him whenever I like. Plus he's single so like s the attention."

Paula stuffed a piece of toast into her mouth whilst attempting to pour some juice at the same time.

"So you need to drop off Buster, go home, pack, and pick me up at one, as we have to be at Manchester airport for three to fly to Heathrow to get our Virgin Atlantic to JFK."

"I better ring Derk and tell him."

"You can do it en route, there's a phone in your car."

"Any more surprises?"

"Yes lots, but you're worth it." Paula was pinching the cheek on his face. "Now go or you'll never be ready."

Dom's head was spinning as he sat himself behind the wheel of his brand new car. Buster was sat on a cover on the back seat obviously sniffing the new leathery smells. The car was a dream to drive, the last time he had driven a car like this he had chased a Porsche, killed someone, saved a life, oh and got shot. That was probably why Paula had bought him the car. It was just about the same as the car that he had chased her Porsche in.

Dom called Derk, who could not believe his friends run of luck.

"Lucky bastard." Were the first words he uttered "Talk about highs and lows," Derk had said to him. Dom was reflecting on this and was not about to let the highs slip by so quickly without really enjoying himself. The good times were here to stay. He promised himself that.

# 26

Several things had happened over the past few weeks in relation to the investigation but they were still no closer to finding the identification of the killer / attacker, or killers / attackers. The main assumptions were that they had two different offenders and although the incidents were curiously linked by their nature no exact link could be put to them other than they had all been prostitutes.

It had been the murder of Sharon Norburn that put the cat among the pigeons, and was causing the most anxiety, because the murder had taken place at the address where she lived. This just did not fit the modus operandi of the other attacks, but they weren't discounting anything at this time. It had a tenuous link to the other crimes and it was an attack that took place on the night that they were expecting it to. They, the police, suspected that the attacker would be a police officer, hence the arrest of Dominic Veil, but he could not be the killer as he was in custody at the time of the murder, although the police, particularly Rossy still believed that he was in some way linked to the other attacks. It was the attack on the police officer that had led him to believe this most of all as it was the night that Veil had triggered a speed a camera going into town but could then not fully account for his whereabouts. In fact there was no fully about it, he could not account for his whereabouts at all that satisfied Rossy that he was innocent, Veil was hiding something, he was connected in some way.

Rossy had had officers trawling through the videos of all petrol station forecourts for the night the detective was attacked, anything that could just give them another fix on Veils position, another clue or a step in the right direction. Rossy was convinced Veil was involved. Bar the Norburn murder it all pointed to Veil, he was the link, but what was the link exactly and how did it all fit together. They were missing something very obvious, they had to be.

A massive boost to everyone's moral had been the start of the recovery of DC Reagle who had recently come out of the coma and was making an excellent progress. Unfortunately however, due to the traumatic nature of the incident the officer had absolutely no recollection of the event. In fact the last recollection she had was coming back from holiday the week before she went to work in

South Yorkshire. It had come as a bit of a surprise to her when she was told where she had been working and what had happened. The psychologist thought that at the present time it was probably not that she was blocking the trauma out but it was more likely to be the result of the head injury that she was suffering which had caused the amnesia. The chances of her ever recovering her memory were 50:50. The doctors just did not know. At the present time she was having no flash backs or nightmares and her general mental health was very good which was probably aiding her physical recovery. The downside to the police was the enquiry was at a dead end, no new clues.

Rossy had put the finishing touches to the press release yesterday afternoon. He wanted to announce that Detective Reagle had come out of the coma. He wanted to go on the offensive. Make the attacker think that the police had new information as to his identity. They wanted him to make another move and make a mistake. They needed to make him think they were closer than they were, because truth be-known they were nowhere.

I t was Sunday morning as Rossy read the morning papers, the article was a good one, it had just the right element of information along with an air of expectancy, and they were playing games.

It also announced that now the officer had been able to give them information they could do a re-enactment that was going to be shown on TV next week. Again it was a ploy to make the attacker think they had more than they did, whilst pleading to the public to come forward. They could roughly put the scene together anyway from what they had already gathered. It would be brief in its nature.

It would reveal absolutely nothing to the public. It was just a tactic, a ploy to turn up the heat.

Rossy sat in his office absolutely knackered, they had filmed it during the night to add authenticity in the exact same spot the attack took place when there was nothing or very little about on the motorway. He needed some sleep but he was still plagued by a dreadful fear, that the killer / attacker would know all this, there were no secrets in the police service and he would be one step ahead of them again. If, to all intents and purposes the attacker was a police officer, then how close was he to knowing everything that was in Rossy's head, the enemy within was putting the fear of God into him because it meant that he ruled the agenda, they were playing his game. It was like playing battleships only your opponent can see your side of the board too. How fair is that?

# 27

At six fifty PM Dom and Paula boarded 'Tinkerbell' the Jumbo 747 Virgin Atlantic flight VS004 to JFK. Dom was lead by Paula and the flight attendant up the stairs to the first class lounge and seating area.

"Wow. Look at the size of these seats………. I've never been in a Virgin before." Paula gave Dom a quizzical and knowing look for that comment. "I meant plane." "Sure you did."

Although the flight was seven hours and forty minutes long, time just disappeared. Dom ate a first class meal and drank several small bottles of wine. He had then watched the latest films on his own screen. In fact he had watched two films. Meanwhile Paula had eaten, drunk a gin and tonic and gone to sleep. She was used to this type of treatment. It was a first for Dom. He was too excited to sleep. It was like taking a kid on his first holiday. The only thing Dom had not said to Paula was "Are we there yet?" Paula kept sneaking a peak under her mask at Dom. She couldn't help smiling to herself at how excited he was. Just like a big kid. Paula never came to America with her new employee's but Dom was different. He was also her friend. But if the look on the others face's were as happy as his then perhaps she should start travelling with them. It was a real tonic.

Due to the fact that they were flying into JFK and not Newark the 747 had passed over the eastern seaboard and Long Island. The difference being that Dom had not had a glimpse of the Manhattan skyline, whereas flying into Newark it was inevitable that you would see the famous skyline. This was a treat yet to come.

Paula noted as they passed through customs that entry into the US was just as officious as it usually was; very few pleasantries from the customs people at the desk. She always found it amusing that they could be really curt with the people coming into the country to spend thousands of pounds on their economy and yet the world trade bombers had just waltzed through customs on a temporary visa. Dom had not noticed much at all apart from that everyone in a uniform had a very large gun.

Dom was carrying both suitcases, which were just about empty. Paula had told him to take next to nothing apart from under wear, as he would get a whole new wardrobe while he was in New York. Paula had done the same as she took every opportunity to buy new clothes. A woman's wardrobe can always extend to fit a new outfit in, or two.

As the two of them walked though the international arrivals lounge to the exit, Paula stopped off at the Virgin desk.

"Parking bay 4." Was what she told Dom.

"Are we driving?" Asked Dom.

"No that's where the limousine is waiting for us."

The Black Lincoln Continental was sat waiting for them, and the Chauffeur was only too keen to oblige. The Limo looked like a brand new one. All curved off, unlike its predecessor.

"What size engines in this beast?" Inquired Dom.

"Six and half litre engine, Sir."

Good job fuels cheap over here thought Dom.

It was just after eleven in New York and the roads in the suburbs seemed reasonably quiet. Paula was pointing out all the areas and attractions.

"I take it you've been before maam," asked the Chauffeur.

"Yes, but I still find it very awe-inspiring every time I see the Manhattan skyline. Reduced me to tears the first time I saw it."

"It is breathtaking maam."

"Could you take us in over the Queens Borough Bridge? I always think that's the best view, and my friend has not seen it before."

"Sure thing maam. In fact when we get close I'll let you know and your friend can stick his head out of the roof and have a better look."

"Thank you."

The limo made its way swiftly along Van Wyck expressway and then headed off onto Queens Boulevard towards Manhattan through the suburb of Queens.

"Isn't this where they filmed *Someone to watch over me?*" asked Dom.

"Well spotted Sir. In fact we're only two blocks away."

The roof on the limo started to open. "Just around the next corner we will be on the bridge." The Limo swept gracefully on to the bridge and both Dom and Paula stuck their head's through the sunroof.

Dom was speechless, partly due to the breeze that took his breath away. Dom glanced at Paula who had tears in her eyes.

"It gets me every time, truly breathtaking."

The East river was like a millpond and the skies were crystal clear.

"It's just like someone has taken the whole nights stars and condensed them to make the Manhattan skyline," said Dom.

"Do you want me to take you straight to the hotel or would you like a quick tour."

"Driver, we're in your hands," replied Paula.

The views from midtown and the Empire state, and the Chrysler building down towards where the twin towers had been left images emblazoned on the heart that would never be forgotten. The other sights of Manhattan became treasured memories.

The Limo completely circled Manhattan heading down Franklyn Roosevelt Drive, under Battery Park and then up West side highway, before cutting across 72$^{nd}$ street, to Central Park West and then down towards Columbus Circle.

In no time at all they had stopped outside Pierre's. Pierre's was situated on Fifth Avenue and East 61$^{st}$ Street. Across the road was Central Park.

"This is a very nice hotel!" said the driver. "Probably the best in Manhattan."

Paula slipped the driver a fifty-dollar bill for the extended trip. He had gone out of his way to show them the sights from the luxurious seats.

"Last time I came here it was Christmas and there was a big ribbon around the hotel. It looked like a present." The hotel did not appear large but part of an apartment building, however looks are deceptive as it extended most of the way down 61$^{st}$ street. "The New York Elite stay here. But I stay here because of the lovely rooms and views of the park. Each room has an individual Character. I hope you don't mind but I booked us a double."

Dom wasn't saying anything. He was just stunned by the whole thing. He was looking around in awe of his surroundings. He was walking in a daze, trying to catch the views of the park as he walked into the hotel. Paula took care of the paperwork at the reception whilst Dom was being nosey. They were booked in for a week at the Pierre and the second week they were stopping above a restaurant owned by one of Paula's friends. Dom had no idea what this was costing, but it certainly wasn't £19.99 B&B.

The bellboy led them to their room which was situated on the top floor at the front of the building overlooking the Park. When the door was opened, Dom could not believe his eyes. It was exquisite. Fit for a King. The size was immense. Really high ceilings, and the decorations, well they were magnificent. It was all too much for him. He walked across to the balcony window and looked left across the park with the skyline of Manhattan as the backdrop. He was a little choked and was unable to say anything for fear of bursting into tears. All hard men have soft centres, and what Paula was doing for him was beginning to get to him. The room was a suite that was bigger than most people's homes in England. Separate lounge, dining area, massive en-suite and both beds were king size.

"Do you like it?" shouted Paula as she waltzed into the bathroom

"I'm not even going to answer that. Do you stop here all the time?"

"I've stayed in a few but this is my favourite."

"Paula…. this treatment, it has to stop. You can't keep treating me like a king. I don't deserve this."

"Look Mr Modest. During my life, I have been raped, kidnapped, shot at, lost my nearest and dearest family in tragic circumstances and the only thing that prevented me from the same fate is you." Paula seemed pretty pissed at him and was really in full swing. "I have more money than I can spend, and yet you." She was shouting now. "You get paid a lousy wage,"

"Got paid," he interjected.

"Worked all hours God sent, was treat like shit, and yet you were quite prepared to lay down your life." Paula was now staring Dom out face to face as if she was about to punch his lights out. "And when you see that person in a hospital bed, shot and injured, you realise that you have got to live for today, otherwise it is all in vein. You risked all to achieve nothing. But this way we get to do it all, have whatever we want, and I have gained the best friend in the world."

Paula had mellowed again and Dom had the perspective. He wasn't about to argue. It was futile. "Okay I give in, but before you kill me with kindness. Can we get something to eat I'm starving?"

This broke the emotional tension that had built up. "I'm sorry."

"For what? Caring!"

Room service was quick and the array of food and the wine was exceptional.

Paula began to tease Dom about the room. "Hope you can cope with a sexy scantily clad women wandering around the room in next to nothing."

"Why are we expecting a guest?"

"Cheeky!"

"I'm used to it, happens all the time." Dom was playing it cool

"Sharon Stone and Julia Roberts do it all the time."

"In your dreams!"

"Funny you should mention that."

"Oh I see."

"I wasn't lying."

"Well I hope you can cope with the sight of a real woman in the flesh."

There was a pause. Dom was pondering his next answer. It was all down to the delivery and just as Paula was having a sip of wine.

"If you're that sexy I'll have a wank."

Paula nearly choked as they both burst out laughing.

"Very funny."

It was nearly three before the two of them got of to bed. It might have been three in the morning but the streets still sounded alive. It truly was a city that never slept.

"What's on the agenda for tomorrow?"

"Barneys, which is just around the back of the hotel, and then a little stroll down Fifth to do a little shopping. A girl can't resist Channel you know and then it's the sights."

"Sounds good to me."

By dinner time the following day Dom had been fitted out with several new suites in Barneys and Paula had purchased several outfits. As they strolled along fifth back towards the hotel Dom spotted the Levi shop just off fifth. It was either 56$^{th}$ or 57$^{th}$ street but Dom had lost count. With several rugby tops and t-shirts under his arm Dom soon came to the top of the second flight of stairs, he looked at what appeared to be a familiar face and without hesitation had said, " Morning," before walking past the man who had very politely returned the greeting. "Good morning." Dom was racking his brains thinking of where he knew the man from when it suddenly hit him. It was Cliff Richards. He was in his T-shirt and jeans. Dom turned to see where Paula was stood. "Pssssst. Pssssst," Dom was trying to get Paula's attention. "What's the matter?"

"Look over there, its Cliff Richards."

"Where?"

"There." With that Paula turned on her heels and headed straight for Sir Cliff. Dom was still frozen to the spot wondering what she was going to do.

Paula instantly greeted Sir Cliff with a kiss on his cheek and said how nice it was to see him again. It was if they were old friends and then Paula introduced Dom to Sir Cliff. Dom was still pretty dumb struck. The conversation was over before he knew he was in one. Dom had more questions than answers.

"Don't tell me he's a client."

"Don't be silly."

"How long have you known him then?"

"About three minutes, I've always wanted to meet him, and now I have. I even managed to kiss him. He'll now be thinking that he must have met me at a function and will feel embarrassed that he can't remember me. What a lovely man." Paula was saying, whilst Dom was in the queue waiting to pay. Then, just as Dom got to the front of the queue, Sir Cliff walked over as he was leaving the shop. "Lovely to see you both, bye."

For the next half an-hour Paula was so giddy at having met him they got absolutely nothing done, so they headed for the nearest Starbucks for caffeine and cookies and to recharge the sugar levels.

The first week flew by. Time just disappeared down a black hole but the sights had been truly amazing. The views of the city had been spectacular from the top of the Empire state building and they had both had tears in their eyes at ground Zero and the sight of the girder crucifix. Dom was impressed at how clean the city was and how safe it had felt. Paula had explained that the new Mayor of New York had operated a Zero Tolerance policy to crime and it appeared to be working.

It had hit home about Dom's own prejudices and stereotypical images when they had got on the Subway one morning. Dom had wanted to go and see the Federal Reserve and so they had gone to the Subway station to catch the green line to take them to the Wall Street district. As it had been peak commuter hour Dom and Paula had been pushed towards the back carriage. Shortly after Dom and Paula had been seated three Rastafarians got into the carriage, all carrying black bin liners and sat themselves on different seats near to Dom and Paula. Unfortunately there was no one else seated in this carriage now and Dom felt particularly vulnerable. It was as if there was an imminent fear of foreboding. The reality was that these fears couldn't have been more unfounded. He had misjudged them badly. As soon as the train had set off the lads where straight into their bin liners, removing small electrical items, electric toothbrushes, hair dryers, gents razors checking that the were in good working order. As they spoke it became apparent that they were street traders. But it was the conversation that stunned Dom the most. Rather than "Yow white boy, why don't you and the bitch put ya motha fuckin money and credit cards and any jewellery in the bag." It went something like this.

"Leo." No reaction as he appeared to be deep in thought

"Leo."

"What man."

"Did you see that program on TV last night?"

"Which one?"

Dom was thinking the one where all the people on the train get robbed.

"The market news program. There was a ten minute slot about street traders."

"Seriously man."

"Yow seriously, did nay paint us in a bad light either. Seein as how we're tryin to make a livin."

"Na I missed it, but I read the article in the economist about this man who was a Street trader that made a million."

"Ya shittin me man."

"Na man I ain't."

"I'll let you read it; I've got it at home."

Paula was digging Dom in the ribs telling him that it was their stop but Dom was totally absorbed. He almost wanted to turn around and apologise to the men for totally misjudging them.

"Funny how images of people cloud your judgement," he said to Paula.

"Mmmm."

"You'd have thought after my treatment at the hands of the press I wouldn't have prejudged someone so easily."

"Oh well, a reminder never hurts. Treat people as you find them."

The second week became more of a working holiday but the experience of New York was still stimulating. Dom and Paula moved in with Kostas at his Italian Restaurant on Mulberry Street, which is situated in Little Italy. Kosta who is half Greek, half Italian was a kind and patient man. He spent hours with Dom imparting his knowledge and love of food and wines that he had built over many years in the catering business. He also gave Dom tips on Etiquette, and how to be the perfect gentlemen. It came easy to Dom, who loved this approach to becoming the complete and perfect dinner partner or host.

Dom had elected to learn French since he had studied it at school. The problem at school was the emphasis had been on writing it and translating it, when it should have been to communicate, 'The spoken word'. Most encounters with French speaking people would result in "Bonjour Monsieur" "Bonjour madam," "Common ca va?" "ça va bien, merci". Not holding a placard up saying good morning, can I have a loaf of bread please? Paula had arranged for Dom to do a distance-learning package that would involve an hour a week with a personal tutor to concentrate on the spoken word.

Dom had learnt a lot over the past two weeks and his friendship with Paula was getting stronger. He loved to talk to her and wished that the two weeks would last forever but there was a job to be done.

Paula and Dom flew back to Heathrow before catching the connecting flight to Manchester airport. Paula had bought a paper whilst waiting for the connecting flight. Dom had only glanced at the headlines on the front page, but it was Paula that had spotted the article on the third page. A fifth prostitute had been attacked and left lying in a pool of blood at the rear of an old derelict railway station. She was currently in intensive care due to massive blood loss and internal injuries from a beating. The article speculated about the murder of Sharon now being a separate matter as the DNA samples and MO (Modus Operandi) were different. Paula chose not to tell Dom. He looked tired, and after all it was nothing to do with him. He had no responsibilities Police wise or other and he had not even been in the country when the attack had happened.

# 28

Maybe it was the calm before the storm, but for Dominic things were beginning to fall into a routine. His new job was going well and he was enjoying himself. He was the fittest he had ever been in his entire life and his circle of friends was increasing rapidly. When he was not working he would probably be at Paula's socialising. He had little money but then again he did not need any money. Paula was taking care of his bills and at night he rarely paid for anything and if he did it was down to the company MasterCard. Anyway five years he kept saying to himself and I will be a millionaire.

However, it was not as if he did not live like a millionaire. He had a brand new car, the best clothes money could buy and mostly he ate in very posh restaurants. It was a good job he had the time to go to the gym else the pounds would have really loaded up around his waist. The only thing that Dom really missed was a night in. He rarely had the opportunity to watch television. Normally it would be a film he had taped the previous night that he would watch early evening before he went out. Although Paula had said he would be working three nights a week, Dom was already working five nights a week and the diary was booked up for the next three months solid. In fact over the Christmas period he could not take a single day off.

Dom had done some recalculations and at this rate the million might come up quicker than he thought. Dom found that ninety percent of the clients only wanted an escort for the night. Someone to flatter them, make them feel good about themselves. What had surprised him however was the number of people who were prepared to pay a thousand pounds per night for the privilege. Even more surprising was the fact that they kept coming back. Dom had taken one particular lady out every week for the last six weeks. Dom's date for tonight was an absolute stunner; and it had been on the fifth date she asked him to join her in the hotel room, for which she gave him another two hundred pounds in cash. Her name was Grace, a beautiful name for a beautiful lady. On every occasion after that Dom had been paid to sleep with Grace, he could not believe his luck. The meetings had always involved meals for two at the same restaurant. Turned out that the lady was a journalist working for a daily tabloid and was intending to do an exposé on escort agencies, she was going to try and reveal the sleazy world of escort agencies. The catch was she found herself being lured and intrigued into the escort world. Dom had sat there with his jaw on the table when she had told him she was a journalist, expecting the worst only to find his jaw still on the table when she had said she wanted him to ask Paula if she could join the agency. Initially Dom and Paula had been very sceptical in case it was just a way of exposing clients to the tabloids and the whole world would come down around them. However when Grace had brought a list of potential new clients that amounted to over one hundred people, some of them public figures and others very well to do the concerns diminished and the risks considered worth taking. Paula had an ace up her sleeve as per usual and had been able to confirm that ties to the paper had been severed.

As Dom had hardly had a day off since joining the company Paula had asked if Dom would like to accompany Grace to New York. Dom described it as being an arduous task but if his boss wanted him to go, who was he to argue. Dom only spent three days with Grace before having to return to England but the break had been a welcome one. What had intrigued Dom was that Paula had booked them into separate suites even though Dom had actually been sleeping with Grace. Dom never gave it a second thought other than the fact that maybe Paula had formed some form of attraction to Grace. That would be a twist, Journalist to Escort Lesbian lover in the space of a few weeks.

Dom was sat lounging around in his dressing gown recovering from jet lag and drinking gallons of coffee when Paula appeared at the door with Buster. "I've brought him home. I think he's been missing you…….. too much female company!" Whilst Dom was busy fussing Buster Paula's phone rang. A series of expletives followed by "Oh bollocks," meant that all was not well. "I'm at Dom's now I'll see what we can do, bye"

Dom had had no particular plans apart from reading about Thursday's date. This client was over in England on business. She was an American lady that was interested in Scuba diving and Archaeology. This was something that Dom had always promised himself he would do but just never got around to it, the diving not the Archaeology. She was called Yasmin and was an international buyer for an engineering company. She was over to attend a convention that spanned two days. The ploy was that she would attend the convention during the daytime and then Dom would pretend to be her boyfriend at the meal. Apparently, the last two occasions she had been in the country, men had forced themselves upon her all evening and it was not a very pleasurable experience for her. From the picture of Yasmin Dom could understand why. This was an unusual one because Yasmin's company were paying the hire fee. Obviously her sales figures more than made up for the expense of hiring Dom for the night. If she was half as talented and charming as she was good looking, then the company would pay handsomely to keep her happy.

"Go on then give me the good news."

It was explained to Dom that David, the other male escort, had been called to Edinburgh at short notice due to an illness in the family and he had just dropped everything and gone. Unfortunately

David dealt with a lady called Mrs Andreas, and he was due to see her this evening. It was one of his regular clients and Paula was sure there would be no problem should Dom be unable to make it, but Dom dutifully agreed to take over the engagement. Paula had left looking rather pleased that the wheel was back on the cart.

Dom had soon changed, grabbed the car keys and Buster's lead and headed off to the office, stopping at the woods on the way. Dom was cursing himself. He should have bought a fax machine then they could just fax all the details through to him instead. No that was a crap idea. Dom liked the glossy magazines that accompanied the package.

Buster accompanied Dom into the office and made his usual rounds so that at least everyone in the office had fussed him twice before he left them alone. Dom was quickly shuffling through the filing cabinets for the paperwork of Mrs Andreas. As he left the building Dom had not noticed that the back page of the plot had fallen from his sheet. After studying the paperwork Dom had surmised that it was a straight forward job. He would go to the ladies home address at eight pm. She would cook a meal for two. He would woo her and then they would retire to the bedroom at exactly eleven pm, this was unusual as exactly 11pm was underlined! Well that all appeared pretty straightforward. The Picture of her revealed that Isobel Andreas was Spanish and Latin in appearance probably in her late forties. In fact she fitted Dom's image of a traditional Flamenco dancer. Unfortunately Dom was not the one that spoke Spanish, but what the hell he was the sub. That was it. Dom never questioned the fact that it made mention of parking his car down the road, discretion was paramount.

At eight pm Dom rang the doorbell. The door opened and Isobel Andreas introduced herself. Dom had learnt not to question why, but this was a true lady. Slender, tall, bronzed with long tousled black hair. She was wearing black leather boots a long flowing black gypsy style skirt cut away to reveal her thigh and a white silk blouse. Clearly she was not wearing any underwear. The house was Georgian and the internal walls all wood panelled with huge tapestries. Isobel had a beautiful Latin accent but spoke perfect English. She flirted constantly with Dom telling him how her husband paid her no attention. He was always out at the Bridge club or Golf club. At the present time he was away on business in Amsterdam. Although Dom had not asked any questions, Isobel volunteered a lot of information about her husbands business, a jeweller that traded in diamonds. It was obvious the moment Dom had walked through the door that they were loaded. Especially when he caught a glimpse of the diamond ring she was wearing. Dom wasn't an expert on carrots but by the look of the ring, and the way it twinkled, even in the dim candlelight he had quickly come to the assumption that Bugs Bunny would have been at home.

At exactly eleven pm Isobel took hold of Dom's hand and started to smooch with him through the hallway to the stairs. She kept hold of his hand and lead him to the bedroom. As Isobel guided Dom to the bed he found that he had been stripped naked, she pointing to the bed whilst she disappeared behind a screen. Dom slipped into the bed whilst observing Isobel in the mirror. What a body. Isobel reappeared from behind the screen with the dim silhouetted light behind her. She was absolutely starkers apart from the leather boots. Boy did she have long legs. Dom had been totally oblivious to the sound of a car pulling up on the gravel drive, the slamming of the car door, or the alarm setting on the Jaguar. It was when the door chime rang as the front door opened that Dom sat upright in bed.

"What was that?"

Isobel was meandering across the bedroom towards the bed. She said nothing, she didn't have to.

"Hi, I'm home, you upstairs?"

"In the bedroom Honey."

'Fuck' thought Dom its Elma Fudd protecting those bloody carrots. Dom was quickly grabbing his clothing and trying to get dressed, but if he had taken the time to look, Isobel was totally composed. She never even flinched. Dom glanced up just long enough to see Isobel swaying to the music.

"Are you mad your husband's downstairs."

"No he's not," she said.

"What do you mean?"

"He's coming up the stairs."

Dom was shouting at Isobel in one of those stage voice whispers, whilst she swayed to the music. To Dom she looked like she was stoned, while he did an impression of a bouncy ball pinging 'round the bedroom picking up his clothes. This was like a bad movie. Dom quickly assessed his options. The wardrobe or the window? Isobel pointed to the wardrobe but Dom was having none of it. He was out of the window. Dom clung onto the window ledge before letting go. It was a good way down to the gravel path. Saying nothing of grazing his elbows on the wall or spraining his ankle on impact with the path. Dom leant against the wall, adrenalin pumping and in total agony. It was like being in the Police force again, only this time he was being pursued.

Dom hopped to the car, realising now why his car was supposed to be parked down the street. It was in case Elma returned. Dom quickly rang Paula to appraise her of what had happened, just in case there should be any complaints from the client.

"Yes, you might laugh."

"No you wouldn't have wanted to see me swinging from the window with my trousers round my ankles."

"What do you mean wait till the others hear about this?"

"You're heartless."

"Will you stop laughing, my ankles killing me?"

"You better come and pick me up."

"What do you mean why, because I'm injured?"

"That stopped you laughing."

"Okay see you in ten."

It was fortunate that the job had been in Sheffield. Dom was sat in the car and beginning to calm down. His heart rate was returning to normal. By the time Paula had arrived they were both in stitches. A quick trip to the hospital revealed no lasting damage, and no broken bones. A couple of days and he would be back on his feet. Paula insisted that he stay with her and they went to collect Buster before retiring for the evening.

Paula had kept smirking all evening and she was obviously finding something amusing. Dom had not been able to put his finger on it, assuming that she had just found it all hilarious. Dom was laid on the bed when there was a tap at the door.

"Only me."

"Come in."

"Dom can I ask you a question?"

"Yes sure, fire away."

"Why did you jump out of the window?"

"You know why. The hubby came home."

"He was supposed to."

"You what?"

"That's the rouse."

"What, that he catches her every Monday in bed with another man?"

· "No, the husband comes home finds her in the mood and they have sex with either you or David watching through the slats in the Wardrobe door. That's their fantasy, they like to do it with an audience and for a free meal and a thousand pounds who am I to argue?"

"You're joking!"

"David says it only lasts about three minutes, he's that excited it's over and done with before she gets the boots off. Dave's normally home for twelve."

"How does he get out?"

"Easy the bloke say's I've left something in the car Dear, and Isobel let's you out of the back door."

"Arggh...... Whoops!"

"No problem, I'll just deduct it from your wages if we lose the client."

Paula winked at him, and put her hand to her heart. "My hero."

Dom threw the cushion at her as she slipped out of the bedroom.

# 29

Whilst Dom had been negotiating gravel landings, Rossy had spent hours going through the statements. Rossy's now almost permanent headache had started again about nine pm. It had been a phone call from the DI. The DS had been making enquiries into Sharon's diary and the list of names. Virtually all the names had been eliminated bar two. One was Kenny Pritchard. The other was Andrew Roberts. 'Keep working on it' the

Superintendent had told the DI, 'and keep me informed.' Rossy had this inexplicable sinking feeling. He had considered going to the scene at the time of the murder but he had feared he may have been recognised. He was sure then that he had done the right thing in not going. Unfortunately he could never use the excuse that a witness might have seen him during the course of the investigation. Now he realised he had made a big mistake. He should have gone. He hoped that he would not live to regret it. But who the bloody hell is Andrew Roberts? It was obvious, if he could have actually got his head around it. But that realisation would come to him later.

Rossy had just gone for one drink, just to calm his nerves, but one became two and three and four and before he realised it he was blitzed. Fortunately the landlord was a friend, who had put him in a taxi; he was in no fit state to drive. The last thing Rossy needed was to have his mug shot plastered on the front page of the paper for drunk driving. It had happened to so many of his colleagues that had just thrown it all away. Career and pension, it really wasn't worth it.

As the front door creaked open to the cottage Rossy tripped over the doormat and collided with the phone table. The crashing sound was enough to wake Abby.

"Keith is that you?"

"Shhh, yep, only me."

"You Okay?"

"I twipped."

"You're pissed again!"

"No I'm not."

Abby was out of bed and across the landing. The light was on and she was stood at the top of the stairs with her dressing gown wrapped around her.

"You bastard, you promised me you were working."

"I was…….. The case broke a little, cot a glue."

"Stick you're hand to the bottle did it? You can't even speak."

"Funny!"

"Well Poirot, you haven't got a fucking clue about how to treat your wife."

Abby was now storming down the stairs to pick the phone up off the floor. As she reached for it, Rossy snapped.

"Who ya ringing?"

"No one, I'm picking it up you drunken bum."

"Gimme that, you're not phoning anyone."

"I know I'm putting it back on the stand."

Rossy grabbed the phone from Abby, pulling on the chord with all his strength. It was a mistake because she just let go of the phone and he fell backwards banging his head on the door.

"You fucking bitch."

It was an instinctive reaction, he was in pain, the red mist had descended and all common sense and reasoning had gone out of the window. The phone flew through the air connecting with the bone just above Abby's right eye. The skin popped like a boxers and a small but deep cut opened above the eye. Blood started to run down her face blurring her vision. Abby collapsed onto the floor holding her eye. Her lilac dressing gown now covered in blood.

"I'm sorry, I'm sorry." was all Rossy could muster. He was just too pissed to be of any use.

After ten minutes with a cold compress on it, Abby could see that the cut would need at least a couple of stitches. She got dressed and threw a blanket over the drunken bum who had collapsed in the lounge and was now snoring his head off.

The roads were quiet as she drove to the hospital, all the time worrying what she was going to say to the Doctor about her injury. She couldn't say that her husband had assaulted her. They might contact the Police. They needed help, not the Police. She knew he was under so much pressure at work but this couldn't continue. He was a good man but at what point do you escape a relationship. They always say that a woman is assaulted on many occasions before she ever contacts the Police, so did that mean there was more to come. Abby was arguing with herself. She had always called women who put up with being beaten weak. This wasn't a beating though, it was an accident, he hadn't meant to hurt her, she was sure of that. She was crying now and the blood was mingling with the tears. She could see the headlines in the paper. Police Superintendent responsible for setting forces domestic violence policy assaults wife. Abby walked into the accident and emergency department and was pleased to see that it was almost empty for once. No drunks she thought, but then again it was Monday not Saturday. She felt sorry for the nurses who had to deal with the drunken yobs that came in from the pub having had a skin full. Then she laughed to herself, no the drunken yob was at home, but he's the reason I'm here. Abby booked herself in explaining to the triage nurse that she had gone to make a coffee. Left the cupboard door open, turned and walked into the edge of the door, cutting her eye. The nurse had looked at her quizzically and then handed to her a form on domestic violence. 'Very convincing' thought Abby.

Abby had gone to sit in the reception room to await treatment. There were three other people in the room. One looked like a bit of a thug and then there was a well-dressed man and woman, laughing and joking at the other end of the room. She went and sat next to them, as she felt a little safer. She'd had enough excitement for one night. She was trying to mind her own business and read the leaflet with one eye. She glanced up to see the man staring at her. He was handsome. He had a kind face. They looked like a nice couple. He smiled at her and without a second thought she smiled back.

"Looks like we're in the same boat!" he said

Abby looked quizzically at him. "How do you work that out then?"

Dom pointed towards the domestic violence form. Paula was looking at him, wondering what on earth he was going to say next.

Dom leant forward and whispered to Abby. "She pushed me out of the window."

Paula digged Dom in the ribs and they set of laughing.

"Mr Veil, please." Shouted the nurse

Abby weakly protested "Oh I walked into a door."

As Paula wheeled Dom into the cubicle, Abby reflected at how her protest had seemed so weak and futile. Was it that obvious? Why was she covering for him? He had hurt her.

Rossy woke with a blinding headache trying to work out why he was lying on the lounge floor. He couldn't even remember getting home last night. His neck was stiff and every part of his body ached. It was then that he noticed the bump on his head. As he walked into the hallway he could see the blood on the carpet. 'Oh my God' he thought. 'What on earth happened here?' Rossy made his way into the bedroom and saw Abby asleep on the bed. Her hair spread across the pillow. She looked so peaceful. She was beautiful. Rossy stared in disbelief as he saw the cut to her eye. The cut was in the centre of her right eyebrow. He could count three butterfly stitches. It was too much for him to take, he instantly new he had something to do with the injury. He just managed to reach the toilet before he vomited. What was happening to him, he was turning into a monster. He needed serious help.

P aula was woken by an early morning telephone call. Before she was able to take the call the answer machine had clicked into place.

"High, this is Isobel Andreas. Thanks for last night. My husband never realised that Dom wasn't in the wardrobe and I found the whole thing just a terrific turn on. Thanks for the new twist."

Dom had also overheard the recording and was now laughing to himself. Poor old Dave he thought. Isobel is going to throw him out of the window next time.

# 30

Dom found it highly amusing that he was attending the Policeman's ball. His invitation had stemmed from Lady Emma Taylor. Her late husband had been a close friend of the previous Chief Constable and he had been a member of the Police Complaints Authority. He had been highly regarded and well respected but although he was a member of the complaints authority he was very pro-police and keen to see the image of the Police go untarnished. Alas it was his lifestyle that had caught up with him. The only exercise he ever got was when his right hand had lifted to his mouth. Usually with a fine malt Scotch in a crystal glass. Sir Roger had never heeded the warnings given to him by the Doctors and so paid the ultimate penalty... Life! The post mortem had revealed that he had sclerosis of the Liver, but it had been a massive heart attack that had killed him.

This particular Policeman's ball was to be held in his honor, but as far as Lady Emma Taylor was concerned, he had no honor. His massive heart attack had occurred whilst humping his new secretary. It was nothing new to Lady Emma and she knew of his string of affairs, he had been less than discreet, and in fact he bragged to his friends of his latest conquests. Lady Emma had always used this angle to make his friends feel as guilty as possible when it came round to collecting for the local charities. Roger had even bragged to her in bed one night that was why he had affairs, to keep his credibility and help her raise money. The only thing she actually raised that night was her knee which had swiftly dealt a blow to Rogers lower anatomy, leaving him somewhat deflated and in agony. That had been six months prior to his death and they had not made love since. Emma had told him she preferred the battery operated device; it was more reliable, harder, bigger, and managed to keep going until she'd had some pleasure. Not just three humps, a groan and a squirt, before the overweight lump collapsed on her with a silly grin on his face. She now thought herself lucky that he had died humping the secretary. It would be the secretary that had the fears of the next man dying in her bed. She could be scarred for life; still she had the ultimate chat up line if ever asked "Are you any good at it?"

"Oh yes.... I shagged the last one to death."

Lady Taylor was a leading fundraiser for several local charities and a total socialite but a working socialite. She always saw her self as fundraiser and that was the reason for her attendance. She sought to attend at least two public functions a week, mostly on her own, however the odd occasion arose when she liked to take a partner. She found it comforting especially at large dinner dances. It was always nice to see a friendly face in the crowd. She had a knack of being able to work a group of people into parting with money or supporting her local schemes. On this occasion Lady Emma particularly wanted an escort. She knew that this had been Sir Rogers's home ground and that all his friends would be there. They all knew what he had been like and she just did not want to cope with the fake and phony on her own. She particularly loathed the Policeman's Ball, local politicians, the upper echelons of the Police Service and local dignitaries. She had never been able to put her finger on what exactly it was that she loathed but the entire experience always made her skin crawl, just like Roger. Perhaps it was the overriding feeling that everyone was there to network, to attain the next rank. Make allies with the local politicians and leading businessmen. As a fundraiser the experience had always proved pointless. Tight bastards with power she had told her husband last time, all empire building.

She found it amusing when Paula had given her the option to take Dom, especially when Paula had filled her in on his background. 'Splendid,' was the word she had used. Lady Taylor was only attending so as not to appear disrespectful. Her late husband had always attended, and one of the senior officers intended to make an honoree gesture to the late Sir Roger Taylor. Hence her hand had been forced.

The Cavendish Hall was the venue for the occasion. Some two hundred and fifty guests were expected to a sit down meal. There would then be the obligatory speeches before the dancing. Carriages were at twelve-thirty. Dom was bang on time to collect Lady Emma Taylor. Dom had been somewhat surprised after Paula had filled him in on the events surrounding her husband's death. He had been expecting a frumpy woman, older than her years. Dom was very pleasantly surprised to find a Lady in her late forties, maturing well and appearing to be more beautiful with age. She was one of those ladies that flourished as she got older. She was almost regal, elegant in stature. Nice legs and a bubbly personality. In fact they looked the perfect couple, Dom wearing his black DJ and dickey whilst Lady Emma was wearing a long flowing petrol blue coloured chiffon dress cut off at the bust. Conversation flowed freely and Lady Emma insisted that Dom just call her Emma. It was too much of a mouthful to keep coming out with the rest. Emma fully briefed Dom about her latest venture, which was a women's refuge on the outskirts of the city. Emma had explained that she was going to try and raise a certain amount of interest and get some financial backing from the people who were attending. She thought that this was a good cause to champion considering the Police's new domestic violence initiative. If I raise five hundred pounds tonight I'll be stunned she had told him.

"Leave it to me. I am pretty sure that when they see me tonight they won't want to be out done when I start."

"What are you going to do?"

"Look upon me as your fundraising manger for tonight."

"Okay I'm in your hands," she said smiling inquisitively.

It had been several months since Dom had left the Police but Superintendent Marsh and Ross recognised him instantly. Several "What's he doing here?" were muttered, but no one had the courage to ask. Lady Emma introduced Dom as a close personal friend that was assisting her in her efforts to raise money for the needy. It was clear for all to see that for men in positions of power they were one; envious, two; jealous, and three; weary of him. Why was he such a threat? They had sacked him, well he'd resigned, it was all the same, but they also knew he had not really done that much wrong. They also knew that he was a real hero, a man of action, who if truth be known they would rather have on their side.

Maybe it was just luck, written in the PG tips, or plain old fate that Dom was sat where he was. On his right was Lady Emma and on his left was Abby Ross. The tables were large and circular with ten people on each. Dom glanced at Abby on several occasions not wanting to appear as if he was staring, but he couldn't help himself, she was certainly striking. He had noted that she was wearing a short, very short, black lace cocktail dress, and from where Dom was sat at the side he could see that the dress easily rode high on Abby's thigh. Well, high enough for him to see the lace top stockings. Abby caught Dom looking and smiled at him. "Eh... Cheeky!"

Dom had seen her somewhere before, and was recounting his recent encounters trying to recall where he had seen the young women. She would be thirty, five foot five, long dark hair, extremely shapely figure. Dom estimated she was a 32D, but it was her eyes that held him transfixed. The clearest emerald green he had ever seen. It was always the eyes that hooked Dom. Eyes speak a thousand words and can hide nothing. To him they are the gateway to your soul. He was always caught staring into Paula's eyes, hers just totally captivate him, but alas she was out of his league, literally, wrong bloody division. Dom snapped out of his thoughts for Paula and back to the real world.

"Forgive me for staring but you have beautiful eyes."

"Home grown...... not even contacts." She said winking at him.

Dom felt like a young schoolboy that had just had his first kiss behind the bike sheds. It was a good job it was dark in there because he was sure he was blushing.

If he wasn't blushing now then he certainly was two seconds later.

"Young man," Abby started, "I find you looking at my stocking tops and then paying compliments to my eyes. One would consider that you were coming onto me."

"I thought I'd seen you some where before."

"Oh that old chestnut, 'I'm sure we've met before routine.'" Abby was playing hardball.

Dom was not about to give in so easily. He had seen her before and at the minute, until he could place her, he was on a hiding to nothing, especially now he'd gone down the line of haven't we met before. It would have been a cop out to change his tactics. He had met her, of that he was sure but where? It would come to him.

Lady Emma was in full flow and was charming the pants of the gents at the table in a vein attempt to encourage them to part with their cash. At the moment she had their attention but not their cash. Prior to Dom's brief flirtation he had noted that Rossy appeared uneasy and that he and Abby did not appear to be communicating at all, in fact she was deliberately ignoring her husband. When the conversation had turned to women's refuge and domestic violence Rossy had appeared distinctly sheepish.

The penny finally dropped and Dom was able to place Abby. The game was about to change direction with the white knight being in the position of power.

"How's your eye?"

Rossy overheard the question and nearly froze. 'How the fuck did he know about Abby's eye?' he thought to himself. Was she seeing this bloke behind his back? Don't be silly he told himself. But the doubts started. He wanted an answer and this was not the place to seek one.

"Fine thanks," Abby, too, seemed stunned at the question. Who was this man?

"Your eyebrow covers the scar."

"Yes, it heeled well."

Abby was confused. Had Rossy told anyone about the incident?

"Excuse me are you a doctor?" asked Abby.

Dom realised that Abby had no idea who he was. He recalled that she had seemed upset on the night and that even if she could recall him at the hospital he had been there with Paula, not Lady Emma. "No nothing like that."

Lady Emma had been intrigued by the conversation she was overhearing whilst selling her ideas. It was an art form doing both at once. Dom could see that Rossy was keeping out of the conversation and when someone said, "Why do they bloody stay with them?"

Abby had feebly offered 'Love' as an answer, but this was quickly swept away. They were referring to battered wives and girlfriends at the time. Anna Gregory, the local MP for Brightside, who was also sat at the table, was now on her soapbox telling the entire table what she would do to a man if he assaulted her. Dom had ascertained that their testicles would be particularly vulnerable. Dom doubted that anyone would want to argue with Mrs Gregory, as she was a formidable fifteen stone. Well that was his guess. It was a brave and strong man that wanted to punch her. It was an even braver man that would kiss her. Dom was suddenly hit with the fear that one day Anna Gregory would require an escort. That just didn't bare thinking about. He would talk to Paula and amend his contract to specifically exclude the retched MP. Dom snapped out of his worst nightmare. It was time to cause a bit of a stir and send out the message that it was time for the other guests to feel uncomfortable. Dom raised his glass, "To Lady Emma Taylor, I wish to pledge Five hundred pounds towards your new venture."

Lady Emma turned to face Dom in a state of shock. "Well thank you." The looks on the others faces were a peach. Dom had backed them right into a corner and knowing Policemen's egos they would not be outdone. Abby elbowed Rossy in the ribs; he was already half way down his second bottle of red wine.

"Yes excellent idea, I'll," correcting himself, "We, would like to pledge five hundred pounds also," stammered Rossy.

The pledge was echoed around the table and by the time the rumour had spread to the other tables Lady Emma had a queue of people wanting to pledge money. No one wanted to be outdone and although some of the pledges were not as outrageously generous as Dom's initial one the evening proved to be very fruitful. By the end of the night and the auction some thirteen thousand seven hundred and fifty pounds was pledged towards the project. Lady Emma took hold of Doms hand and requested that he dance with her. Once on the dance floor she whispered in his ear. "I owe you one. Thank you."

"Anytime, that was fun."

It had not escaped anyone's notice that Keith Pemberton Ross was drunk. Most had drunk a large amount but nothing like Rossy, they were amateurs as far as he was concerned, playing at it. Arthur Ross had come over to see if Abby was okay but she told him it was easier to ignore her husband rather than deal with him. Although he had not hit her since the incident with the phone he was still drinking. It was embarrassing.

"You like that girl. Don't you?" Asked Emma

"Yes very much.......but"

"But what?"

"Oh I don't know, there's something...I can't put my finger on it."

"Don't let that stop you........ go after her."

"I can't."

"Why not?"

"Well for one I am here with you, and secondly her husband is sat next to her."

"Dom my boy, ask her to dance, she needs cheering up."

"Are you sure?"

"Something tells me that Mrs Ross won't be Mrs Ross for much longer, she won't put up with that. Well not if she has any sense."

Dom wasted no time in going over to Abby when the Chief Constable had cut in and asked to dance with Lady Emma. She had given him the wink and told him to 'go for it.' Who was he to argue with a real lady!

"Would you like to dance?"

Dom could see Rossy mimicking his words to Abby.

"I'd Love to, just one second."

Abby leant over and whispered something in Rossy's ear. From what Dom could over hear, there were a few expletives and the general hint was that he go home and leave her be. What ever she did say to him appeared to work, as he stood up almost immediately and went to the door, exchanging a brief word with his father on the way out.

"Well that took care of that drunken pillock," said Abby.

Dom was not sure what to say for the best.

"Have you remembered yet, how we met?"

"You're the window cleaner."

"What and I've seen you in the flesh."

"Oh you wish" she said tongue in cheek.

The two were now smooching to some George Michael song.

"Yes, I suppose you're right."

Dom knew as soon as he had said it, it was the wrong thing to say, and normally he was so careful.

"Suppose," she said laughing at him.

"One should never reveal their hand too soon," he retorted.

For the first time in ages Abby had that feeling of being protected, she was in a man's arms that were strong and completely wrapped around her, her head resting on his shoulder. It was a funny feeling, like nothing she had ever felt before.

"The hospital," she whispered, "how's your ankle?"

"Well remembered," and the balance of power slipped again, it was now stalemate.

"Where's your wife tonight?"

"She's with her new boyfriend."

"You looked so happy."

"Oh that wasn't my wife that was my boss."

"Good looking boss."

"Yes she is rather," Dom quickly added, "Nearly as good looking as you."

"Charmer."

They swayed to the music just happy to be holding each other. Lady Emma managed a quick wink of approval as she sauntered past. Dom plucked up enough courage and decided to go for broke.

"Has he hit you since?"

"No not since, but as you've seen tonight he is still drinking heavy. He's an alcoholic but he just won't admit it." For the first time Abby had admitted to someone that Rossy had hit her. Why had she done that? She never intended to let it slip.

"Why stay with him?"

"Love."

"I didn't really want to hear that."

"Why?"

"You certainly go for the jugular, don't you?"

"Sometimes a girl needs to know where she stands."

"Well put it this way do you believe in lust at first sight?"

"I refuse to answer that one on the grounds that it might incriminate me."

Abby was starting to get the stare from her father in-law, "Look I have to go."

"Don't settle for second best. Don't let the bastard hurt you."

Dom had hit home. He had unnerved Abby. She knew he was right and she also knew that she was attracted to him, but she had a husband to deal with first. Dom took out his wallet and gave her his card. "Ring me anytime……. and I mean anytime." All too quickly she was gone. Dom felt giddy like a schoolboy, she would be his, but was it love or lust? His was struggling to reconcile his feelings. Something was nagging at his heartstrings, but what? What was causing him so much concern? Before he could consider his own thoughts Lady Emma was on him in a flash. "How did it go? You looked cosy together."

"I'm not sure Emma, but it's been one hell of a night. We conned them out of a few grand and made them feel uncomfortable on their home ground, and I think I've just met the girl of my dreams."

Lady Emma paused and considered his answer. "Adda boy, come on take this old bird home. A Lady needs her beauty sleep you know."

As Dom drove home, Emma was very quiet and as he opened the door to help her to her feet she kissed him tenderly on the cheek and gave him a big hug. "Thank you again for all your help tonight."

"You're welcome, anytime, I really enjoyed it."

"Oh Dom...... one other thing. She's not the one"

Dom looked quizzical at her

You said "I think."

She kissed him lightly again and left him standing on the pavement.

# 31

Arthur Ross was sat in his office reading the morning paper and drinking a cup of sludge that was supposed to be coffee. In fact the coffee was only hindering his headache and adding to his bad mood. Art was reading a local piece on the women's refuge and the benefits it would provide for women in need and the local community. Art was also contemplating the fact that he had pledged five hundred pound's to Lady Emma's work.

Boy what a sucker, between his son and himself they had put up a thousand pounds. Art berated himself, stuff 'em was what he was thinking but it was all too late. That damn Veil was having a laugh at their expense.

It was now nine-thirty am and still no sign of his son. Art was beginning to worry about him. He was kicking himself for pushing him so hard. He knew the boy was good, damn good, better than he had ever been or ever could be, yet all he could do was shout at him and give him a hard time over Abby. He thought he ought to give Abby a ring to see if they were both okay only he couldn't get anyone to answer the phone. Art knew that Abby had got home safely as he had dropped her off. Oh well Keith was probably on his way to work. He tried his mobile but that was switched off. Art gave up worrying about it; he was a grown man for God's sake. He had got to forty without him interfering so he wasn't about to start now, it was just one of those funny feelings, he felt something was wrong but what exactly he had no idea.

Art's thoughts were broken by the sound of the phone ringing. Art instantly new who it was and did not particularly want to talk to the Chief especially after his belittling comments the night before?

"Argh good morning Sir."

"Yes it was a good night."

"Yes Lady Emma did an excellent job."

"Good idea, yes that would go down well with the press."

The pleasantries shifted from the previous night to the real reason he had rung.

"No Sir I haven't forgotten about the presentation to the federation."

"No I am fully up to speed with the new designs for the protection vests."

"In hand, leave it with me."

"Bye Sir."

"Arsehole, now where did I put the file on ballistic vests?"

No sooner had Art stood up to find the folder with his notes in, the phone rang again. Now what he thought?

"Good morning Detective Inspector."

"Oh." Followed by stunned silence.

"Where?"

"When?"

"Have you spoken to my Son?"

"No, I can't find him either."

"I'll be down in two minutes."

It took the Detective Inspector and the ACC five minutes to get to the scene.

"Who found the body?" asked the DI to the PC guarding the scene.

"The caretaker Sir. He's over there in the school. Oh and Sir, he's in shock."

The officer took their names and added it to the incident log. It was just protocol, to ascertain who had been to the scene in case any evidence needed to be eliminated, and it also kept people away from the scene to protect it from those that had just come for a nosey. Art and DI Jones were experienced officers with fifty years Policing experience between them but neither had seen a body so badly beaten. It was not mutilated but the injuries were excessive.

The scene was a hive of activity and the protection tent was just being erected. It would prevent nosey onlookers and allow the officers to work at a pace that meant it wasn't a race against the elements, as rain appeared a distinct possibility. Three task force teams appeared; drafted in to start on the local enquires. One team conducting a finger tip search of the school grounds the other the adjacent paths and streets while the third team went door-to-door. The kids loved it, they had been sent home for the day, for the parents a nightmare rearranging their days to accommodate.

The school was situated on the outskirts of the town centre smack in the middle of the red light district. Most of the surrounding area was commercial, industrial units and shops, very few houses. All the video surveillance of the city had been seized and detectives were being instructed on tasks to complete. Most were based on tracing all known prostitutes in the area whilst other teams of detectives were contacting taxi companies. This was the second murder and seventh attack.

The police surgeon was on the scene, assessing the position of the body and the surrounding environment. It would be his job to piece together the chronological sequence of events in terms of how the young girl died and ultimately give a cause of death. The DI was looking to the police surgeon for some initial guidance. Normally police surgeons tended to closely guard any assessment for fear of getting it wrong, but Dr Lamkins was very helpful. He made it clear to the DI it was only his initial assessment and the conversation was taped. Not to protect anyone but purely to assist the Doctor in his prognosis.

"Sir it appears that the deceased and the assailant have come onto the school premises for privacy. Up until this point I would suggest that no violence has been proffered, as there is no trail of blood to the scene. It is extremely concentrated, tending to suggest this was the spot. You can see the pooling from the head, towards the drain."

The DI and ACC were glancing around to see for themselves and nodded in agreement with the Doctor.

"Secondly I would say that the girl came totally voluntarily and was even participating in a sexual act when the assault occurred. Look at the girls clothing," the Dr was pointing to the girl's clothes.

"You can see from the way the top is rolled down towards the girls middle and the fact that she is not wearing a bra would tend to suggest she has just rolled the top down around her middle, so that whom ever could see or fondle her breasts. Next you can see the skirt doing the same thing rolled up over her top around her middle revealing her bottom and again if you look closely without touching, it appears that there is no damage to either garment, suggesting at this stage that she was compliant and no struggle had taken place. Her knickers are on the floor, again in one piece. I'm a little confused by this as most don't wear any or they just slip them to one side to allow penetration, so I'd rather not speculate on this."

"So basically you're saying that the pick up and the sexual act if any up to this point had no violence attached to it."

"Just about, but I won't be sure whether they had intercourse until the post mortem, but my guess is that they did"

"Okay, so what happened next?"

"I'm only surmising but I think that at the point of ejaculation and I must stress this is purely speculation, the attacker has flipped, inflicting extensive injuries to the head. It could be consistent with a kicking looking at the disfigurement of the face. Her torso looks pretty much intact, as there are no external markings to her chest or breast region. The next region of massive trauma is that of the vagina. Her pelvic plate looks totally crushed, probably caused by repeated kicking and stamping in this area. Death, I would say, due to trauma caused to the head. Extensive head injuries and blood loss possibly linked to shock. The girl would probably have been unconscious within seconds and had no chance to summons any assistance."

"Thank you," said Art

"If you want my opinion, this is the killer's first murder."

The DI and the ACC looked at the medical examiner, wanting further information.

"What does that mean?"

"Well all the assaults on prostitutes to date have all had the same MO. The injuries are all consistent with it being the same person, even this attack, although the injuries are a little more severe. But the murder of the prostitute in her home, that one baffles me. At the minute, I would go out on a limb and say that you are looking for two killers. That first killing had no sexual connotations, purely a single blow to the head and a minor scuffle. This was an intense attack of rage and hatred."

Art was very quiet. All he was thinking was the Chief is going to love this. We couldn't even solve it when we thought there was one killer, now we have two. But then again, they had known for a while that the DNA samples had been different. It didn't alter things that much, well, he hoped it wouldn't! Art was suddenly thinking back to the days of the Yorkshire Ripper. This needed sorting, and quickly.

# 32

It was just after eleven thirty when Rossy made it into his office. He was already aware that there had been another murder. He had heard it on the news although the radio broadcast had been a little bit sketchy to say the least. All it had said was that the body of a young woman had been found in the school grounds and the Police were treating it as suspicious.

As soon as he sat down his phone began to ring.

"Good morning Detective Superintendent Ross speaking"

"Where the fuck've you been all morning?" bellowed Art.

"Morning."

"Don't 'morning' me, get yourself upstairs now."

Art hung up. He was in no mood to humour his son. It was time for a rant.

The onslaught began the moment Rossy walked through the door. It was unpleasant, abusive and totally uncalled for, but it was making Art feel better. He was doing his job, he was telling his boy how it was and how it was going to be. Rossy just sat down and listened and after five minutes the shouting stopped. His ears were ringing. Art was looking at his son who was saying nothing.

There was one of those really unpleasant voids, a vacuum in sound that made Art feel really uncomfortable so he decided to fill the gap and started shouting again.

Two minutes later the shouting stopped. Rossy still said nothing. This was winding Art up even more.

"What's the matter with you?"

"Oh, does that mean you're going to listen to me now."

Art was taken aback by his son's nerve.

"Well listen up. I'm sick of being treat like shit, by you, Abby and anyone else that thinks I am their rubbing rag. I've got my own problems, not just Police ones, personal ones, and if I don't sort myself out, I will lose everything. Dad, I'm an alcoholic and this morning I went to an emergency counselling session."

Art was actually quiet for once; he had no idea what to say or how to react. Rossy continued. "If I can get myself sorted out, then maybe, just maybe I can work a bit of that magic I used to have and try and sort this mess out. Oh and a women from the university is coming to see me this afternoon to try and assist with the Psychological profile evaluation."

Art was, to say the least, somewhat stunned by his son's confession and also surprised that he had the foresight to seek assistance now with the attacker. Hindsight is a wonderful thing and maybe this should have been done much sooner but now that they were sure that they were looking for two different murderers, they needed all the help they could get. Feelings of guilt hit Art. He had done nothing to help, he had shouted at the one person that probably could sort this out. Why do people always try and hurt the ones they love? He was an old fool and he knew it. This had made his mind up for him, at the end of this case he would retire, with thirty-two years service he would take his lump sum and run. The last calculation was in excess of £120,000 and then his monthly income. Humility was flowing freely through his thoughts and veins, his fatherly instinct was taking over, he ought to try and help his son get a retirement package too, he now had twenty years service, but maybe he could wangle him a medical pension on ill health grounds. He wouldn't say anything for now he would just try and be more supportive and help him through this.

"Son, I'm Sorry for going off the deep end."

Rossy interrupted, "It's okay."

"It's not okay, I'm an idiot."

"It was just the job speaking," said Rossy, defending his Father who appeared to be regretting the way he had reacted.

"I'm your Dad first and foremost, I lost sight of that, blood is thicker than water."

Rossy smiled at his Dad who winked at him as he left the room. For the first time in ages they had connected as Father and Son. Art was sat at his desk wondering what on earth he could do to help; he knew that what his Son had just told him had taken a lot of courage. In his way he was telling Art he needed help.

<br>

After dinner the consultant psychologist arrived. The DS, DI, Rossy and Art were all sat in the conference room discussing what they knew with Doctor Cassi Rehman. Phil, BSc (hons). Cassi had worked with Rossy before and they were old acquaintances. All the evidence to date was summarised very succinctly and very accurately by the DI, maps were laid out by the DS showing the exact place of the attacks and where the victims were found. Photographs were shown to Cassi of the victims. It was explained that until very recently they could not be sure whether the murder of Sharon Norburn and been connected to the attacks on prostitutes but after this morning's incident they were almost 100% convinced that they were dealing with two separate unrelated crimes. Cassi was a very thorough women and asked many questions, she passed no comment just trying to absorb what information she was being given. After an hour of constant bombardment of information they broke for a coffee break. Cassi had heard the tape of the women. Rossy cringed every time the tape was played, for fear of someone else recognising her voice. He had been watching Art when the tape was played but there was no flicker of recognition on his face, and if anyone was going to recognise the voice it would be him. After the break Cassi asked to be left alone for an hour, she wanted to review her notes and look at the evidence again.

At four the group reconvened to hear what Cassi had gleaned so far.

"Gentlemen, I concur that at the present time, from the evidence you have put before me, there would appear to be two killers with very different motives." Her opening statement was a cover all in case she got it wrong and also in case the police were holding back.

"The crux of the first murder lies with the telephone call. Identify the caller and maybe, just maybe she can give you the name of a possible killer."

"It all sounds very easy but every possible avenue to trace the girl have failed, our next port of call with that is a national appeal for her to come forward, Crime Watch, Crime stoppers etc," said the DI.

"Our reluctance to date though has been that the killer may then turn on the caller if she is known to him and hence loose a possible witness and have another murder on our hands," said Rossy. He was holding out on this argument, because the last thing he wanted was Abby's voice on national TV. Someone would recognise it for sure. And to date he was just assuming that due to his outbursts she thought it was him.

Art chirped up "I agree. We don't want to release that tape and put the girl's life in danger."

Cassi continued, "The other problem you have is that the caller may have been referring to something completely different. You hooked Dominic Veil and maybe this interfered with the plans of an unknown third party, our prostitute attacker. As I said, that call is the key. My gut instincts tell me that the lady called Sharon Norburn was killed by someone that intended her to die. Whether it is one of your unidentified clients Mr Kenny Pritchard or Mr Andrew Roberts is another matter. Maybe she had a rich client that she was trying to blackmail. Maybe someone got some sexually transmitted disease, gave it the Mrs and hence something's gone wrong from that angle. The style of attack also suggests that Mrs Norburn was the intended victim. Now, with the other attacks, they have been a victim of circumstance, randomly picked, because they were there at the time." Cassi had a quick drink of her water before continuing. "The person responsible for this is a male, confirmed by the DNA. He hates prostitutes, but it appears that at the point of ejaculation he flips. None of your witnesses have stated that they felt in any danger right up until that point and even at that point they didn't even see the attack coming. From descriptions we are looking for a man that appears to be in a position of power, possibly a Police Officer. He is possibly a wealthy man as he drives a big car with leather interior. A Company Director, Ambulance Officers, Fire Officers, Prison Officers, but it has to be that kind of combination. I think it's unlikely that the uniform is stolen because if the chap gets stopped he has nowhere to hide, no reasonable get out clause. No, your man is in a position of responsibility, but above all, power."

"So why's he doing it then, what's the motive?" asked Art

"Good question," said Cassi. "I think this all stems back to childhood."

"Don't they all?"

"No, trauma in later life can cause pressure and a person to change, but my gut reaction with this one is that it is linked to childhood. Maybe abuse from a parent, maybe his Mother was a prostitute, something like that. But the danger is, now that he has killed, well, that was just the beginning, he has taken this to the next level."

"Have you any good news Doctor?" asked Rossy

"Yes you have his DNA, there is a pattern and this man is very catch-able. Since the very first assault he has changed his MO very little, only the uniform has disappeared. But you need to catch him soon, because that kill will have given him strength, power, and confidence to go on. He wants you to stop him. He's a man in power who has lost all sense and reasoning."

Rossy was looking at his Dad, thinking, I know a man like that but no serious thought to the fact that he was just about to try and label him.

"Sounds like you Dad."

"Very funny."

"If you get any further information don't hesitate to contact me, day or night and I will do what I can gents."

Rossy showed Cassi out of the building and thanked her for her assistance. She had provided him with a new focus. He had been guilty of dropping the ball, maybe he had been juggling too many, but he felt invigorated, with a new sense of purpose. The Abby issue had clouded his judgement; maybe he was wrong, maybe it wasn't Abby on the phone. Rossy made a conscious effort to concentrate on the serial attacker. The other murder was to be put on the back burner. It looked like a one off, motive unknown; maybe they would stumble across it whilst looking at this one.

Rossy arranged to speak with all involved in the case at six pm. He would give a briefing, and all officers would be on 12-14 hour days. Overtime was not an issue. He would stand the barracking from the Chief.

Rossi's opening remarks had everyone's attention, the room was silent and yet there were over thirty detectives in the room.

"This has now been designated a major incident and as such I am giving you notice that there will be some long shifts until this offender is caught." This was music to the ears. Most of them lived for the overtime. It had been a major factor why some had gone into CID. They had no home life, this was what they did and this is what they did best.

"The victim found this morning was just sixteen years old, a baby, a child." Rossy paused for effect. Most had kids of varying ages. "From what we have gathered so far she had been on the streets since she was fourteen years old and by all accounts making a decent living. She had no pimp or enemies that we know of. She was last seen at ten past twelve this morning by another working girl. A customer picked her up and she left our victim stood at the junction of Chapel Road with School Road. Apparently the victim was last seen heading down School Road. That was the last sighting of her until this morning, when she was found in the school grounds by the caretaker. The post mortem has now been completed and basically nothing new has come to light since this morning. For those of you that where not briefed earlier this afternoon, it appears that the victim has gone voluntarily to the spot where she was killed. It also appears that a sexual act has been performed. At the point of ejaculation the attacker has rendered the victim unconscious before totally obliterating her skull and pelvic girdle. At this time it appears that no instrument was used only his feet.

From the pathologist report, semen was found in the victim's mouth, and bruising around her vagina and anus. That just about brings you up to date on the act and the victim. This afternoon we have had a psychological input from Dr Rehman and the result of what she has told us will form the backbone of your actions for the next few days. Basically one team is to speak to all the prostitutes again. Another team is to work on the vehicles of all Police Officers, every car, what they drive including second cars, wife's, girlfriends and the type of upholstery. I want another team looking at special constables, they wear the same uniforms, check their vehicles and what they do for a living, access to company cars etc. I want the last team to revisit all the people that have been attacked take them samples of uniforms. I want to know what Fire Officers wear, Ambulance Officers wear, surrounding forces and Prison Service. And ladies and gentlemen, it goes without saying that I want it done like yesterday. All the actions are now to be issued by the computer and every action is to be written off properly on the computer before you conduct the next action. No short cuts. From the information we have to hand it won't be long before the attacker strikes again. Any questions?"

There was silence in the room. Rossy had been in full flow. The gaffer of old.

Wardy raised his hand.

"Yes son."

"What about chauffeurs? Bloody good question." That had caught Rossy on the hop, why hadn't he thought of them?

"The team that's looking at police officers own vehicles can take on this aspect as well. Well done." Aiming his praise at Wardy. "This is a team effort, and if anyone has any idea's like that I want to hear them. Right then, as from six am tomorrow the computer will be up and running. Clear up any commitments you have or have 'em reassigned, and we'll start afresh tomorrow." With that Rossy made for the door. He needed a drink. It had been a long day. As he was just about to get to the door Art, appeared by his side.

"Excellent briefing son, very informative, you had the edge, made me want to go and do the enquiries right now."

"This bastards going down, she was a sixteen year old girl, someone's baby, she never stood a chance."

"Come on, I'm buying."

Rossy turned giving his father a quizzical look.

"Not that sort of drink, a meal at the feathers and a coffee, how's that sound?"

"Sounds good to me."

"What about Abby?"

"Forget it. We're not on speaking terms and anyway she went to Nottingham today to see a client, she's staying over."

# 33

Three days had elapsed since the murder of 16 year old Claire Aldridge. The papers had a field day on this story, covering child prostitution, an inept Police Service, but above all the family had been in for a rough ride. Many questions had been asked about the parental responsibility and speculation was rife surrounding the possible attacker and the motive. The good thing had been that Art had taken the heat from the publicity angle;

he had actually done a very good job in dealing with the press. He had been on radio talk shows and a television broadcast which had allowed Rossy to get on with his job.

The teams had been working long days and evenings and several promising leads meant that the enquiry was heading in the right direction.

The first team had been tasked with speaking to all the prostitutes in the area. Cassi Rehman had given them an idea that perhaps this man liked a particular sexual act. They had pursued this angle to see if anything out of the ordinary came up. The Police had actually found two girls that recalled a man wanting exactly the same thing and it was not the normal run of the mill stuff. It was just another line of enquiry. They had said he was a bit of an overbearing man, very pompous. The style of sex had been just as described, with the women giving the man oral sex whilst he used his hands to grope at their bottoms. One of the women stated he definitely penetrated her bottom with his finger, she had retaliated by biting on his cock. Neither woman could recall any uniform, although both said he had a flash car with leather interior, and on both occasions the sexual act had been performed in the car. Unfortunately this was approximately three months ago they had not seen the man since. Both of these women were now assisting the officers with an E-fit of the man they had seen. It was start and a bloody good start even if it was several months into the enquiry.

The second team had spent three days trawling through thousands of computer checks to verify who used and owned what car. The job had proved more difficult than initially thought as checks had to be completed on all cars within the household and most families had two or even three cars. At the present time there were 198 officers out of nearly three thousand who had cars with leather upholstery.

Of those, all but eight had been discounted, as they had cast iron alibis due to various timings of the assaults. If, on the date of any of the assaults, the officer in question had been working then they had been discounted instantly from the enquiry. Unfortunately eight had not been working on any of the occasions. Three of those had been discounted due to holidays, three more due to illness, which left two officers. One was an Inspector who worked at Sheffield and appeared to have been bloody unlucky not to have any alibi. The other and most unbelievable of all was the Chief Constable. That had caused a laugh and a few raised eyebrows. There was one Special Constable who was the managing director of a motor company and due to this affiliation it was thought that he could have access to any kind of vehicle he liked. Leather interior obviously would be his preferred choice especially if he was seeing prostitutes as the seats could be cleaned easier. He was also a family man, married for eighteen years with two children aged seven and nine.

Specially trained investigators in a safe, calm environment had spoken to the victims again. The interviews had been recorded on video should the procedures ever be challenged at court and any insinuation that words had been put into the victims mind could be rebutted. The main findings had been that both girls that had been assaulted by the man wearing the uniform recalled that he was wearing a belt around his middle, which would later prove to be very significant. Also the girl that had been assaulted having had sex in the rear of the vehicle recalled seeing a flat cap under the driver's seat whilst she was knelt over. The only varying factor was that one of the girls recalled him as being quiet, slightly charming and handsome for his age. Every one of the witnesses had put the attacker in his late forties to early fifties. The discrepancies in the man's demeanour was a minor issue, moods vary every second of the day depending on what preceded that moment.

Following the interviews the officers had been to the Fire Service, the Ambulance Service and the Prison Service. The upshot of these enquiries revealed that only the officers in the Fire Service wore tunics with belts and flat caps. Enquiries on the whereabouts of these officers had found all to be in the clear.

The same could be said for the Prison Service, everyone was in the clear because the uniform just wasn't right. By far the most interesting revelation had been the Ambulance Service. Paramedics wear green uniforms but the senior officers wear what can only be described as a Police uniforms. This had been a conscious choice by the Ambulance Service to have a uniform that resembles that of the Police. One of the previous Directors had always wanted to be a Policeman on the sly and so when the issue of uniform arose they adopted a similar style. The uniform included a belt and a flat cap. Enquiries had been more discreet at the Ambulance Service as officers had met with a certain amount of resistance and scepticism. However, of all those that could wear that type of uniform, only two had no alibi's at all. One was a control room manager, a bit of a jack the lad type who was certainly known for his antics and the other, well, that was a shocker. It was the Chief Executive Officer himself. Both of these two had large company cars and both had leather interior. One was a Scorpio and the other a Mondeo; both were the same colour with the same colour interior. This proved to be fascinating news.

Once Rossy had heard the news a quick recap was made of the possible suspects. It was at that point that further more intriguing news broke. The Chauffeur theory was not totally dead and buried. The Chief Constables driver had no alibi. In fact on the nights in question the vehicle a dark blue Jaguar had been used. And although the driver was a PC, he wore a flat cap like the Chief and a tunic with a belt. The car had been instantly taken to the drying room to try and confirm one way or the other if the car had been the one used and if any forensic evidence was available to confirm the suspicions. The officer had been contacted and was coming into the station voluntarily to provide a DNA sample for comparison. It was of his own free will, which tended to suggest he was innocent.

Once the chief had heard that he was also a possible suspect he quickly volunteered to have his DNA compared along with the inspector who was unable to furnish an alibi. This certainly made the job easier and took a definite three suspects out of the equation, providing that they came back negative. Fast track DNA also cost an absolute fortune at £3,000 a time, and hence the Chief was not going to be impressed with that, but he had to show unequivocally that the Police's house was in order before they cast their net elsewhere.

That left three suspects, the Special Constable, the CEO (Chief Executive officer) of the Ambulance service and the Operations Manger of the Ambulance Service. The immediate authorisation was given for surveillance to be carried out. Three days had now lapsed since the murder of Claire Aldridge and there was a feeling that now the man had killed, the next attack would come sooner rather that later and hence there was a nervous feeling that one was due. Tomorrow background checks would be done on all three. Rossy knew they were close, damn close but he just didn't realise how close. Before leaving his office he consulted with Doctor Rehman and told her of the three possible suspects. Cassi had informed him that she knew two of the suspects and had worked closely with them on a project. They were of course the two from the Ambulance Service. She had told him she was reserving judgement but in her heart of hearts one of the men was certainly not the person they were looking for. His profile from what she knew of him was all wrong, but the other, well, she was intrigued. By the time Rossy left his office it was nine thirty pm and he had missed a session at the AA. He was kicking himself, but things were a lot better. He was sure he could beat it on his own. He had just been depressed because he had a lot on his mind of late and hence it was just a comforter. He could take it or leave it. Things were back on track.

As Rossy pulled into The Feather's car park just after ten, he was just going to have one, to show that he could handle his beer. It was a mistake, a big and very costly mistake. By the time Rossy got home it was just after twelve. Fortunately the landlord had taken his car keys from him again. Rossy had insisted that he was okay to drive, but the licensee had insisted as he was a mate and a good customer. Someone in the pub obviously wasn't a mate. Rossy noticed the marked police vehicle discreetly parked up the lane as soon as he left the pub. He would have been history if he had got in his car. Rossy mulled over the idea of finding out who had rung the call in, before he realised it was a neighbouring force that he lived in. He had no chance of finding out and the information would probably have been anonymous.

He had escaped. 'Fuck 'em,' he thought. By the time he had got the key in the door he had got himself quite wound up that someone had tried to dobb him in to the Police. Rossy hadn't noticed that Abby's car was parked on the road and she was back from her trip. He noticed she was back though when he fell over her briefcase in the hall.

"Is that you Keith?"

"No it's a burglar," he said sarcastically

"Pissed again?"

"Pissed again," he said mimimoking her.

"Go to hell you drunken bum."

That was it, he just snapped. Rossy was up the stairs bouncing off the banister rail and the paintings on the wall as he went. To Abby it must have sounded like a baby elephant coming upstairs. The bedroom door just about flew off it's hinges, smacked the rubber door stop on the floor and shot back, twice as quick, smacking Rossy full in the face. That just made him even madder. He dove onto the bed, although he had no idea what he was going to do. Abby was absolutely terrified, he was like a wild animal that had been caged and prodded with sticks, and he had literally flipped. As he dove at the bed, Rossy never saw it coming. Abby had been reading when he had come in, the works of Hitler and Stalin, a hardback book that was at least three inches thick. With both hands on the base of the book, she took a double-handed back hand sweep from the bedside table across her self in an arc. It had power, but above all, venom. The trajectory of the book and the forward momentum of Rossy increased the impact two fold. The flat back part of the book timed perfectly to collide with the left side of Rossy's temple. His head recoiled as he was swept off the bed and lay in a heap on the floor, lifeless. If Abby had been a cricketer then that would have been a six. In fact the ball would have left the ground. Abby calmly leant across the bed, book poised for a second stinger strike. She almost felt disappointed that he was unconscious.

"Not so clever now are you?"

A few seconds passed before Abby suddenly felt a slight tinge of guilt, and tested to see if he had a pulse. He was alive, but Abby wasn't exactly sure whether that was a good thing or not. As she sat back on the bed, she had no idea what to do next. What if he came too, he might kill her. Abby quickly put Rossy into the recovery position and just for good measure taped his legs together so he couldn't chase her, should he come to. She then rang Art and told him to come and collect his son.

By the time Art had got to the cottage, Abby had packed three suitcases. She had packed every single piece of clothing she could find, including the dirty stuff. As Art walked into the house he was concerned as to what had happened. All the pictures on the stairs were wonky. The contents of a briefcase had spilt across the hall floor. The suitcases were on the doorstep.

"Are you alright?" Art said putting his arm around Abby and giving her a big hug.

"No, no I'm not alright, he's a maniac."

"What happened?"

"He came home drunk again, and just flew off the planet. He went berserk."

"Are you hurt?"

"No not this time."

"What does that mean?"

"Exactly what it sounds like."

"The cut, the cupboard, that was him, wasn't it?"

"Yes, that was him. I can't take it anymore. Just take him away from here, tell him to get ready for the injunction."

"Abby, is that absolutely necessary?"

"I'd hoped not but things are getting worse."

"What about his career?"

"If I hadn't have knocked him out tonight he might have killed me, then what would've happened to his career?"

"Point taken. Where is he?"

"Upstairs on the floor, tied up."

"Tied up!" Art shouted.

"You've obviously never been scared to death have you?"

Abby lead Art to the bedroom without another word being exchanged. The sight of his son, laid in the recovery position, legs bound, stinking of booze, was hard to accept. Art felt old, for the first time in his life, things were becoming too much for him. His thoughts of the previous few days came back with a vengeance. He needed to retire and he needed to get his boy some help before it was too late.

As Abby helped Art put Keith in the back of the car, she leant in and took her house keys from his pocket.

"Tell him, It's over, were finished, the house is mine, I'll pay him off. If he comes anywhere near me I'll go to the papers and ruin him."

Art said nothing in retort to that, just, "Look after yourself Abby. I'm sorry."

"It's not your fault."

Art drove home with sadness in his heart, his boy had everything, a beautiful wife, home and career and he'd thrown it all away, well nearly, the career was intact, just. At least they still had each other. Art was going to have to be more of a father now that he had ever been. Keith had been unconscious for just over an hour. Art really didn't want to take him to hospital, as they would ask too many questions, but if he didn't come round soon he would be forced into taking him. Art had rung a family friend who was a retired medical practitioner who came quickly to check him out. By the time the two of them had stuck the smelling salts under his nose, he came too heaving all over the floor. Art was covered as the liquid just sprayed everywhere.

'Oh please God, let this night end' he thought.

The old Doctor friend had advised that he keep him under constant supervision, the blow to the head could have caused concussion, which could be extremely dangerous. "You need to watch him very closely," the doctor warned. "When he comes around properly, if he feels dizzy at all or sick and he doesn't think it is the alcohol then take him to the hospital immediately."

Art pulled up a reclining leather chair alongside the bed, found his latest novel and settled in. It was now two thirty in the morning. This was going to be a long night. By three thirty the vigil was at an end, Art was asleep.

At five thirty Rossy awoke. Vesuvius had erupted in his head, and he felt like he was going to be sick again. A quick scan of his surroundings revealed that all was not well. What was Dad doing asleep in the chair? Where was Abby? Why was he at his Dad's house? And why, oh why, did it feel like he had been hit with a steamroller? Rossy tried to remember, had he been involved in an accident. He remembered the police car and he could recall speaking to Doctor Rehman. Then nothing, it was a void. Rossy was suddenly very frightened, he couldn't remember, what the hell had he done this time?

# 34

The brief to the two surveillance teams had been simple. Don't get caught and go and dig some dirt, but after two days glued to their respective targets they had had no joy. It had been decided that due to there being two suspects the teams would swap over just to keep them focused so that they didn't become bored.

Whilst the follows had been ongoing the CID teams had been conducting background checks on the two suspects. Officers had gained names and addresses from regional office of people that had worked for the service but were now employed elsewhere. That way it would not raise suspicion in the work place. On this occasion the Police had been in luck. There were three people that had all left recently and all would have worked closely with the two people under investigation. One was a secretary, who was working for another agency and an appointment had already been made to see her later that day. The other two were both ex Finance Directors. One now lived in Devon and had left the Service under a cloud. Two detectives were already on the road to Devon. The last Finance Director had left to do her own consultancy work for the NHS, but unfortunately she was currently at a conference in London. She would be back tomorrow and already an appointment had been made to go and see her at home.

At six pm the swap had taken place on both targets. On each of the targets were two unmarked vehicles and a high-powered motorbike. It had been thought that surveillance in the work place was unnecessary and they would commence once they left work.

John Pilgrim and Dale Pike were sat in the unmarked VW VR6 inspecting the pictures of Steve Lordourail. He was approximately fifty years of age. About six foot one, fourteen stone, distinguished grey hair, quite a rugged looking guy. He certainly appeared fit for his age, no middle age spread, but he appeared perhaps just a little too confident almost smooth but smug with it.

"Bloody hell, that's him." John was looking at the main door to the control room. Dale was right. The target was walking towards the car park. This had been unexpected. He was due to finish work at ten and it was only ten past six. They were bloody lucky, the teams had only just managed to get into position.

"Perhaps he's just going for something to eat."

Not two seconds later the Blue Mondeo emerged from the car park heading towards the main road, the driver blissfully unaware of his surroundings. Steve was merrily singing away to his Aretha Franklin disc and ringing the Mrs on the mobile.

"Be advised target is on the move and heading towards the main road, you will have visual in five, four, three, two...."

"Yes Roger, we have him."

The mobiles were all interlinked with a voice activated system and hence no one needed to speak into the radio. To anyone on the outside it would just look like two people in a car having a conversation. All officers were equipped with their own hands free kit should they end up on foot conducting a ground follow.

After five minutes, it was clear that Mr Lordourail was not going for something to eat as he was already on the motorway-heading north bound.

Dale picked up the mobile phone and rang the control room for the Ambulance service.

A very professional sounding young woman answered the phone.

Dale wasted no time. "Yes gooday mate, is me owd mate Steve Lourdapants in? It's his mate from Oz."

John was trying to concentrate on the driving but it was proving increasingly difficult when all he wanted to do was burst out laughing.

"No, I'm sorry you've just missed him."

"No worries mate, I'll ring him at home."

"Can I take a message?"

"No thanks mate, like I say I'll ring at home."

As Dale pressed the end call button, John burst out laughing. The next thing Les the Sergeant cut in. "That was the worst fucking Australian accent I've ever heard." Dale turned to John. "You bastard you switched to voice activated didn't you?"

"Soz mate." He said, in his own Aussie accent.

"You bastards."

Fortunately the follow was easy. Steve was driving like Miss Daisy. Seventy-five miles an hour max. In fact it was quite hard holding back, so that they didn't go flying past. They were approaching the exit that Steve would normally take to go home. Three hundred yard marker, no indicator, two hundred yard marker, no indicator, and then he indicated and moved to the middle lane to overtake a slow wagon and went past the junction which would have taken him home.

"Very intriguing," came a voice over the VAS (Voice activated system)

Two junctions further north the Mondeo came off onto the slip road. He was heading towards Worsborough Village. Near the Park and the small lake in the old village the Mondeo indicated right and turned into a walled courtyard, which was a complex of renovated barns and a mill. Carol was on foot and walking past the entrance to the courtyard, just as Steve pressed the doorbell on Wheel cottage.

By the time Dale made his pass of the courtyard they had four registered numbers of the vehicles in the courtyard. The check on the voters register verified who lived at the address. It was a Derek Goodridge, Fran Goodridge and Ross Goodridge. The last vehicle check that was done via the communications room came up with a marker. The details of the owner were protected. The Ops room Inspector asked for verification prior to passing out the details, which were done, via a secure telephone line. The car is registered to a Police officer Derek Goodridge. The Wheel Cottage, Worsborough. There was silence in the car. Dale had realised who Derek aka Derk to his friends, was.

The Team all convened in the local car park with a view of the Courtyard. Les got off the phone with the operations room Inspector.

"PC Goodridge is booked on six-two evenings," he said to the team.

"The cheeky fucking bastard, he's shagging his Mrs behind his back," Dale was not happy to say the least.

"Let's not jump to any conclusions, they may be friends, this could be perfectly innocent," Les said trying to calm Dale down a little.

Les grabbed the high-powered Minolta camera with a zoom lens the size of a trumpet. "Back in two-ticks."

Les skirted around the edge of the courtyard and across the small footbridge that led over a little weir. The topography was perfect. A steep hill to the rear of the premises, covered in huge conker trees. Les was not the most athletic of men but he managed to get himself into a perfect position overlooking the rear of the cottage. One of the rooms had the curtains drawn. Les assumed this must be the child's room. The lens found its target. At first there was a blur, then rapidly homing in on the pure clear shot which can only ever destroy lives. There was a man, shielded by the window ledge, who appeared to be naked, as his bare knee could be seen, obviously laid on his back. Then a woman walked into the bedroom wearing absolutely nothing. The camera rattled a full film off; Les's finger was stuck on the automatic button. Thirty-six incriminating photographs that would never see the light of day. They were intrusive pictures and against peoples rights to privacy, under the Human Rights Act. This type of surveillance was taboo unless authorised. Les knew they would never need to go that far, but he had them all the same, just in case he needed to apply a little unofficial pressure to this man. Les returned to the car. He trusted the team with this information but really he had no choice as they had seen it for themselves. It was just like any other job, in that they had to keep their personal prejudices out of this. They would report as normal and let the ACC decide on the appropriate course of action.

At ten pm, the Mondeo left the courtyard, heading for home, and just like any other working day he arrived home twenty minutes later as normal. One of the team was left in situ while the others retired for some rest. Les had made an appointment to see the ACC and was heading to the ACC's home. He was surprised to see Rossy at the house but then again he was his Son. Why shouldn't he be there? Probably came around for a drink. While Les was at Art's house his mobile rang. They had found out where Fran Goodridge worked. She was a part time control room worker for the Ambulance Service and things just fell into place. Les briefed Art and Rossy on the night's events. Art was storming up and down, pacing, he was furious.

"Her husband's out risking life and limb and she's up to her neck in cock," Art was shaking his head, "poor lad." Art paused for a minute having a couple of slurps of his coffee. He felt like having a malt, but with Rossy in the room it would have been unfair.

"Right this is the way we are going to play it. The film will never see the light of day unless we need to use it as leverage. Arrest him tomorrow, we can use our powers under the suspicion part and let him provide an Alibi for all the nights when the assaults have taken place. Pound to a pinch of shite he was with her on one of those occasions. Let's make that little fucker squirm a little. Then he will have to tell the police that he was sleeping with a Policeman's wife whilst he was at work. After he has sweated a bit offer him a the option to give DNA and lets sort him one way or the other. Obviously we will not tell PC Goodridge anything, if he finds out, well, so be it, but I am making myself perfectly clear here, no one tells him anything."

"What if he wants a brief?" asked Les.

"I doubt he will, he will think he is helping us with our enquiries, and if he is innocent he will not hide anything. If he asks for a brief, well, we'll just have to be less sarcastic, and he might have something to hide."

The next morning the team reconvened and was fully briefed as to the discussions with the ACC. It was unusual for the surveillance team to do an arrest or interview, but under the circumstances the cover was to be blown. If they needed to follow him again they would use the other team, but the fewer people that new about this, or were involved the better.

Carol and John were to carry out the arrest. Les and Dale would do a house search. Les was pleased that there had not been an attack overnight, but he almost wished there had been so he could make Lordourail squirm on his own front door step. The night's man was sent home to get some sleep. Carol and John stood on the front door step whilst Les and Dale went to the rear. It was amazing how many times they'd go to arrest someone or go for an enquiry and they'd leg it out of the back door. Les heard the banging on the front door.

"What a stupid name Lordourail." Said Dale.

"Sounds like God's own rail network."

"Wonder if he comes on time."

"Steady there, young Dale."

Bloody sods law, Steve Lordourail came to the back door.

"Good morning Mr Lordourail, I'm Detective Sergeant Les Crowe and this is my colleague DC Dale Pike. There are another two of our colleagues at your front door."

"Come in."

Pleasantries were quickly exchanged and Les managed to get on first name terms with Steve. That helped. Mrs Lordourail was making the kid's breakfast, and wandering around in her dressing gown, clucking like all good mothers at her two teenage daughters. Les instantly noticed the calendar on the wall with his shift patterns on and the corresponding pattern of what his wife was working. That would be perfect. Les took no time in explaining that they were investigating a series of attacks on prostitutes and a murder. He explained that unfortunately Steve's uniform, car and his shift patterns had not provided him with an alibi and that they needed to eliminate him from their enquiries but due to the fact that he would need to be released on Police bail, he would be arrested, it was nothing to worry about. Oh, so matter of fact. Steve appeared calm, and very helpful, nothing was a problem or too much trouble. Carol Stepped forward and cautioned Steve and then arrested him on suspicion of assault and murder. Steve never flinched. He turned to his wife.

"I'll be back in a few hours, there really is nothing to worry about, just a matter of elimination purposes as the Sergeant said."

It was then that the sucker punch came and the calm exterior that Steve had been portraying was completely wiped out. Les was thinking 'you don't mess with a Policeman's family, or you mess with each and every one of us.'

"We went to speak with you last night at work at about seven, but we just missed you." The comment was innocent enough but what a bombshell, the quizzical look from Steve's wife,

"You were at work last night. You told me all about it when you got in."

Steve's face and mind were in a shear frozen panic, he had no answers and he had just been cautioned. He said nothing, but his wife had seen it in his face, his eyes, she knew.

Les was really pleased with himself. It had been a cruel blow without even having to break into a sweat. In fact Les was a little disappointed that Steve had rolled over so easy. There was never any doubt in Les's mind that Steve was innocent of the attacks, but he was guilty of fucking with the Police. Les had no remorse and during the interview he toyed and played with Steve until he had filled them in on the full picture. The interview had been artistry; it was stylish and had shown all the guile of an experienced detective. He had made Steve want to talk, no oppression just cleverly worded questions. The full truth of the matter was that Fran had been seeing Steve for years and Ross was the bi-product of a night of passion at work. Steve was the father. By the end of the interview Steve was in tears. Les even felt slightly guilty, but not for very long. If, or when, Derk ever found out it would break his heart. He would be devastated. At the end of the interview the tapes were sealed and they all sat in silence. It took no time at all to verify Steve's story and a sample of DNA was taken but only as a matter of procedure for elimination purposes. Steve was guilty of a lot of things but not murder.

# 35

Rossy had taken a couple of days off sick. Well, it was kind of an enforced sickness. His father had suggested he take a few days to get his head together, attend a couple of AA meetings if at all possible. It had been good advice, and having found the courage to speak at the meetings, listen to others he realised that he was not on his own with this terrible affliction. There were in fact millions of people out there all suffering in silence, but not Rossy, he had found help and he was going to take what was offered to him. He had worked too hard to throw it all away. He had even decided to pay for a one on one session and had just got back from the session. He had tried to ring Abby to see if she was alright, tentatively find out how the land lay between them, but he had been unable to speak with her. Her mobile was turned off and the answer machine at the house just kept clicking in. After the events that had taken place a few nights previous, which had been described by his father he could understand her reluctance to want to speak with him, but they needed to sort things out and find out if they had a future together. It was much too soon for her to take him back and Rossy decided to leave it until he was feeling a little stronger in mind before broaching the subject with Abby.

Art had kept Rossy up to date with the case, but to all intents and purposes, Art had taken up the lead role as the senior investigating officer. It was a short stop gap until his Son was well enough to take over again. Art had just had a short conversation with the DI, who was quite optimistic about the trip the officers had been on to Devon. They were due back shortly and it was then that the DI would fully brief Art on there findings.

Art had just got off the phone with his son at three in the afternoon when Detective Inspector Jones came into the office with a silly grin on his face.

"Take a seat," offered Art with a sweeping motion of his right arm, "would you like a drink?"

"Love one." Art could see the pleasure on the face of the DI, which obviously meant in turn he would feel a lot happier about the whole thing if it were good news. Art was almost savouring the moment; he could do with some good news about now. Art sank back into his large reclining leather chair, having just served up two cups of percolated coffee, "Give me the good news then."

"Right," said the DI. He shuffled through the statements that had been obtained to the parts that had been highlighted in fluorescent pen.

"Although they are not direct evidence of anything," he began, "they give us an extremely good description of this bloke's character. The secretary that left said the man was a nasty bully. He used to go into her office if she had made a typing mistake screaming and shouting, waving his arms about like a wailing banshee. It was quite frightening, then, two minutes later he would come in all nice and calm like he was her best friend in the world, putting his arm around her. She thought he was a bit creepy. In the end she left because the other secretary got a seven thousand pound pay rise."

"How much?" screamed Art

"Seven grand!"

"That's got to be either hush money or shag money."

"Well, when the secretary challenged the amount, he just screamed at her that his personal secretary had been underpaid for years, and it was to fetch her pay in line and that he was the boss and that if she didn't like it she could leave. Apparently he was banging his fist on the desk."

"Sounds like a dictator........Sounds like me."

The DI was thinking the exact same thing, but thought it best not to mention it.

"As a result of that the secretary could take no more and found herself another job. Everyone in the organisation that sucked up to him got what they wanted even if it wasn't in the best interests of the service, but anyone that spoke out against any of his idea's, well, they were in for a rough ride. The same was echoed from the two previous Finance Directors. In law there are two statutory posts required to run a public service. One is the Chief Executive Officer and the other the Finance Director. Apparently, they both said there used to be massive bust ups with the CEO, especially when they didn't agree with his ideas. Both sought assistance from higher office but got no help at all due to the fact that they kept managing to balance the books. It put them both in extremely difficult positions. In the end the man in Devon said enough was enough and left to set up his own business. He described the CEO as a 'small-minded egotistical bigot.' The last female director went further than that, in her assessment of him. As well as describing him in exactly the same way, she had said she was going to take a grievance out against him, for harassment and bullying, but as soon as she confronted him with it, he changed tactics. He became smarmy, touchy feely and in the end rather than create a stink she just left. There was one thing she said though, something about a rumour. The rumour had been that he went to see ladies of the night. And that one of his ambulance crews had clocked him kerb crawling whilst they were on standby in Sheffield. She also said he used to stay late at night and go home in his uniform. But this however was months ago."

Art sat pondering what he had been told. It was unusual for three separate character witnesses to be so cutting in their assessment of a man's temperament. Usually most people feel some kind of loyalty to an ex-colleague, but not to this man. They appeared to hate, despise and loathe the man. Art was also thinking that on the odd occasions that he had met him at various functions that he couldn't say he had taken to him in any way. He was an odd ball.

"Do you want us to lift him?"

"No, I want him to get the full humiliation treatment. If it is Krell, I want him nailing in the act. Set too with the statistical analysis. Look at patterns, strike patterns, did the dates coincide with any functions, likely dates for the next attack and I want a full team of decoys ready to go at a moments notice. Use our own prostitutes, hook him that way." There was a pause in the conversation, "You know! Now I come to think of it I can recall him at the Policeman's ball the night Claire Aldridge was murdered. He could be the man we are looking for."

"We're already on with the stats' analysis."

"Keep me informed and make sure the Surveillance teams don't lose him, or someone might get hurt. Oh, and give Dr Rehman a ring, see what she thinks of the statements but don't let on who the target is just yet." Art was unaware that his Son had already fully briefed the Doctor as to who the possible suspects were, it was pointless holding back on the information.

Art took no time at all in ringing his son. He wanted him to hear the good news, thought it might help him out.

"Fantastic, maybe a step in the right direction." Rossy had said when he was briefed about the statements. "You're doing well Dad." He had said in an encouraging tone.

"No, it's nothing to do with me, you'd set it all in motion. I just hope we nail him."

"Fetch him in then, arrest him now."

"It could be embarrassing if we are wrong, especially considering his position, and if it is him I want him caught in the act, besides the Chief is a bit worried. He wants us to have a bit of concrete evidence before we start arresting a leading public figure."

"Yes, I see your point."

Art attempted to change the subject enquiring about the afternoon's session that Rossy had with his councillor. Alas he didn't get very far when he quizzed his son. The door had been firmly shut on that topic. Truth be-known the session had gone very well. Rossy had been made to face up to his fears, his hopes and expectations. He had been told it was going to be a long process but at least he had recognised that he did need help with his addiction. The realisation that you actually need help is the hardest part and now he was actually helping himself the road to recovery would be an easier one, but not easy and probably a long one. He had been surprised to hear himself talk so frankly about his problems and realised that there was a lot bottled up inside of him that he needed to get off his chest. The councillor had advised him to write his feelings down, and be truthful and frank with himself and then a couple of days later read what he had written. Rossy had thought it amusing at the time, but it was explained to him that you tend to be frighteningly honest with yourself when committing thoughts to paper and so it may help you understand what it is that you are concerned about, and learn about your inner most feelings and fears. Rossy had tried the exercise when he got home and wrote it all down on paper. He had then made himself a cup of tea and sat down and read the piece of paper. It read.

I have failed my wife, my father and myself.

I have cheated on my wife.

I have hit my wife.

I am a drunken bum.

I am holding back on a murder investigation for personal reasons.

I am a joke.

I am tired with this life.

I need to escape.

Rossy felt depressed, but he wasn't thinking of doing anything stupid. He was tired with his life the way it was but not tired of living. He would take this piece of paper to the next session. It would help to get these items into context. He needed help in regaining his focus, the term life balance sprang to mind and at the present time it was out of kilter.

# 36

The Nokia was merrily beeping to itself as Dom was drinking his morning coffee. Dom needed his caffeine injection before he could make any meaning-full sense of the day. Dom picked up the phone. Messages, select.

Inbox.... select.

+447974244 Read

Pick me up tonight at 7.30 if you want to wine and dine me.

ABBY

Dom clicked to options; well he eventually got to options after a few tours of the phones menu. He still hadn't got used to his new phone, he was definitely not a technophobe and to Dom a phone should be used for phone calls. Eventually, Reply

Write message.

Love to C U. Please send address. Dom.

At least he had got the abbreviations sorted, and this time when he was offered a night out, he remembered to ask the all important question. Always important to learn from your mistakes!

Send message.

Dom took no time at all in ringing Paula.

"It's me"

"What time is it"?

"Late."

"Don't lie, what time is it?"

"8.00 am."

"Jesus Dom, what are you trying to do to me I was out while three this morning."

"Not my fault you old chicks can't hack it."

"Cheeky monkey....... What can I do for you at this time in the morning?"

"Need a favour."

"Wow it must be important, you never ask for a favour, so what is it?"

"I've got a message from the lady I met the other night .The one I told you about the one we met in the hospital."

"What's it say?"

"Nothing much, pick me up at 7.30 to wine and dine me."

"You're really taken with this woman aren't you?"

"I don't know. There's something about her, maybe a helpless vulnerable sort and she's a bit of a sex kitten,......She intrigues me." Dom paused and then started again. "She's not in your league, and nowhere near as good looking as you, but then, you and I are in different divisions."

Paula was smiling to herself, if only he knew.

"Then my boy I will cancel tonight's appointment for you. David can take her out, he was looking for some work this evening and besides he owes you one after the window incident. Hey listen give me an hour and I will come and pick you up and take you shopping. New outfit, my treat, and then you can take me for lunch."

"You really are the best."

"No you are, and I will always be there for you and don't you ever forget it. You are the closest thing to a brother and my guardian angel. So be ready. Love you."

Paula had rung off before he could say it but he loved her too. There was a special bond between them that would never be broken.

The Porsche was gleaming; it was after all her baby. She loved it to bits, nearly as much as Dom liked to drive it.

"Car looks well!"

"It should do, it cost me eighty quid for a full valet and polish yesterday."

"Ouch…. I'd have done it for you. Obviously I'd have had to borrow it for the day."

"I take it you'd like to drive then?"

"Of course."

Dom never offered, after all it wasn't his place but Paula liked his driving and it was nice to be driven, especially in this car.

"Get your foot down and take us to York, there are a few nice shops up there and I know a great little place for lunch."

"Oh Paula I for got to tell you something."

"When?"

"When you hung up on me."

"What?"

"I love you too."

She smiled at him; put her hand on his knee. "I know you do silly, I never doubted it."

Some five hours later the two returned to Dom's place and collapsed. Talk about shop till you drop.

"Do you know how much you've spent?"

"Don't care, I can't take it with me. Anyway get the kettle on and make me a drink and I'll give you a pep talk for tonight. Oh, and don't forget the chocolate biscuits."

"I know what you're up to. You're making the day go quickly, so I don't spend all day getting too giddy about it."

"Arrgh.... you've found me out, but really I just needed a chauffeur for the day."

"Bullshit, you'd still be in bed." Dom said laughing and smiling at her.

Both settled down to watch the afternoons five nations rugby or six as it's now called, and within no time at all Dom fell asleep on the sofa with his head on her lap. Everything was just so right, relaxed and comfortable with each other's company. Dom was having some sort of dream and twitching. Paula loved him so much, but telling him, well that was a whole new ball game. Dom's dream felt so real, it was as if he was actually living it. It involved two women, lust, love and passion and he had to decide between the two. It was the easiest decision in the world, but as with all good dreams, something was pulling his dreamy unconscious state into the real world. At five thirty he was woken when he felt a gentle stroking of his ear. "Come on Casanova, time to get ready for your big date. I've ironed your new shirt and trousers, so you just need the shit, shave, shower and shampoo routine."

"Oh........ well put."

"I'll put the music on to get you in the mood and leave you to it."

Two minutes later Dom was howling to some Phil Collins track whilst shaving. Paula burst in on him, planted a big kiss on his face, which meant she too was covered in shaving foam. "Good luck, have a good night, ring me in the morning. And be careful. You've still got a fragile heart don't let her hurt you, or she'll have me to contend with."

"Bye, Love ya."

And she was gone. Dom continued his well versed howling and was really in the mood for his night out. Paula had primed him on where to take her and had made the phone calls and reservation to assure the best table at a little restaurant in Hathersage. Dom came walking into the kitchen to pick up the keys. He was wearing a casual black single-breasted jacket, grey shirt, grey slacks and black shoes. When Paula had picked them that afternoon she assured him that he could not fail to pull looking like that. He was also wearing his favourite Cologne... Channel for men. He was ready. As Dom searched for his car keys he found a note left by Paula. It read.

Borrowed you're car, taking my Mum and Dad out.

Need a back seat.

Use mine tonight

Love

P

Dom knew for sure that she wasn't taking her parents out, but it was a lovely gesture.

# 37

Dom was ten minutes early as he pulled up outside Abby's house. The lights were on upstairs and Dom could see her in the mirror putting on her earrings. As Dom started to get out of the car, the front door burst open and out came one irate husband, even if he was soon to be an ex-husband.

"Oh, so you're the bastard she's seeing tonight are you." Dom was not exactly prepared for the onslaught and was taken aback by the tirade of abuse.

Abby flounced out of the front door, her long flowing hair swept back by the breeze. She was wearing a tight fitting long black dress with a shawl around her slender shoulders. She slammed the door behind her and walked towards her husband. Without any warning or change in stride pattern she punched him right on the side of the face, knocking him into the bushes.

"I've told you, we're finished so please leave me alone and stop annoying me."

The door to the house was locked and Rossy was out on the street. His car keys were inside the house in his jacket.

"You'd better ring Daddikins to come and rescue you"

Dom was still half in the car and half on the pavement watching the proceedings. He hadn't spoken once, a little overawed by the situation. "You look great," he stammered.

"Nice car." she said

"Borrowed!"

"Stolen?"

"No. Just borrowed."

"Who cares, take me out and show me a good time." It was not a request, but a definite instruction, which he was not about to disobey. "What about green fingers?"

"You're right, I shouldn't leave him there just in case he does try and break in."

Abby picked her mobile. "Yes. Police please. Oh good evening I've just seen a prowler at 34 Primrose cottages. I think he saw me because he was hiding in the flowers."

The question must have been what's your name? As Abby said, "Sorry you're breaking up, damn mobiles." And she pressed the end key. She turned to Dom and winked at him. "Oh, I really did want to leave my details she added." Laughing at her own little scam.

"My you do look handsome tonight," she said. "Oh and thanks for the compliment. It wasn't the type of greeting I had anticipated but what the hell it'll give us a laugh or two later over dinner."

"You left him then?"

"Right after the night I met you."

Dom smiled. He was flattered. Well at least he thought it was flattering.

"Where are you taking me?"

"Oh my friends recommended a little place out at Hathersage."

"Would that be Paula?"

"Yes that's right."

"What is it with you two?"

"Oh I did a favour for her once and since then she has been doing little things for me, like give me a job, a car, a house and the most gracious and loving friend I could ever wish for."

"Must have been a big favour you did for her?"

"No not really I was just in the right place at the right time."

"I'm intrigued, do tell."

Dom managed to skilfully change the subject but knew it would not be long before he would be questioned further about his relationship with Paula.

It seemed no time at all before Dom was pulling up in the car park of the Partridge Hotel. Dom was swiftly out of the car and round to the passenger door.

"Wow I can't remember the last time somebody opened a door for me."

"It's just a cheap way of trying to get a glance up your skirt."

"Should've known!" she said smirking at him, and flashing her thighs.

Dom took Abby's arm as they strode into the restaurant.

"Good evening Sir," said the Mâtre De, in his Italian accent.

"Good evening."

"And madam, may I take your shawl?"

"Thank you"

"I have a reservation for two. Mr Veil."

"Would that be Dominic?"

"Yes, but just call me Dom."

The Mâtre De continued. "That was my father's name, Dominique. It's Latin meaning 'Of the Lord' and quite often given to people born on a Sunday."

Dom was wracking his brain, but yes, he was sure he had been born on a Sunday.

"We have been expecting you sir. This way please, we have a very special table for you." Dom and Abby were led to a table for two in a quite secluded alcove. It overlooked the fireplace and the roaring fire on one side and to the other was a window that gave a view of a lit garden. The garden vista extended down across the lawns to a fast flowing river that cut through the grounds.

"Will this be satisfactory sir?"

"It's lovely, thank you."

"Can I get you any drinks?"

"A gin and tonic for me," said Abby

"And for me a glass of red wine, thank you."

"I was surprised to here from you," said Dom.

"Why's that?"

"Well, that night at the dinner dance I thought you were telling me to keep my nose out, or at least that was the impression I got."

"No, I think I was just so stunned to hear someone talk so frankly about my problem and it was then that I realised that I could not put up with the beatings any longer and as soon as I got home that night I new I needed to start divorce proceedings. Things got even worse two days later when he again came home rolling drunk wanting to rip my head off, only this time I knocked him out instead, Hitler and Stalin struck again, tied him up and then got his Dad to come and remove him. Since then I haven't spoken to him until this evening when he just turned up on spec. Then we started rowing the moment he saw I was going out. It's not gone down very well as you can see. His father keeps ringing me. They are scared to death I am going to tell all about the beatings. It is the last thing either of them need, both high-ranking Police Officers, and complaints of wife battery would not look good set against their new domestic violence policy."

"I'm glad I'm out of it."

"That sounds like an interesting story?"

"It's one I will tell you when I get to know you better. I don't want you running a mile just yet." Dom paused temporarily trying to gauge Abby's facial expressions before continuing. "You're the first person I've been out with in a long time, other than work."

"Date!" said Abby rolling the word around her tongue as she said it.

"You're teasing me now. Behave yourself."

"Oh no, I don't intend to behave at all."

Timing is everything and the waiter arrived with the starters. He glanced at Dom obviously having just heard the last sentence in the conversation and smiled raising his eyebrows. Dom blushed but fortunately the lighting was dim enough for the waiter not to notice.

"I say," said Abby as the waiter was walking away. "You're blushing."

Abby was still in fact finding mode and whilst Dom was still looking flush she hit him with the follow up.

"So how come you and Paula aren't an item?" Abby certainly went for the heart. If she wanted to know, she pulled no punches.

"We are, but not in the way you think. Paula's had a few tragedies in her past and hardly anyone notices that she is gay. She lost her partner and brother in a car accident a few years ago. Neither of them was to blame for the accident it was or appeared to be a blown tyre, which blew out on the motorway. The car went across all three lanes of the motorway and down the embankment into a ditch. Both died at the scene." As far as Dom was concerned it was the truth, the reality was slightly different. It was Paula's best friend, not girlfriend and yes she was female but it was her brother's girlfriend, not hers.

"How awful... Is she alright?"

"Yes and no. That's why we are such good friends, we are very close"

"Don't you want her though?"

"Of course..... she is beautiful but I love Paula just the way she is."

"I'm glad about that because the competition looked a little stiff from my point of view."

"You're revealing your hand some what."

"Well I am certainly interested in you, shall we say. Unfortunately hubby now thinks that you are the reason I want a divorce."

"And am I?"

"I'm not saying. That would be giving too much away, especially on the first date. Anyway how did you and Paula meet and what was the favour you did for her?"

"You are getting brave, two questions in one."

"Don't ask, don't get."

"I'll remember that."

"You won't need to. So come on, tell all."

"Oh it was nothing really, Paula just had trouble with one of her cars, it was misfiring shall we say, and I helped out."

"Oh you're good with cars."

"No not at all, this was just one of those problems that needed to be dealt with quickly."

Abby obviously had no idea what Dom was on about which suited Dom just fine. He was trying to woo her on his own merits not on his heroic past, but Abby seemed to have a problem with Paula, all questions led to that door and their relationship.

Dom subtly tried to swap the conversation back to the irate husband but before he went too far down that line he realised that he was history and swiftly changed the subject. The conversation was effortless with Abby and he was utterly smitten. It had been a long time since he had sat down with someone and had a candle lit dinner and not got paid to do it. Boy there was a craving inside him. Was it just lust? Or did he have real feelings for her. There was a feeling deep inside, an inner magic and he loved everything about this woman. She had seemed fragile, but now, different, almost overtly confident, or was she just putting on a facade. She was charming and forthright, yet she knew exactly what she wanted. That was obvious. Yet there was still that vulnerability in her that Dom loved. He was hoping that he was her weak point. Yet he also realised that this woman was just breaking up from her marriage, which would ordinarily mean she was on the rebound, alas he would work around that little problem later. This after all was only their first date.

Abby excused her self after the main course and left Dom to ponder and mull over his glass of Chateau Larmande. This was truly an excellent red wine.

Abby was gone a good few minutes. Dom suddenly felt anxious, thinking that she had left him there on his own. Abby breezed back into the dining room and up to the table. She was certainly a head turner. There wasn't one man in the room that had not glanced in her direction on the way back to the table. Dom smiled to himself. It had been a long time since he had been lucky in love. Not since his wife had run off with the old bastard, but things were certainly looking up at this moment in time.

"Thought you'd left me?"

"You're not that lucky!"

"Do you fancy anything else?"

"Well actually now you come to mention it…"

"Off the menu I mean."

"Actually I'd like another glass of this excellent wine and maybe a brandy with coffee."

"Me too, but I think I'll just have the coffee."

Dom glanced at Abby who was smiling at him and swinging what appeared to be a key in her right hand.

"Oh I don't think so. The manager has just given me the keys to the best room in the hotel, so I thought you might like to stay and keep me company."

"Red wine and brandies all round then."

It was at that point that Abby's mobile phone rang. Abby looked stunned and was wishing that she had remembered to turn the damn thing off.

"You fucking bitch," screamed the voice on the other end of the phone.

"Who is it? I can hear them screaming from over here!"

"Hubby." Abby just ended the call.

"Look Sergeant I'm Superintendent Ross from South Yorkshire."

"Yes sir and I'm Lord Lucan said the custody Sergeant. This is Derbyshire and until I clarify that you had authority to try and enter the premises and verify who you are you will be staying with us."

"Can I have another phone call?"

"You've just had one."

"But she just hung up on me."

"Looks like Sir really did piss her off!"

"Go screw yourself Sergeant."

"Put him in Cell M2 that's the coldest."

"I want a phone call."

"You've just had one. Drunks are my favourite. When you're sober you can tell us who you really are."

Rossy was not having a good night. As soon as Abby had left him with the tulips stuck up his arse he had wasted no time in attempting to get into the house. He was attempting to force the louvre window out of the kitchen when the Police arrived. He had been unable to show them any identification as his warrant card was in his jacket which was in the house, and in view of the phone call and what the neighbour had said he was screwed, literally. He was regretting not having the house put in joint names when they got married, but Abby had lived there for two years before they were wed, and he had always been too busy to worry about it. The biggest mistake had been to go around and attempt to sort the matter out. It had been the sight of her all dressed up to go out that had caused him to flip, and start on the bottle of malt in the lounge. God only knows what he had been thinking. He had just needed a drink for comfort, steady his nerves. As he sat in the cell he was annoyed with himself. He had worked hard all week at staying dry, then the first time he'd seen Abby he'd lost the plot and dove into the nearest bottle of scotch. What had he been thinking? Abby had called him a drunken bum, what an idiot. He was supposed to be showing her that he was trying to get help, not just turn up, get into an argument and then get pissed before her very eyes. As the cell door clanked shut he sat on the cold wooden bench. Veil of all people, he thought to himself. It was ironic that he had put Veil in a cell and now the boot was on the other foot although he had kind of put himself in it. The stench in the cell was horrendous. The previous customer must have had a serious foot odour problem. Rossy wanted to vomit. He was feeling extremely ill. The view into the metal loo was even worse, he wanted to be violently sick and now he was face to face with the world's hugest turd. That was just too much for him to take, his stomach rolled twice before he heaved everywhere. The retching just about took out his stomach lining. Rossy rolled back onto the wooden bench. Jesus what had happened to him, what had he done to deserve this? His mind was in turmoil and the image of Veil refused to let him settle. He was out with his wife and at that point he realised his marriage had just flat lined. Not only had he ruined his marriage there was something else nagging at him. Rossy was searching his ever hazy and spinning mind. What was it that Abby had said? It was something about prostitutes.

"Was it you and those fucking prostitutes?" did she mean the work or was she referring to Sharon, had she found out? Or had she said, "It's you that's fucked those prostitutes," inferring that he was the attacker and the murderer. Rossy fell into a disturbed and fitful sleep.

As the restaurant had got warmer there was a beautiful aroma of percolated coffee, burning logs on the fire and the occasional whiff of Abby's perfume, Chloe. Wow, it was intoxicating. It was well past eleven when the two left the dining room and headed for their room. The hotel was one of rustic charm, with beautiful rugs and hundreds of watercolour paintings hung on the walls. It also had one of those double twisted landings with a beautiful landscape mural that went all the way up the stairs.

As Abby led Dom by the hand into the bedroom, it was a lovely cosy room with soft lighting and its own log fire. Imitation, but it looked good turned down low. What a perfect setting. She turned to him and kissed Dom gently on each cheek and then the chin and then the forehead before kissing him on the lips. This was a private moment and all that went after was not to be disclosed.

A few hours later Dom awoke. Abby was wrapped around him and her arm draped across his chest. Dom reflected, on the last few hours, he felt so protected. She was like a shroud of silk wrapped around him. Gentle, warm, and the depth of his feelings for her were immense. She had rescued him. It was ironic to think that a few months ago he was out in the cold. Emotional turmoil, wife left him for an older man, esteem on rock bottom, then getting arrested, losing his job, and yet how quickly things had turned around. A special woman now adored him. Paula, and then there was Abby. Where would the next few months take him? Only fate would decide and seeing as it had not let him down recently he decided it best not to worry about things like that and just let events take their natural course. Abby stirred squeezing ever tighter and pulled herself towards him. Dom just closed his eyes and let his mind relax, this must be heaven.

# 38

Dom was still in his own little dream world as the Porsches flat six howled along the country lane, as he hit every apex of a bend he was in heaven. Approach speed to the bend on the side of caution, slip into third gear, just sustaining the revs, hit the apex and bam. Floor the accelerator and the car would squat at the rear and growl. Rubber would cut into the tarmac and he would fly to the next bend and do the same thing all over again. It was now deep into autumn and the leaves had all turned. It was Dom's favourite time of the year. The deep rich bronzed and reddened leaves that littered the landscape. The edges of the roads were strewn with decaying detritus. He recalled that the first wet day after the leaves had fallen would always lead to a high number of accidents. People just never accounted for the fact that they couldn't stop on wet leaves and invariably they would end up face down in a field awaiting the emergency services. The window was fully down and the earthy smell of a freshly ploughed field was one of the best things about the countryside. Dom had dropped Abby at home insisting that she contact the police and sort out the previous night's incident with her husband. Dom had explained that Rossy wouldn't want to make too much of it due to the embarrassment factor. He would also be fearful of what Abby could tell them about the assaults. It's amazing how eighty-five miles an hour; the wind in your hair and the roar of a fabulous car can refresh the sensors.

"**S**on of a bitch!" How could he have been so blind? Why hadn't he spotted it before? Dom grabbed the mobile phone and rang Paula. After he had explained that he was sorry for keeping the car for a few more hours he let her in on his thoughts. Paula's response had been similar to Dom's "Bloody hell." Dom hung up, spun the car around and floored it to whence he had just come from. Abby's house. Dom just about burst in through the front door of the cottage, to find Abby sat on the floor looking through some old photo albums. Abby was startled to say the least.

"Ever tried knocking?"

"Over rated….. Is he here?"

"Who?"

"You know who, hubby?"

"No, his Dad went to pick him up from the Police Station when I said I didn't want to make a complaint."

"Why didn't you tell me it was you that phoned the Police?"

"What are you on about?"

"The night I was arrested, there was a phone call to the police, a woman saying someone would be attacked. I'd always assumed, wrongly it now seems, that the phone call was made by my malicious ex-wife, trying to get back at me, but it was you………… You made the call." Dom was verbally assaulting Abby with all his thoughts without giving himself chance to contemplate his theories. Dom continued. "Somehow I think you thought or think that Rossy is involved in the assaults on the prostitutes and you were trying to warn the Police, only the little trap snared the wrong man. Me!"

There was a long pause as Abby looked at the photo's searching for some kind of inspiration, then she appeared to be cross with herself that it was all coming out.

"How did you know it was me?"

"I was on my way home today and I was thinking about something you said last night. It was the tone that you had said it in that made me think. I'd heard it said before, but where? Something had been nagging at my sub-conscience all night and I hadn't got a clue what it was. I've been racking my brain trying to think where? It was then that I realised it was the voice. I'd heard your voice before and not at the ball. It was played to me when I was interviewed, the night Sharon was murdered."

Both were silent for a moment, trying to get to grips with each other's realisations.

Abby spoke first, "I thought he had been seeing a prostitute and a couple of the nights that the assaults had taken place, like the murder of the young girl last week, I have no idea where he was. I thought that he was involved so I tried to tip them off."

"Why not go to the Police now?"

"Because I don't know who to trust, both my husband and father-in law are in charge of the investigation."

Dom was deep in thought, he was trying to hatch a plan, but Abby was right, it was finding a person they could trust with the information, without being dismissed as a jealous wife, wife's lover or a vengeful ex- policeman.

Dom dropped down to Abby's height and put his arm around her. "I have an idea, but I need to make a few calls first, meanwhile I want you to search the house, we need something that was your husbands, a razor, blood, hairbrush or something like that. If your hubby is involved then the police already have a couple of DNA profiles because they took mine to compare, so we can have it compared.

Dom spent the next hour on the phone. He knew the scientist that worked at the lab as he had worked on the shooting incident when Dom had scrunched Skunk. He had worked on the ballistic reports for the Police Complaints Authority, to show that Dom's actions had been justifiable and that shots had been fired. It was unnecessary really in view of the video evidence and the eyewitness statements but all eventualities had been covered in case the family tried to sue the Police at a later date. Four bullet holes in two Police Officers can easily justify lethal force. At the Inquest Skunk's father had remarked that he had wished it had been he that had been driving the Police car. No love lost there then.

Dom had eventually spoken to Bill on his mobile phone whilst the recipient of the call was half way up a cliff face in North Yorkshire. That must have been one hell of a sight seeing a rock climber hanging from a near vertical ledge, just taking five to answer his mobile. The scientist had been extremely reluctant at first but since he had already arranged to meet someone else at the labs at seven, there was no harm in doing what Dom was asking, especially when he was being offered five hundred pounds for a bit of moonlighting. As Dom came off the phone he shouted to Abby that he had sorted the meeting, all they needed now was a good sample. Dom wasn't too keen when it had been explained to him that the sample would take at least four hours to analyse, but what the hell, this needed sorting one way or another, and Police Forces pay a fortune to get their samples done. As Dom made his way back into the hall Abby was stood waving around a large bundle of grey tape. "Will this do?" She asked, with a smile of deep satisfaction on her face.

"What is it?"

"Well the other night when I knocked him out, I bound his legs with this grey binding tape but it appears when I helped take it off the tape pulled half of his hairs out of his legs........... Whoops." What a cheeky grin she had.

"Perfect."

Rossy had spent the morning eating humble pie apologising to his father and the officers at the station for the misunderstanding. After they left the Police station Rossy had insisted that they go into work. It was a Sunday morning but something was nagging him, and he needed to get it sorted in his own mind. Obviously the time in the cells had been well spent and given him some clear thinking time. Art had dropped Rossy off at the station. Rossy was sat in the deserted incident room reviewing all the evidence in relation to the prostitute assaults and the Murder. At ten the skeleton staff arrived to start on the Sunday mornings actions but truth be-known there was very little for them to do this morning. Everyone was on standby. After an hour he was happy with the target that they had, the CEO. It was the murder of the other prostitute Sharon that was puzzling him. He looked at the address book several times and then he took the address book to his father's office. He read the two names that had not been identified. He knew who one of them was. Kenny Pritchard was obviously himself, Keith Pemberton Ross; Sharon had used a cover name for him.

Rossy hoped he was wrong, he wanted to be way off the mark with the thoughts that were flooding into his brain but he wasn't and he knew he wasn't. That sixth sense of his was back and he was in full flow. He just needed a little verification to show that Andrew Roberts the other unidentified name was Arthur Ross, his own bloody Father. They'd both been banging the same women. Rossy was now wondering if Art had found out about himself and Sharon and a fight had taken place over it, or was she blackmailing him? No that couldn't be it they were both gentle people at heart, his Dad shouted a lot but he was always a gent around women. Oh what a bleedin' mess. This was the last thing that he needed right now. Not only was he up to his nuts in trouble, so was his father. It took no time at all looking at Arts desk diary and verifying his worst nightmare. The soft idiot had even pencilled Sharon's initial into his diary. He hadn't even had the common sense to remove them. He was obviously confident that no one knew of his involvement. Rossy quickly seized the diary and took it to his office and placed it in the safe. It was evidence, and it was also his Father's life he held in his safe. He quickly returned to the office. He needed a sample. That was easy; the electric shaver in the toilet provided all the test material he needed. A brief phone call to his mate Bill and everything was arranged. Seven pm at Whetherby. Rossy hoped he was wrong; he needed to have lost his touch on this one, but for whatever reason there was something to this, and he knew it. Rossy had not told Bill whose sample it was and he'd never asked.

# 39

Les and his crew had joined forces with the other active surveillance team on the sole target. Allen Krell the Chief executive officer of the Ambulance Service. At the beginning of the weekend the other team had followed the target to Oxford. It had been a quick trip and late Saturday night the target, closely followed by the team had returned to South Yorkshire and Krell's home. It was at 8am on the Sunday morning that Dale had taken over with Carol on the surveillance. Team one had all gone home to bed but was still on standby should anything occur. The rest of Les's team was coming on at two pm. By now all appropriate authorities had been sort in respect of the intrusive surveillance and the team had listening devices on the phones and an observation point from a house that was for sale across the street. Since Allen Krell had become the target his lifestyle to those looking in from the outside appeared very normal and in fact almost boring. He appeared on the surface of things to be a lonely hard working executive who spent a lot of his time at his desk on the computer. There had been no evidence of him doing anything sexual in the house. No dirty magazines or any suggestion of self-abuse. He had spoken to certain colleagues on the phone, all very business like. There were no lady friends that were known to the Police, and he appeared to have very little to do with his family. The only person he had any contact with was the brother in Oxford that he had just visited.

The truth of it was that since the breaking news of Steve Lordourail, nothing had happened, and the team was beginning to doubt that they had the right suspect; however there had been no attacks whilst he was under surveillance. Everything conveniently pointed to this man, so why didn't they just arrest him and take him out of the game, take his DNA and have it compared. It was bloody frustrating, but then again they wanted to be sure, minimum embarrassment to the man if it wasn't him and the lid to the coffin, glued, nailed and bound if he was the killer.

Dale was bored. Carol had been out for breakfast and returned with two of the biggest all day breakfast sandwiches he had ever seen. Dale had broken out the flask of tea and the two had set too having a good Sunday morning breakie whilst reading the Sunday papers. They almost missed Krell leaving the house, but fortunately

Dale was sat in the right position. Both jumped up in a hurry, abandoning everything in haste. Dale was soon behind the large Scorpio in the VR6 and some three hundred yards behind was Carol on the Fireblade, Dale enjoyed seeing Carol in the leathers most of all! The journey was a short one. A quick trip to the garage to fill the car with fuel and then through the car wash. Krell stood for a short time on the forecourt exchanging pleasantries with someone that had recognised him but then they were soon off again heading back towards the house. The Scorpio then pulled up outside St Catherine's Church, and Krell made his way inside. He was going to the Sunday morning service. Bloody marvellous thought Dale, we have breakfast at the house and here we are stuck outside the church waiting for Krell.

Carol's thoughts were different, she was wondering if this was new to Krell, or had he got something he needed to get off his chest, was he praying for forgiveness? Carol couldn't remember the last time she had been to church, other than for a wedding or a funeral, and for the first time ever she felt guilty. In her own way she believed, well she wanted to believe, maybe she needed proof. Agnostic is the word that she would use to describe her own feelings towards the church. She slipped from the bike and made her way into the Church grounds. What magnificent architecture she thought. The church was very well kept and all the grounds in beautiful condition. The grasses were cut and all the graves appeared to have been tended to recently. As she strolled between the gravestones she read the epitaphs on each one. Her heart was suddenly filled with sadness and inside she felt like crying. She knelt down at the side of a headstone with a little angel on the top. The name of a boy, Philip and he had died at the age of five. The wording read 'Mummy and Daddy's little Angel. Always in our hearts.' Eternal love. Mum and Dad. There was a little picture of the boy in a frame on the headstone. Carol remembered him well. Carol had been the first one at the scene of the car accident, it was no ones fault, the little boy had just run out between two parked cars, and in an instance, Philip had entered the afterlife. It suddenly became personal and a tear tolled down her face, a tragic loss without reason. She stroked the picture of the little boy and tried to smile. She stood up briefly and glanced around, the graveyard was full of tragic stories. She desperately wanted to believe they had been taken for a reason. She thought of Krell and began to prey, if he was getting help and asking forgiveness then so could the good guys. As she began to prey the church bells rang for the eleven o'clock service. By the time Carol had said Amen, her tears had dried, she had recovered her composure and she smiled at the picture of the little boy.

"Thank you Philip" With a saddened heart that felt heavy she turned and went back to the bike. She had been rejuvenated and humbled in one go. One thing for sure, she knew in her heart that they were going to catch this evil man and today was going to be the day, she could just feel it.

By two in the afternoon the status quo had returned. Krell was at home reading the Sunday papers and tinkering on his computer. The full team was now on and the entire house was surrounded. The team settled in for the afternoon, it was going to be a long one.

# 40

Dom had insisted on travelling up to Whetherby on his own. Bill might be uncomfortable with a stranger in the lab especially when what he was being asked to do was a little underhand. Abby had been concerned at being left on her own especially now they considered Rossy to be a possible suspect. He could be capable of anything and so Dom had driven her across to Paula's, she would be safe there. It had also given him the opportunity to swap back into his own car. As much as he loved driving the Porsche he had an affinity to the T5. It had been a present and it was his little baby. The journey up the A1 was a short one and as Dom pulled into the complex he saw two other cars in the car park. One was obviously Bill's and the other must be the other client he had mentioned on the phone. Dom pulled alongside the other car. He had seen this car before, but he couldn't remember for the life of him where from. Dom sat in his car and rang Bill on his mobile to let him know he was outside waiting. It was safer than banging on the door for ten minutes arousing suspicion. Bill quickly appeared at the front and let Dom into the building. It was a modern purpose built building. To all intents and purposes it was just another unit on an industrial estate, apart from the fact that the security was state of the art. The front of the building was all glass and the reception areas could be seen from outside. The laboratories were in the back. Much of the work done here was top secret and as a result of a recent arson attack, the scientific support centre had been split and moved to different sites. Now each unit had a different function, and it meant that all the samples weren't on one site, preventing the 'eggs in one basket syndrome'. The number of investigations that had been compromised as a result of the fire was tragic and they were adamant it would not happen again.

Bill had graduated from Liverpool University with a first in Genetics and then went onto to do his doctorate in molecular genetics. Bill's specialty was Gene splitting, but at the present time he was at the forefront of any work being done on DNA profiling. This area of scientific study was making advances on a daily basis and the quality of the results and validity were improving all the time. The new advances described as Low copy Number DNA was a massive step in the profiling of DNA and was beginning to help

Police in cases that were at one time considered dead and buried. This type of DNA is ultra sensitive and the amount of genetic material required is negligible but the down side is that this type of procedure is state of the art and expensive, hence it is only used as a last resort or where others have failed. Maybe in the not too distant future our DNA footprint will show everywhere that we have been, like a snail trail through the garden.

Bill was six foot two tall, extremely athletic in appearance, almost wiry but well defined. It was all the rock climbing he did. He had naturally curly shoulder length flame red hair tied back into a ponytail. His face was covered in freckles and a day's stubble. He was wearing sandals, Bermuda shorts and an abusive Hawaiian shirt that was in flagrant violation and contravention of the Colour Code Act. In fact Bill looked more like a beach bum than a scientist.

Bill stuck out his hand gripping Dom's with the natural force of a climber that makes you shake your own hand after just to get the blood back into it.

"Nice hand shake," Said Dom.

"Thanks, good to see ya! How you keeping?" asked Bill.

"Not too bad, I've left the job you know."

"I'd heard, well I read it in the papers actually."

"I'm surprised you're going out on limb for me then."

"Don't be silly, you're a paying customer."

Bill was deftly charging along the corridors and stairways leading Dom to the Lab. It was at the point they went into Bill's office that Dom was struck by shear terror. Sat behind Bill's desk was Rossy. Dom tried to grab Bills hand and pull him out of the office as he spun so that Rossy couldn't see him. Bill was already in the office and turned to see that Dom had disappeared. Bill stepped back out looking to see if he had lost Dom in the corridors. Dom was leant against the office wall quickly assessing his options. Should he retreat or should he go in and confront Rossy. He was an intelligent man. He would soon realise that the sample that Bill was going to test was his. This was a shit awful dilemma and further more what was he doing here? Dom's decision was made for him as soon as Bill stuck his head out of his office. "Dom, come in there's one of your ex colleagues in here."

As Dom walked into the office the look of horror on Rossy's face was comparable with that of his own thirty seconds earlier. Both looked at each other in stunned silence wondering what the hell was happening. Bill took one look at the both of them and realised there was a history to this, he was astute and looking at the pair of them it wasn't a good history.

"I'll put the kettle on," said Bill "This looks like it's going to be a long night."

Just as he was about to step from the office Bill stepped back in to issue the warning. "If either of you step out of line in here, you're out and I'll bin your sample and take the money."

Dom's mind was racing, what sample had Rossy got that he wanted checking? He knew it wasn't his.

Rossy's thoughts were easier to sort out; he knew it was his sample that Dom had. In someway that was a good thing; he could be proven innocent to Abby who he knew was adamant that he was embroiled in all this.

"It's my sample isn't it?" asked Rossy.

Dom thought long and hard before answering, should he reveal his hand. There was little point in holding back, who else could it be. He was seeing his wife for God's sake. The answer was obvious.

"Yes," was all he could muster.

"For which murder do you think I am responsible?"

That was a low-ball question. Dom had never thought about it from any other aspect than that of the serial attacker and murder of the prostitute in the school ground, but now, the question had been asked and it made him wonder.

"Could be both," Dom said rather lamely.

"Argh, Abby told you that the night Sharon died I assaulted her and she had a shiner, I was the bad guy. You then think I've gone and killed a prostitute. Truth is Dom, I was out of my box that night and I have no recollection of that night at all and hence if I killed Sharon it will be news to me too."

That took the wind out of Dom's sail. On the face of it Rossy had nothing to hide.

"Actually it's the prostitute attacks and murder in the school I'd got you lined up for," said Dom.

"Yes I can see your logic, I've been hitting Abby, and the night the prostitute was murdered in the school, my whereabouts can't be accounted for."

Dom interrupted. "And don't forget the phone call."

That hurt, Dom had worked out that Abby had phoned the police the night she had thought there was going to be an attack. The room fell silent as they both thought out the motives, arguments and rebuttals. It was like a trial without evidence. Something had to give.

Bill returned with a tray of coffee. "Have you boys sorted your differences yet, or is it handbags at five paces?"

Dom sensed that Rossy did not appear unduly concerned about having his sample compared.

"Compare my DNA with any sample you like. Like you I know I am innocent of any crime." The comment hit home and for the first time Dom believed what Rossy was saying. He wasn't trying to hide anything. Why should he? He had nothing to hide. Bill asked for the samples and Rossy handed over the shavings of his father. On no account would he reveal just yet the source of the sample just in case. Dom pulled out of his pocket the grey tape. Rossy set off laughing on seeing the tape. He knew his leg had been sore and until now he couldn't work out why there were no hairs on the bottom part of his calves? Well now he knew. Both men appeared to warm to each other's company and settled down to the fact it was going to be a long night. Bill left them to exchange pleasantries. The point of fisticuffs had long since abated, and it was safe for him to go to the lab and set about the task of trying to put each man's fears to rest.

# 41

Les was on obs in the house whilst the rest of the team sat at the back of the room playing cards, eating and drinking crap and generally taking the piss out of everyone. It had been along day without any progress or excitement. Another hour and Krell would be in bed. Perhaps they did have wrong target. Les had the high-powered binoculars focused on the desk where Krell was working. Krell stood and turned and went to the bookcase. He came back with what appeared to be a photograph album.

For Krell it had been like any other weekend. He had spent Friday night with his brother in Oxford, before retuning late Saturday. He spent most of Sunday working, apart from the trip out to the church in the morning. He had just finished a report on emergency dispatch and standby procedures for his ambulances. It was a touchy subject within the service. The management and public needed the Ambulances on standby so they could get to the patients quickly and reach the set government activity targets, and yet the Unions hated the idea of standby and were fighting it all the way. Industrial action was a distinct possibility. He was sick of their unprofessional approach and militant behaviour, but he knew it was only a few of them that were causing the majority of bad feelings. Krell dropped the report into the bottom of his briefcase and went to stand and leave his desk. He saw the picture of his Mum on the desk. What a wonderful woman she had been. He went and picked up the photograph album and brought it back to the desk. He was merrily flicking through the pages and having the fondest of memories of his Mum. As he turned the next page the picture that he hated most in the world, like the devil himself stared at him. The demon was there in front of him playing mind games with Krell, laughing at him, sneering at him. Krell was transfixed on a black and white photograph of his Father, a man that he had hated for the last forty-two years. He had been a man that had destroyed his family and sent his wife to an early grave. It was a battle now as to who won the staring competition. There was only ever one winner, his Father, as the evil eyes tried to burn out Krell's retinas. Krell had hoped that he had taught his father a lesson, but no, he hadn't, the hate was as fierce as ever. His Father needed to be taught another lesson, and another one of the devils little helpers would perish. These bastards of the devil could not be allowed to multiply. Krell looked at his Mum in the photograph on the desk. How could he have done it to her? He had blatantly played away from home with the ladies of the night, hookers, prostitutes, hoars or whatever local name they had for slags. He had treated his Mother like shit and these women, if that's what they could be called, like royalty. He was always out on the town with a different woman on his arm. Mother had caught endless diseases and infections and was always at the doctors for some pills or lotions. She was a laughing stock but she stuck to the old traditional family values. She stood by her man while he did what the hell he wanted. Krell had always sort to seek revenge, it was his destiny, and as soon as he was big enough he was going to kill his father, alas fate played its part and he had been denied the opportunity. His father had caught a nasty dose of hepatitis, the really contagious one and then gone home and given it to his wife. On the same day that Krell buried his Mum, they buried his Father too, and not two graves away was one of the town's hookers that had died of a similar illness. The family never disclosed what she had died of saying it must have been a broken heart, but Krell knew, it had been that tart that had given the disease to his Father and then his Mum. Krell was horrified at the thought that she was so close to his mother in the ground but consoled himself with the knowledge that the cow would have gone to hell with his Father whilst his Mum would now be at the right hand of God as there was no other place for her to go.

Krell was seeking to wreak havoc among these demons. He knew that if they were beaten in the way he had been beating them there would be no children of the devil running around. He had also accepted his fate. God may spare him, he may let him into Heaven for killing the demons, but he also knew there was a chance he would be frowned upon for doing what he was doing. Deep down he knew he would go to Hell, but that was what he wanted, to be able to confront and torment his Father as he had tormented him. Always in his nightmares, tricking him and hurting his Mum, well no more, he would have to kill another one. He wasn't going to stop until he was stopped. It was his mission, his destiny. He also knew that one day he would be caught, and that was inevitable. The police were good and would eventually track him down. He would save the taxpayers an expensive trial, he knew where the next battle lay, and that was with the Devil and his Father and he would take his own life to continue the fight in Hell and Damnation. As far as Krell was concerned he had always tried to save lives, being an Ambulance man since he was seventeen years old, but in this case there was only ever going to be one outcome. Death.

Les observed through the lens, his eyes drawn to Krells, was he crying? Something was wrong; his entire facial composition had changed. He was staring, his eyes set on the photograph album. He was transfixed to the picture of something; he had not turned the page in the album for at least five minutes. What was happening? Then Krell looked up from the book and stared out of the window.

"Holy fuck."

"What is it?" the team was paying attention.

Les had seen hatred, in the eyes of many a criminal but this man, wow; he was looking into the eyes of pure evil.

"Get ready quick, he's lost it."

# 42

Rossy was quite philosophical about the whole situation. He knew that he was not the serial attacker but understood why Dom thought he could be. Soon everything would be out in the open and no one would need to worry about who did what. Rossy decided that Dom wasn't such a bad guy after all even though he was seeing his wife. Even that was understandable under the circumstances. He knew he had been a complete shit, and when it comes down to it no woman in her right mind is going to stop with a bloke that keeps beating her, especially when he can't even remember doing it most of the time due to him being in a drunken stupor.

"You're barking up the wrong tree you know?"

"Good, I'd hate it if another good guy lost his job." It was a cheap jibe but it hit home.

Rossy decided to take a chance and tell Dom what was happening in relation to the investigation, although he left out the bit about Lordourail as he knew Derk and Dom were best of friends. He was taking a chance but he knew it was a small one. Dom listened intently to the whole story, including the fact that certain Police officers had given DNA for comparison. After nearly an hour and a very comprehensive account from Rossy, Dom knew that he just wasted five hundred pounds. He almost apologised but thought better of it. Dom sat quietly pondering the whole scenario. If the Police were so confident about the target for the serial attacks then Rossy had to be here in relation to the murder of Sharon, and he was doing it unofficially because the person was very important, a friend or relative. If Rossy thought that he had controlled the situation up to that moment he was just about to lose the initiative.

"So you think your Dad had something to do with the murder of Sharon?"

Dom always thought it amazing how the brain could react and answer the really shitty questions but the body; the physical appearance always let the brain down badly.

The answer was,

"Don't be silly!" but Rossi's facial expression and body language was in pain and torment. His brow was furrowed, his shoulders twitched and he immediately crossed his arms in a defensive position.

His foot started nervously tapping on the floor. What a massive give away thought Dom. No need to question that one any further.

When Krell drove off his drive the rubber on his Scorpio melted like a Le-Mans start. His driving was aggressive, and he was blatantly flaunting the speed limits. If staying with Lordourail had been easy then this was proving to be a bit more of a challenge. In fact the speed at which he was driving was positively dangerous. Les was concerned that the limited amount of traffic on the roads would give them away. There was a mad man in a Scorpio, a VR6 doing warp factors to stay with it, a Fireblade and a Subaru Impreza. Anyone using his or her rear view mirror would have spotted the team frantically trying to keep up. But this was not rational driving and Krell wasn't using his mirror. Les was still concerned and contacted the air support unit via a secure channel. He was sure from what he had seen so far that something was about to happen. They were already nearing the edge of town and needed to stay close. If they lost him now it could cost someone their life. Les also contacted the other team, he was pushing the panic button, something was going down and it was going down now. It had been the look in Krell's eyes that had told him.

Rossy had calmed himself after Dom had stuck the dagger blow in his back. He knew that he had answered the question but he might as well have told the truth. Dom had seen straight through him. Out of the blue Rossy said.

"I do love her, but I know that she will never love me again," Dom did not respond. What could he say without sounding contrite?

"Just tell her I'm sorry."

Dom was still feeling awkward and decided not to respond. The two had been in each other's company for nearly five hours and the strain was beginning to show. Both men were tired, it had been like a world championship chess game. Dom had clearly come away with the most information, but at least they both had an understanding of each other's position.

Bill came back into the office just after midnight just as Rossi's mobile began to ring. Bill didn't mess around and if the results were to have been private he blew that within seconds of walking into the room.

"Both negative chaps, neither sample correlates in any way with the two outstanding samples from the two murder scenes." he continued, "even the part sample we have from the Sharon Norburn murder scene can be discounted, what bit we do have doesn't match in any way shape or form."

Rossy was relieved but was grappling to unclip his mobile from his belt. The realisation was just sinking in. He needed to talk to his Father. He needed to clear the air and get the matter resolved properly, especially now he was happy he was not the main suspect. Both men had learnt in a matter of seconds that they had not solved either crime. The phone call that Rossy took made it clear in no uncertain terms that they had solved one mystery. Rossy left in a rush, he had to be somewhere else and quickly. As he left the room he told Bill to get ready in the morning, they had the killer and he wanted it confirming one hundred percent he was the man.

Interviewing him was pointless unless they convened a séance. He was dead.

# 43

Krell was now cruising around town, the aggression had gone from his driving and he was now on the prowl. His mind was a cauldron of evil thoughts; he was going to cleanse another bitch. It had only been a few weeks since the last attack but the girls were back on the streets. Had they ever gone away? Preying on the innocent, casting their evil spells on people and infecting them with disease. The Devil had now given them the deadliest of diseases to pass on. Trick or treat? Aids. Krell was on another mission of mercy he needed to protect the innocent from these vile creatures.

Les could see from his vantage point that the chosen victim was a woman in her late forties. She was an experienced hooker, probably a real looker when she was younger but the years had not been kind. Her face was weathered, her hair bleach blonde with dark roots, like she was fraying at the edges. What gave her away were her hands. They were old woman's hands, wrinkled, and chapped, with an excessive number of cheap trashy rings on each hand. Standing for several hours a night on street corners, in the cold, wet, damp conditions does nothing for a girl's complexion. Les could clearly see her through the binoculars. The air support unit was a mile away but with the high-powered lenses they had they had a clear view of the whole proceedings. The only thing that surprised Les was that this women was older, all the other victims had been young. Something was different, something was wrong.

Krell had picked this woman especially, all the other women had been chosen because they were young, and it was preventative medicine. They would not go back to bagging, and hence he had been right to stop them, they could not pass on their deadly diseases. But this one was probably the oldest bag out there. This was a revenge attack for all those that she had infected over the years. Looking at her it was going to be a mercy killing; she wanted putting out of her misery.

Krell cruised past her for the third time as the woman glanced over toward him. She knew he was trying to pluck up courage. It was always the same for the first timers; they would keep cruising past trying to steel their nerves, like the first time a juvenile buys condoms, or any other time for that matter. How wrong she was.

Krell was waiting for just the right moment. When the streets were safe and no one would miss her. Lucky for her, big brother was watching. Not something she would normally have approved of but on this occasion the whole fucking world could have watched her give head if it would save her life.

As the car stopped alongside her she stepped away from the wall from which she had been leaning. As she opened the door she asked him what he wanted. Krell wasn't listening; he could just see the end result. Her body lying dead in a pool of the Devils blood as it drained away into the gutter.

"I said what do you want luv'?"

Krell shrugged his shoulders.

This was nothing new; they are all embarrassed to ask for what they want, especially the first time.

"Hand job's a tenner, blow job's twenty-five, same for a shag, finger fucks are twenty."

Very descriptive thought Krell, he was going to enjoy every moment of this.

"What about a blow job and a finger fuck at the same time?"

"Cost you forty."

Macy, as she was called, got into the car. Well that was the name she used, whether it was her real name would never be known. Krell drove half a mile to the rear of an old sausage factory. It had closed down several years previous and was the perfect place. What Krell hadn't appreciated, was that it was a perfect place for the surveillance team to get close to. The helicopter had repositioned itself and was recording the events in infrared.

The helicopter was relaying the pictures via the satellite down link back to the operations Inspector. It had been an hour since Krell had left his house. It had only taken ten minutes to get into town but nearly fifty minutes to select the target, by which time just about the whole police operation was in place. The decoys had not been an option. The DI was on his way to the control room and the armed response vehicle was on standby. This was purely a precautionary phase but it was considered and they were near by. The second surveillance team was now in position or at least en-route to a rendezvous point. If Les had called it wrong, then this was just about to be the most expensive peep show ever. At this point in the proceedings they had to let the unknown prostitute go ahead with the act, they needed to know one way or the other before they would pounce. They probably had enough to reveal themselves now and arrest on suspicion but they wanted the lot, shit or bust. The helicopter had been instructed the moment they thought that Krell was about to strike they were to light up the entire scene and pin Krell. Wherever he went, the million watt candle bulb would follow. It was another subjective call but the officer in charge of the procedure was ready.

Somewhere in the region of twelve witnesses watched Macy perform oral sex on Krell whilst he groped at her bottom and between her legs. He had positioned the Scorpio near to a drain. This had been intentional. He was surrounded on three sides by disused buildings, his car in the middle of what had been the car park, and he lent over the bonnet, his back arched over the long bonnet as Macy went to work. At the point of ejaculation Krell's elbow was already arcing round to strike the victims head. His elbow struck cleanly on Macy's cheekbone and down she went. As the elbow was en-route to the target the entire compound was lit up. The light blinded Krell, but it was too late, contact had been made, the game was up. Les ran towards the car as Krell tried to compose himself and fasten his trousers. There was no time to get in the car he had to run. He had to complete his task. He could not be taken alive. By now the helicopter was swooping in on its target and was virtually directly overhead. Les was thirty yards behind Krell as he set off running between the buildings. It was futile he would be stopped within a short distance. As Krell broke from the rear of the unit he was near the main road. He could see his salvation some three hundred yards away coming up the hill. He had pegged the distance to a steady thirty yards as Carol joined Les and they ran stride for stride after Krell. The other cars in the location could be heard screaming into life, rubber was burning, springs bouncing as everyone tried to converge on the attacker. Krell's lungs were at the point of exploding, he was unfit, what did he expect he was fifty for God's sake. Everything was aching, creaking groaning, but he wasn't about to be denied his destiny, he had earned that. His saviour was now one hundred and fifty yards away. Fortunately he was running down hill at it, he had all the momentum he needed, no one was going to stop him now, and the result was inevitable. Carol was pulling away from Les, but only a few feet, she was still some twenty yards to the rear of Krell. The helicopter was directly above relaying the entire proceedings back to the control room. Other units were being directed to intercept Krell. The VR6 was coming up the hill at Krell on the same side of the carriageway. It was travelling up hill at over one hundred miles an hour; he would be with Krell in seconds. Dale was flooring the VR6 and he could see the target coming at him, closely followed by the two officers. The only thing in the way was the tram traveling up the hill at a steady thirty miles an hour.

Fifty yards to the tram, no way would they catch him. Krell glanced back to see that one of the officers was just about on him, maybe five yards behind him. It was the surge of adrenalin that he needed to just push himself that little bit harder. He was running on empty, there was nothing left in the tanks, his lungs burned. The tram was maybe twenty yards away; the timing was going to be perfect. Krell took two lengthened strides, like he was doing the long jump. The tram was maybe ten yards in front. Now was the time to meet his Father again. Krell dove like the legendry Gordon Banks, a beautiful high dive to his left fully extending into the path of the oncoming tram.

Carol was closing him down, she was only a couple of yards to the rear, one more yard and she would dive at him, it would be her arrest, but then she was too late. As she prepared herself to dive at the legs of Krell, she saw his body arc off to the left into the path of the oncoming tram. There was nothing she could do. The punishment was swift, but it was clear to see that Krell had taken his own life. Carol had not interfered in any way. As Krell landed, his body literally went straight under the nose cone of the tram. The body instantly dissected, dismembered and strewn across the tracks. It was just a six-piece jigsaw puzzle that was left lying in the road.

By the time Rossy got to the scene just about everything had been done. The road had been secured and the scene preserved. Scenes of crime were present along with the accident investigation branch. The medical examiner was en-route. As it turned out there was only one thing to be done. Rossy needed to speak to Krell's brother and inform him of his death. The house search had revealed nothing, no letter, but then he wasn't expecting to die, well not today. Rossy decided it was best to wait until the morning, he would grab a few hours sleep, be briefed at six and try and be in Oxford for nine, this needed to be done in person.

By the time Rossy returned to Sheffield the following evening he had all the answers he needed. Although Krell's brother had never known how deep the hatred for prostitutes was, he knew how much Krell had hated his Father. The scar had never healed and if anything ever rose in conversation about his father then Krell's tongue had always been wicked. This chapter was finally closed, another public figure falls by the wayside. Rossy reflected on his own situation and that of Sharon. He needed to speak to his own Father and let him know what he now knew. They had both been silly boys and hopefully their secret would not come out.

# 44

In the weeks following the death of Krell much had been publicised in the papers relating to motive and the reasons why Krell had done what he did. Prostitution became a bit of a political hotcake. Certain MP's were screaming for prostitution to be legalised, and hence it could be governed and controlled, brought within the realms of the government, they could be taxed, the industry could be cleaned up, and it was an industry.

Governmental control would also mean a greater degree of safety for the working girls. In essence the government would be the pimp and take a cut. They could get whatever treatment they needed; help, advice, regular medical checkups and blood tests. In the long run decrease the burden to the NHS.

Dom sat reading the Sunday papers intrigued by the political uncertainty of it all. Since the case had been finalised a degree of normality had returned to his life and he was working harder than ever as Christmas approached. In the morality stakes he could well and truly argue the case from both sides, but his overall view was if a woman wants to offer a service, and as a result of that, one less frustrated man is on the streets, which in reality probably meant the chances of one innocent unsuspecting woman being attacked would be reduced.

Unfortunately this was a view that was not shared by Abby and since the incident with Krell and Rossy the relationship with Dom had gone very cool. They saw each other often and enjoyed each others company immensely but invariably the conversation would come around to Rossy or Krell or what Dom did for a living and then the barriers would come crashing down and the conflict would start. Dom had been convinced since the moment he had met her that she could be the one. If he could have just looked into his heart a little deeper he would have seen the truth, but he didn't trust himself to be hurt so soon after his wife, rejection for the second time was not an option.

Αs far as the Police were concerned the two names that were in Sharon's diary remained unidentified. Rossy had spoken to his Father about the matter. Art had naturally denied any involvement and considering that only Rossy knew for definite, and perhaps Dom, that it was not Art's DNA, other than mere suspicion that he had been seeing Sharon, he had nothing on his Father. If only his Father would trust him enough to tell him the whole story then maybe they could take the case further forward but until that time they were no closer to catching Sharon's killer.

Bill had received further samples from the crime scene; they were looking at the new LCN ( Low copy number) technique and trying to build up a full genetic code just in case the killer was already in the Police system. At this time it was the only avenue of investigation available to them.

Dom had been working for Paula for nearly four months and the trade was excellent. There was real money in the business of providing personal services but it never ceased to amaze Dom that people would pay a thousand pounds a night for whatever service they wanted. This was a job that he really enjoyed and, it gave all the freedom he wanted meeting some very special and nice people at the same time. His job was actually an education in life, in people and their needs and desires. Dom was concerned however that he wasn't looking after his own interests and his relationship with Abby was suffering as a consequence.

It was a bad time of year for taking time off but Paula had been unable to refuse Dom, she was too soft with him, but that's how you behave when you're totally and utterly in love with that person. The only problem was that Dom was unaware of how she really felt towards him. Paula had seen how the relationship had gone somewhat frosty between Dom and Abby and she was hoping that it was only a matter of time before the two split up. She desperately wanted them to break so that she could have a chance; the funny thing was she knew that they were so right for each other. That being her and Dom. Paula had been careful not to reveal that she was not really a lesbian, she wanted him to find his feet after the separation and most of all she wanted them to be friends, she would not lose him under any circumstances and if just meant being good friends then so be it, friends it would be, you don't let go of someone like Dominic Veil, there aren't that many good guys about. The one thing that Paula could not be responsible for was the two of them breaking up otherwise Dom may never forgive her. It's the old adage; if a Father says do one thing then nine times out of ten the child does the opposite. It was cheap child psychology but Paula was playing the game. She had time, money, looks, but above all, no one, but no one would ever love Dom like she did. His wife had been a fool, to walk away from that kind of love. Her new man must be a bloody super hero to have thrown it all away, but more fool her. Paula's only problem now was to dispose of Abby some way or another, but tactfully.

Paula had made out that Dom would be doing her a favour if he went to New York to collect a couple of new suits that she had ordered the last time she was over. They could collect the suits and then have a two day cruise on the new Pheonix liner, Sundance, sail from New York to Boston before flying back from Boston. It was only a five-day trip, two days shopping and a couple of days on the boat. The cost was extortionate, nearly fifteen hundred pounds a piece but Paula had covered the cost. She really was being too kind to the both of them. Paula was just hoping that at some point over the next five days they really would reach breaking point and come back single. She had even driven them to the airport. The atmosphere in the car had been particularly frosty. Dom just put it down to the fact that Abby saw Paula as a constant threat. Paula gave Dom a kiss and hug as she left them at terminal one, she really didn't want to let go and wished it was her that was going with him. Call it woman's intuition but she sensed that something was seriously wrong.

# 45

Derk was mulling over what the DI had said in briefing. 'Be extra vigilant, stop check absolutely every vehicle out after 11pm with single males in. Pass all details through to the incident room.' Although Krell had been caught there was still an unsolved murder and at the present time no one had any clues. The actions had stopped and the trail was cold. No motive, no suspects, so they were on a fishing expedition.

Derk was working a six two evening shift, which he hated. It always meant waking everybody up when he went home. It was unavoidable, the dog would bark on seeing the car pull onto the drive. This in turn would wake his Son, who would then wake Fran who would then give it him in the neck when he got into bed. It was literally a no win situation.

Derk had been disheartened when Dom left the job, but he was starting to get back into the swing of things. His new partner on the response car was Mac, the dark destroyer. He was of black West Indian origin. Athletic build, very muscular and well defined and the quickest thing Derk had seen on two legs. Nothing escaped in a straight foot chase, not even those that had a head start, but most of all he had a sense of humour, he was good at his job, had a way with the public and he was a total flirt with all women. Derk was the calming influence of the two, and the more sedate behind the wheel. Derk still hadn't been able to work out who was the fastest between Dom and Mac. Mac was a loose cannon behind the wheel, very aggressive, almost pushing people off the road. Dom had always been smooth and calculating. There was nothing to separate either of them of that he was sure. He always preferred Dom's driving however because he always thought he would be going home at the end of the shift.

The two were parked in a lay-bye on Brightside lane watching the junction. Mac was busy bragging about his recent conquests, whilst Derk tried to get his pocket book up to date.

"Is it true Love?"

They both started laughing.

"Kinky sex, more like."

"Here we go............ brag brag."

"You're only jealous."

"Don't even try and make out it's a black thing."

Flash

Flash

"Whoops she'll be happy."

The GATSO had instantly claimed another victim.

"They both looked like babes to me."

"Do you want to stop them and give them the good news?"

Mac was busy pushing all the buttons on the console, lights camera, wail and whelp, action.

Half a mile down the road the small clapped out Fiat stopped in a bus lay-by.

"Fetch her back to the car Mac."

Before Mac had got his backside off the seat she was out and walking towards them. Derk could see she was a giggly student, perhaps twenty years of age. Wearing flip-flops, a very short denim skirt that only went half way to reaching her knees. A tight fitting white top with 'Kookai' emblazoned across her chest. 'More like cookies' Derk was thinking. She was very fresh faced, no makeup, long flowing blonde hair. What a cheeky face. Mac pointed to the rear seat on the passenger side and Leah Bunting made her way to the door and slipped into the car. Mac sat back in the front passenger seat. Both Derk and Mac were straining to look at the girl but they needn't have worried, she made it very easy for them to look at her. She slid into the middle and sat hanging onto the rear of the front seats leaning forward. Her legs were slightly parted and Derk couldn't help but sneak a quick glance. It was like Basic Instinct only the view was better.

Derk began with. "Do you know the reason why we have stopped you?"

Leah smiled at him and paused for a second considering her answer. "Cos I'm a young good looking chic"

"Good answer."

They were all laughing. Sod that, they were all flirting. Leah spoke in a beautiful clear soft Irish accent. She re-answered the question. "Those flashes."

"Yes, I am afraid you have just gone through a red light."

"Is there anything I can do?" asked Leah

Mac was thinking of several things but nothing that was going to get her off with the GATSO Ticket.

"It might not have had a film in the camera," Derk proffered with some degree of optimism.

"Do I pay you?"

"No I'm afraid it doesn't work like that," Derk had taken an instant liking to the girl and decided it was time to help her out of her little dilemma. "If we decide to help you out of this little fopar, which was short for 'fuck up' you will have to agree to do what ever punishment we see fit."

Mac was looking at Derk wondering what the hell they could do, but hey just play along with it.

"Sounds intriguing."

"Okay to get off with the GATSO camera you must sing a nursery rhyme in full from start to finish. If you manage it, I will give you the answer, if you fail, well that just doesn't bare thinking about."

There were very few people that could be dealt with like this, most froze in the presence of the police and couldn't hold any form of conversation with a Police officer but this girl was so relaxed. It was the Irish blarney.

"Okay I agree."

316

"Right, I must caution you first and tell you that you don't have to sing a nursery rhyme, but it may harm your well being if you fail to sing one in full. Any thing you do sing maybe taken down and used against you to take the piss."

"That was the rarer version of our caution!" said Mac.

Leah slumped back into the seat thinking for a second. Oh I can't think of one.

"What about three blind mice?"

"Yes okay I can do that one."

Leah cleared her throat. "Three blind mice, three blind mice see how they run, see how they run, one run after the farmer's wife, dum de dum di dum dumm dum de dumm de de dum dum dum three blind mice."

By this time Derk and Mac were in hysterics. The girl who was sat in Leah's car was straining her neck to see what was happening.

"There you are I've done it."

"That was a fail, we need to hear all the words."

"I don't know all the words, didn't you like my dum de dums instead."

"No, a deal's a deal."

"What if I sing Humpty Dumpty?"

"Brill, go for it"

Leah then rattled of a perfect rendition of Humpty Dumpty, followed by a fake bow in the back seat of the car. Derk turned, smiling again and said I think everyone enjoyed that we had an open mike out of the car. Leah instantly blushed.

"Only kidding."

Mac decided to go and see if the other girl in the car was okay and just explain the delay. Derk took out his pad, which would require Leah to produce her documents at the Police station. He then wrote on the ticket the exact time and date of the offence and that she had received a verbal caution for going through a red traffic light.

Leah looked puzzled.

Derk took all her details, address, and date of birth and wrote down her description.

"How will this work?"

"It's easy, have you ever heard of double jeopardy."

"Yes."

"Well you can't be found guilty of the same offence twice and as I have used my discretion to formally caution you, hence you have received your punishment. So if the photograph appears on your doorstep with a fine send it back with a copy of this ticket attached saying you've had a warning for the offence.

"Fab, thanks."

Boy the Irish accent was a turn on.

"Just sign on the bottom of the form to say you will produce your documents for me."

Derk handed Leah the Pad. Leah signed the pad and then closed the pad shut writing on the front.

RING ME 01142765677. TONIGHT.

Leah handed the pad back to Derk and winked at him.

Derk glanced at the pad. Very professionally he reopened it at the page of the ticket. "You have seven days from midnight tonight to produce your driving licence, insurance and MOT at Valley Police station. I must warn you that if you fail to produce them you will be reported on summons for those offences and any other offences that come to light. Do you understand?"

"Yes officer," There was a pause, "But you can check my documents when you come around later, can't you?"

Derk was not normally stuck for words but on this occasion it was he that had been hunted not the other way around.

"Officer, what's your name?"

"Derk, short for." "Derek," she said finishing his sentence.

"See you later Derk."

With that, Leah slipped from the vehicle and was halfway back to her car when Mac got back in the vehicle. Mac was full of himself; he had managed to get the passengers telephone number. Derk lifted the pad and showed Mac what was written.

"Good lad......Are you going?"

Derk was quiet. He was fighting with his conscience. There was Frannie at home with the baby and there was he up to his old tricks, or at least contemplating getting up to his old tricks. The two drove around until mealtime at 9pm. It had been a quiet evening on the whole. They had been to a domestic dispute and arrested the husband to prevent a breach of the peace. They had then gone to a non-injury road traffic accident, where an old bloke had driven into a wall. Derk and Mac had still not managed to work out how he had done it, but at least it was only the metal and the brickwork that were damaged. All the time Derk had been tugging away at his own conscience. Should he? Shouldn't he? "Mac will you cover for me if Fran rings?"

"Yes sure."

"I'll ring her now and tell her I'm doing four hours overtime. I'm sick of going in at two and waking her." It was obvious that Derk was trying to justify it to himself.

The call was quickly made and within the space of ten minutes Derk had spoken to Leah who was expecting him. The sergeant had given him four hours off. Mac was very impressed with the skulduggery and he was even a little jealous. But hell, the number of times that Derk had covered for him recently, it was the least he could do.

By ten twenty Derk had changed out of uniform and was on his way out of the building. On his way out of the back door the new Police gazette had just been delivered and Derk grabbed a copy. The address had sounded familiar to him when she had told him on the phone and now he knew why. It was the road where Sharon had lived, although he couldn't remember which house it was. It was close to here though, the picture of Dom on the front page of the newspaper sprang to mind, and he was very close to where the picture had been taken. Derk walked the short distance to the building. He could see that the large Victorian house had been split up into flats.

Derk pressed the Buzzer for Leah's flat. Inside the pit of his stomach he had butterfly's' he was excited and apprehensive all in one go. He felt like a kid on his first date. The door clicked and Derk was in. Tentatively he walked to the top floor where Leah's flat was situated. The door was already ajar. Derk could here music emanating from the room. Tom Jones and the Cardigans singing burning down the house. As Derk knocked lightly on the door it just swung open.

"Come in."

Leah was stood on the middle of the room. She was wearing one of those wrap around skirts that tied off, very short, making her legs look longer than he remembered. Derk could see a small tattoo of a dolphin around her belly button, due to the crop top revealing her midriff. Leah stood holding two bottles of Stella extending her arm and handing one to Derk as a welcome.

"How long have you got?"

"Six at the latest."

"Great I thought you'd say an hour. I'll pop a pizza in the oven, you must be starving?"

"Sorry, I forgot to fetch a bottle."

"Oh don't be silly."

"Hope you don't mind, I've brought a police magazine by mistake and didn't want to leave it in the car."

"You can show me later. I love a man in uniform."

Derk collapsed onto the sofa. The flat was small but very cosy. From what he could see it consisted of a kitchen, bathroom and lounge / bedroom. Leah had got the place really well sorted. Her desk and laptop were over towards the main window, which overlooked the main road. To the side of the desk were hundreds of books, many of which were old and appeared second hand, some even leather bound. The bed was a large pine bed with white quilt and lots of cushions. In front of that was a large sofa which Derk was sat on and a coffee table on which sat the TV and stereo system. The walls were covered in posters of dolphins and whales and two certificates that had pride of place showing that she had adopted Orpheus a dolphin and Snowcap a Killer Whale. There were no lights on only several well-placed candles that added to the ambience. Derks assessment of the flat was disturbed by Leah diving over the back of the sofa and landing next to him.

"Didn't think you'd come!"

"Neither did I."

"Saw the gold-band."

"Well I won't tell her if you won't."

"Deal."

That was the last conversation they had in relation to Derks domestic situation. Neither wanted to discuss it or spoil the occasion.

"Where are you from then little Miss Irish?"

"Lisdonvarna, it's on the west coast of Ireland in a place called County Clare."

"The home of Guinness and the Cliffs of Moher."

"I am impressed."

"So was I........ with the cliffs."

"You've been?"

"Yes..... but along time ago, twenty years or so. It was a family touring holiday around Ireland. It is a truly beautiful place."

"Oh... the Pizza,"

Leah flew from the sofa to the kitchen. Within minutes she was back with a small Caesar salad a large Pizza and two more Stella's.

"Thought you students were supposed to be poor."

"Big overdraft,"

Leah put the food on the coffee table. "Do you mind if I put this film on she asked? Only my friend wants it back tomorrow and I haven't watched it yet."

"No not at all, what is it?"

"Thomas Crown Affair,"

"Brilliant film, I saw it at the pictures."

Leah popped the film on and both sat munching away on a hickory steak pizza and Caesar salad. No sooner had the film started than the pizza was finished. Leah was nestled into Derks body with her arm across his middle, whilst Derks arm was draped around her shoulders. She sure did have soft skin. He couldn't remember the last time he had sat down with his arm around anyone; this sort of intimacy had just disappeared when he got married.

Leah started to stroke the inside of Derks thigh at the same time kissing him on the neck. Derk took the hint, she wanted to play.

"What about the film?"

"I can hear it."

Playful, joyful, explosive and passionate, neither of them saw the credits to the film. They were both asleep in the most romantic position of all, as one as Derk lay inside her. Derk was awoken at four thirty by Leah fetching him a cup of coffee. Boy she was beautiful. Twelve years his junior but this was something special. Dare he push his luck?

"Leah, where do I stand?"

She smiled at him and put her hand on his face. "I know what I want, but you are married. I will put no pressure on you. I am here if you want me."

"What do you want?" asked Derk

"You, you're the one."

Derk was stunned. Not just by the comment but by absolutely everything. He loved everything about her. Surely he wasn't going to leave Fran, but he knew deep down he would. You can't help who you fall in love with and he wasn't about to live a lie. Little did he know he'd been living one for the past eighteen months. Leah picked up the Police gazette and jumped into Derks lap and started flicking through the pages. On the back page was a picture like the one you would have taken at a wedding. It was actually a picture of everyone who attended the Policeman's ball. Derk spotted Dom's face on the middle row. Derk pointed to Dom. "He's my best friend."

"I've seen him before."

"Very probably he's been on the front page of the papers a few times over the last year."

"No not in the paper. I saw him once or twice when he came to see Sharon. I remember him smiling at me and saying hello as he walked past me."

Derk was pointing at Krell. "Look at that mad bastard there, that photograph was taken just about two hours before he went out and brutally murdered that young girl."

Leah was now scrutinizing the picture. "I know quite a few of them," She said nonchalantly. Derk was suddenly very interested in which ones she knew.

"Those three."

"How do you know them?"

"They've all been to Sharon's on several occasions, apart from that one. I only saw that person a couple of times."

Derk was wondering if the Police had already spoken to Leah, but of course they would have.

"People used to come and go all the time, I never thought anything of it and obviously I never knew any of them."

"You do now."

"I take it we're talking about before the murder?"

"Oh yes."

"JESUS CHRIST." Derks mind had gone into overdrive.

# 46

Just after five in the morning Derk was braying like hell on Paula's door. As soon as she opened the door she knew something was badly wrong, she could just tell by the look of panic on his face. "Where is he?"

"Who?......... Dom!"

"Yes Dom, I can't get him at home or on his mobile."

"Why? What's the matter?"

"Is he with Abby?

"He's in New York, left yesterday."

"Tell me he's not with Abby."

"Why, tell me why?"

Now Paula was beginning to sound distressed and agitated; she wanted a straight answer to a simple question. Derk quickly explained about Leah and what had happened. Paula would neither judge him or do anything to hinder his happiness, in fact she also thought a lot of Derk, as he was the other man that had helped save her life. The disturbing news was about Rossy and Art who had been seen at Sharon's. Paula tried to put Derks mind at ease as she knew that neither of them were killers due to the DNA tests. Derk was talking but she was unable to take it in, she was too busy trying to tell him whom it was not whilst he was trying to tell her who he thought it was. Derk let her ramble on for a few more seconds before screaming at her.

"Is Dom with Abby?" He had shouted it so loud it startled Paula.

"Yes."

"Right listen, can we contact him because Abby has just been pointed out to me as being at Sharon's on two occasions prior to the murder? Now that's strange and it's never been mentioned before."

Paula was musing over what she had been told and thinking back to what happened. "That would make sense, Dom had found out that Rossy thought his Dad had been involved with Sharon but maybe he was looking at the wrong family member."

"Who do we go to?" asked Paula

"You try and contact Dom and I'll go and see Mr Ross when he arrives at work."

Paula was not just about to ring Dom and tell him that the women he loved was possibly a murderer. That is not the sort of news you give to someone and then ask them to love you. No she needed to find him personally. Paula checked her clock. It was now Five fifty am here, which meant it was about one am in New York. No she had to get to New York and quickly, where's bloody Concorde when you need it? He had protected her. It was her turn to protect him.

By the time Derk managed to track down Rossy it was just after nine. Unbeknown to Derk, Paula was just taking her seat on a Continental flight from Manchester. Derk quickly briefed Rossy on what he knew. Rossy new that judgement day had arrived and things were going to get messy, but first they had to catch a killer, his wife. On the desk was a report from Bill, which stated that they had been able to build a complete DNA profile of the killer or what they believed to be the killer. The one important ingredient that had been missing from the last sample was the gender of the killer due to the damage to the sample. Everyone had just assumed that the killer was a male. The evidence was now overwhelming, and it pointed to the fact that it was actually a female killer. Timing is everything, maybe it was coincidence but he was sure in his heart he would never have in his wildest nightmares accused Abby of murder. Rossy also knew he would have to answer the question, why he had never disclosed that he had been sleeping with Sharon and that he had hindered the murder investigation. It had now been confirmed for definite that his Father had been seeing Sharon and there was nothing he could say either. It looked like it was time for him to retire; maybe they would both be going. Rossy had attended all his AA meetings and was dry at the present time but this was enough to push anyone over the edge.

"Where is Abby now?" he knew that Derk would know where his mate was.

"New York."

Rossy was deep in thought. He was mulling over his options, should he contact the authorities in New York or wait for her to return. There was no reason to think that she would not return. She had no idea that she was now the new prime suspect in the case. He had a couple of days at best to put his own house in order before they returned. It would give him chance to keep a little dignity.

'How blind am I' he thought. "I should have spotted it a mile off. People become very emotive where relationships with prostitutes are involved. I must have been careless and Abby must have found out."

"Looks like she might have found out about both you and Art and decided to do something about it."

"The answer is so simple when you have all the pieces to the jig-saw. They just fall into place." Rossy was thinking out loud." The phone call had been a red herring to make us look for a man. She had been watching the house, uncanny Dom was arrested there, it should have been me later, but the call meant I was busy all night, God I bet she was going to set me up. We arrest one of our own and she slips in the back door, and if we had missed Dom or anyone else there would have still been the body and we would have been looking for one of our own. That was the night she accused me of giving her a black eye and I couldn't remember a thing about it. Still can't, but I bet she got it off Sharon." Rossy was shaking his head. What had he done? What had made her do it?

"Can your mate take care of himself for a couple of days do you think?"

"Two Psycho's in New York. I hope so."

Rossy had listened to Derk and the events that had unfolded with Leah the night before. Derk had intimated that he was worried how the evidence would come out and it would put him at Leah's. He wasn't unduly worried he just wanted it handling tactfully. He was about to give up his whole life and walk away to a new one, but he wanted to do it with some decorum.

Rossy opened his filing cabinet and leant into the safe that was buried deep in the back. Rossy carefully opened the safe and removed an envelope containing thirty-six pictures and a tape transcript. Rossy held out his hand.

"Are you sure you want a new life with Leah?"

"Why?"

"After just one night?"

"Yes, sometimes you just know"

"This envelope would never have seen the light of day if I wasn't sure that you wanted to leave your wife. Well maybe now you won't feel so bad about it."

Rossy dropped the envelope in Derk's lap. All that was written on the envelope was Lordourail.

# 47

The 747 touched down at exactly four twenty pm English time, which was eleven am New York time. This had been a long day already. By the time Paula had cleared customs and jumped into a cab she hit the busy Manhattan traffic which was bedlam. As she left JFK she was hoping to get to the hotel before they checked out however it took over an hour to get to the Radisson Empire which overlooks Broadway and the Lincoln centre. If Paula had not run into the foyer she would have perhaps seen the couple strolling off in the direction of central park. The concierge was very helpful but unfortunately they had checked out. Their luggage was still at the hotel but this was being sent on to the port and put in their cabin on board the ship.

Paula had been in hot pursuit for the last twelve hours, and she was tired. It had never occurred to her what she would actually say if she caught up with Dom. She was there to protect him not to confront him. Paula left the Radisson and jumped on the subway coming off at Little Italy, she needed some food and a couple of hours sleep and Kostas was just the man to look after her, build her strength back up and plan her next move. Something told Paula that she was about to go on a cruise.

After some light refreshment, Paula made several phone calls. Derk appraised her of what Rossy had said but that had provided no comfort to Paula. As far as she was concerned Dom could be in real danger. Derk was surprised to hear that Paula was now on the other side of the Atlantic. Derk had frowned upon the idea of playing chaperone as this might alert Abby to the fact that something was wrong. Paula had promised to play it cool and just look on from a distance. The second phone call had been to the Pheonix Cruise line. She was in luck and there were a couple cancellations due to illness. Paula had told the booking agent that some friends were also on the cruise and that it was to be a surprise and could she have a room nowhere near the other couples. Paula had managed to book herself an inside cabin on F deck whilst Dom's room was on D Deck. Another plus was that they were dining in different restaurants

Paula came off the phone and sat back reflecting on her good fortune at being able to get herself on the ship. Kostas placed an espresso on the table and gave Paula a quizzical look.

"What....... what have I done?" Paula said in a pleading way

"Have you got any plan?"

"No not at all, but that's not the point, I can wing it."

"So you drive at break neck speeds in one of the worlds fastest super cars, fly two and half thousand miles, to then hitch a ride on Pheonix's newest 76,000 tonne super liner, without a plan and no cocktail dress."

Paula sat and listened scrunching her face up as the facts were relayed to her. What was she doing?

"I think it means I love him?" she said nodding at Kostas.

"I think it means you've got too much money." He said with a knowing look.

"Oh shut up."

Paula needed a cocktail dress and she needed it quickly, she also needed a change of hairstyle, a shorter more radical cut was required, so that if she were seen no one would give her a second glance. By four thirty Paula boarded the Sundance and made her way to her cabin. This was the most nerve-racking part as she could bump into them just as she was registering, but as luck would have it she made it to her cabin without being seen. She had enquired as to whether her friends were aboard the ship but at the present time they were not. The kind young receptionist had promised to let Paula know when they were aboard, but without letting on that she was on board the ship.

Prior to Dom and Abby joining the ship they had had a couple of hours shopping on their own in the afternoon. Abby had intimated that she wanted to buy Dom a present while he had decided to go and collect the dresses for Paula. The ship set sail at seven pm, leaving pier 19 and heading down the Hudson River before heading out to sea and travelling up the Eastern seaboard. The departure from New York was dramatic to say the least. The band playing at the dockside, streamers and air horns followed by the rasping deep tones of the ships horns. Wow what a sight as the majestic liner slipped away gracefully from New York. The view back to the skyline was stunning and moving. The absence of the Twin Towers left a lump in Doms throat. The reflection of the skyline shimmered from the icy cool but still waters as the Hudson converged with the East River. Lady Liberty was waving farewell and bidding them a safe journey. Both Dom and Abby returned to their room to dress for dinner and adorn all their finery. At eight Dom and Abby left their room for a brief stroll to the Crows Nest for a cocktail before dining. Abby was wearing a short red cocktail dress with a low halter neck whilst Dom was looking devilishly handsome in his tuxedo. The pair of them looked a million dollars and yet there was an atmosphere between them, they still weren't gelling. Abby quickly downed two G&T's which did little to chill her attitude towards Dom. Dom meanwhile was working his way down the cocktail list and had just had an Arabian cooler. By the time the two of them reached the Alexandria restaurant conversation was minimal. Fortunately they were seated at a table for eight and the company provided by the other diners made for an enjoyable evening.

Paula meanwhile, had a lucky escape as she too had been to the cocktail bar in the Crows Nest. She had soon attracted several admiring glances and it had not been long before two men whom had obviously managed to slip from the claws of their wives had moved in to keep her company. It had been these two gents that had blocked the view of Dom and prevented him from seeing Paula.

It was uncanny and certainly one of those mysterious things that when Paula was seated at her table in the luxurious opulent Atlas Restaurant that the two men were seated on either side of her, and as it turned out wife free, the men appeared to be travelling together. Both utterly charming, and Paula was keen to find out their story but neither was letting anything slip. Leo Aspen and Charlie Teuce proved to be the perfect dinner partners and Paula settled down to enjoy what was a first class meal.

The setting at the rear of the ship could not have been more romantic. The table at which Dom and Abby where seated had sweeping ocean views, although in the darkness the view was limited. Abby was sat adjacent to Lord Tavenor who was a retired Peer and who was nearly eight-five years old. Abby had commented to Dom that he was a frisky little bugger. Dom was next to the wife of an American Banker. Dom had thought he was an American Wanker and his title had got lost in the crossfire. His wife on the other hand was a true gem, and spent most of the time apologising for her over exuberant and obnoxious husband. Abby meanwhile had not eased back on the G&T's and it was clear to Dom that her mood was becoming more cantankerous and churlish towards him but she was sweetness personified to the other people at the table. By the time Dom had finished his coffee he was ready for some fresh air and a stroll onto the prom deck. Abby reluctantly joined him, but Dom had made his mind up to sort this one way or the other.

In contrast Paula had really enjoyed the company provided by Leo and Charlie. They were both men of the world and had experienced life and yet Paula could still not work out what they did for a living. At one point she thought they were businessmen and then she thought they were some kind of investigators for big banks. She was close but they would not let her know just yet who they where. Leo was a Detective 1st Grade with the NYPD and Charlie was a Detective Sergeant. They had been dispatched to keep an eye on proceedings taking place on the boat. Rossy had been happy to leave the matter until Dom and Abby returned to England but when he was made aware that Paula was now in New York he feared that she may tip Abby over the edge and they would lose the element of surprise on her return to England. That unknown factor, the X factor, had caused him to reconsider carefully his position. He had neglected to act earlier in the investigation and if he failed again it would be very costly and hugely embarrassing to the service. As a result of this Rossy had spoken to the NYPD and told them what he had. The situation was deemed to be under control if they could keep an eye on Paula, and hence with a little co-operation from the Pheonix management and Captain of the ship suitable protection was in place. They were under strict instruction not to declare who they were and to leave matters to run their natural course. Intervention was only to be adopted in extreme circumstances.

Leo and Charlie had just finished what they had considered a shit assignment; baby-sitting a federal prisoner about to give evidence and for once they were in the right place at the right time. Now they were sat dining with a beautiful woman on one of the Worlds finest ships ever to set sail for two whole days. Things don't get much better than that.

Dom had made his way up onto the Prom deck and proceeded to walk in a clockwise direction around the ship, along the Port side and the back down the starboard side of the ship to the aft. Dom was stood looking out to the ocean. The air was fresh and cool. Abby looked cold as Dom slipped his DJ around her shoulders. Dom wanted to clear the air, but it was Abby that started the conversation. Her tone was harsh and unforgiving.

"Who do you think about when you're on the job?"

That was a nasty question and Dom was hoping he could give a politician's answer, one that didn't answer the question.

"Well it depends; you should always try and concentrate on the person your escorting."

"Yes, but what about when you have to bed them?"

"I don't think I like these questions Abby, why are you doing this?

Paula had made her way onto the prom deck and little did she realise that she was on a collision course at the back of the boat with Dom and Abby. What she had not spotted was the two detectives playing catch up behind her. It was the sound of Dom's voice telling Abby to "cut that out."

Paula froze on the spot, literally twenty foot from where they were stood, just out of sight on the Port side. She hoped the voices remained slightly raised so that she could here them above the sound of the engines and the cutting of the ship through the sea.

"Come on who do you think about, me, Paula, or the hussy that's paying?"

"That's enough."

"You're just like the rest of them, you're all the fucking same. You break up marriages and screw them for money."

Abby's entire demeanour had changed; she was aggressive and was clearly over stepping the mark.

"Look if that's how you feel we can end this now"

"Oh we can end this now alright," the anger and venom in Abby's voice was clear to hear.

"Fucking prostitutes, Paula, Sharon you."

"What's Sharon got to do with this?" Dom was trawling the depths of his memory banks, why had she mentioned Sharon.

Abby wasn't answering that question. Sharon's name had not intended to slip out but she was bloody furious with the lot of them. By this time Paula was still pressed against the side of the ship ear wigging. Leo and Charlie who made light of bumping into her joined her. Paula pretended she had come across a lovers tiff and rather than interrupting she was leaving them to it, although it had got a little heated.

For Dom the penny had finally dropped and he had slowly pieced the bits together.

"You knew that your husband wasn't the attacker, or the murderer. It was just convenient for you that someone was attacking prostitutes. We were all looking in the wrong direction. You phoned the police anticipating that it would be Rossy going to see Sharon that night and regardless of whether anyone was attacked you wanted to humiliate him like he was humiliating you. That's why the press was there. You called them, only it was me. Your little rouse to expose him had failed so you decided to confront Sharon, you were there all along and as soon as the Police left you went in and killed her."

"You were all shagging her, my husband and even my father in-law. None of you have any morals. I knew he was seeing someone. So one night I followed him from work. I sat outside for two hours in the car. I was stunned, at first I thought it was his bit on the side, a mistress, but while I was sat crying in the car after he left I saw Art pull up and go in. God how disgusting, the disease infested bitch. I knew then I wanted her dead, but I wanted to humiliate him first."

"So it was all just a set up?"

"You have no idea how much your kind disgusts me."

"Get a grip; you're a wacko like Krell. No one's forcing anyone to do anything here"

Paula had listened intently but was surprised to say the least when the two detectives pulled firearms and showed her their badges. Leo quickly made his way to the other side of the boat to see if he could creep up on her blind side.

Dom continued. "How did I miss that you were the biggest wacko?" He was really annoyed at himself for missing this one.

"Simple! Like you really, you just wanted to be loved, you'd been hurt and you were easy meat, a gullible fool."

Dom looked at Abby who was deadly serious and now pointing what appeared to be a very small gun at him. That was about it for Dom's limited knowledge, but it looked real enough.

"A ship full of people, nearly two thousand and you're going to kill me. I don't think so."

"It's easy, you jump and take your chances, or, I fill you with little holes. Don't you just love America? Two hours and you can buy anything you want."

"I fetch dresses while you're buying Smith and Wesson or what ever it is."

Dom was now feeling pretty foolish, he hadn't seen this coming. While he was still stood stunned, maybe his eyes were playing tricks on him or maybe he had been shot. Dom quickly glanced down at his shirt. No blood, no holes. Dom glanced back up to the port side and saw Paula walking towards them. Well it certainly looked like Paula apart from the fact that her hair was exceptionally short. She was wearing a beautiful long fishtailed black silk dress that was held up by her bosom. Boy was she a sight for sore eyes in more ways than one.

"Did I miss anything?"

Abby swung around to see Paula winking at Dom. Abby was stuck in the middle, two targets and one gun.

"Aren't you pleased to see me?"

"Oh it's the little dike, the Madam. This should be more fun than I imagined two for the price of one."

"Don't kid yourself dip shit, as soon as you get back to England its goodbye. To prison you will go."

"They have no idea?"

"Don't count on it."

Abby was now not really in control of the situation, she was waving the gun between the two, rather than getting them to stand together.

"Oh and another thing, I'm living on borrowed time. You see that hunk in front of you that you're about to kill, well he went to great lengths to save my life from a mad man with a gun. He's done it once he can do it again."

Abby was swaying from one to the other pointing the gun at them, who should she aim at? Paula had rattled Abby's cage and although she had the gun Paula had the psychological advantage.

"This time I'm quite prepared to die to save his life. Having said that, last time there was one nutter and three targets, now there are only two targets. Guess who lost?"

Paula answered her own question, "The Nutter," she screamed at Abby.

Dom could see that Paula was running the show; Abby was floundering and losing her composure.

"You'll not get us both you vengeful, twisted fuck." Nice words thought Dom as Paula continued to push her luck.

Abby was just about in a frenzy waving the gun from side to side. Paula was slowly moving towards Dom, and the arc of the swing that Abby was making had narrowed. Dom had noticed that Paula was also trying to position herself between Abby and himself. It was at this point that Dom realised the enormity of Paula's love for him. When he had saved Paula it had been a split second decision. This was a calculated move; she would lay down her own life before any harm came to him.

"Freeze, drop your weapon ma'am," said Leo, who was on the Port side with a clear shot of Abby. At that point Abby heard a noise behind her, and spun to see Charlie on the other side with a firearm levelled at her.

Abby immediately backed up to the stern of the ship, which made it difficult for either to shoot, it was a crossfire situation with Paula and Dom in the firing line. In that instance Abby new what she had to do. If she dropped the weapon they would not shoot. The gun clunked against the hardwood decking. Abby dropped her head but refocused her anger and energy. The game wasn't over yet. Abby started to run at Paula and whether you're an American football fan or English rugby fan the tackle was hard and high into Paula's chest instantly lifting her from the floor and driving her towards the railing. The adrenalin surge had meant she had the power of an ox and the speed of a bullet. Before Dom could blink Abby was going head first into the ocean their bodies twisting in mid air. Paula meanwhile was doing a high back dive over the railings. Winded and with no concept of her surroundings Paula too was heading to an icy grave.

It was the desperate act of a man in love; he had the agility of a pouncing panther as he too dove for the railings. His entire mid rift was suspended over the top rail with his feet in mid hair. His hand reached into the darkness and grabbed. It was a clean hold of a woman's ankle, Paula's ankle. It was funny but Paula knew there was no way she was going to fall. That vice like grip was not about to let go. She was safe.

As she was swung back on deck she managed to recover her composure and pull the dress back down to cover her underwear. They sat entwined on the deck with their arms round each other neither wanting to let go.

".........Lesbian eh?"

"Sorry............I just........well I didn't.........You know........"

"Good speech"

Paula recovered her composure it was time to get down to the real deal.

"I have a new business venture"

"Go on, I'm listening"

"Lots of hard work"

"And the job description?"

"Love and Sex..................But with one woman"

"And obviously this would be a full time job"

"Obviously!"

"Do I know her?"

"Not properly......yet...but she does love you."

"I never doubted that."

"But does he love the girl?"

"Lady...so much it hurts, but that could just be the bullet holes."

# Epilogue

Abby's body was never recovered, three miles out to sea in icy cold waters the survival time for the body is not long. She now rests in a watery grave several miles off the eastern seaboard of America. Abby's death meant so many new beginnings.

Rossy and his father Art had to answer some difficult questions relating to the investigation and the withholding of information.

Both Art and Rossy retired, Art's retirement was well overdue and Rossy took a reduced one for finishing early. His philosophy was that if he kept this pace up the job would kill him and he needed to rebuild his life. Rossy also inherited the remainder of Abby's estate, which more than compensated for the short fall in his pension. Art sold his house and between them they bought a cottage near Killarney in Southern Ireland with its own private stretch of river for fly-fishing. The nearest golf course only a few miles away and life for the two of them is just idyllic. Rossy is a recovering alcoholic but every now and again succumbs to the odd pint of the finest Guinness. The difference being there are no pressures to drive him to it.

For Dom Paula, Leah and Derk, fate had brought them together, but it would be love that would keep it that way, unless the tides of destiny turned again. As for Paula's business, it was under new management.

Printed in the United Kingdom
by Lightning Source UK Ltd.
111244UKS00001B/169-267